Doctor Co:
The Living Dead Man
by Perley Poore Sheehan

Introduction
by John Wooley

Off-Trail Publications

Elkhorn, California

A thik slice of krazy kolored kake to Bill Blackbeard
for indispensable assistance in kompiling this kollection.

"Doctor Coffin: The Living Dead Man,"
Copyright © 1932, Metropolitan Magazines, Inc.
"The Murdered Wife," Copyright © 1932, Metropolitan Magazines, Inc.
"Dead Man Blues," Copyright © 1932, Metropolitan Magazines, Inc.
"Seven Seconds to Die," Copyright © 1932, Metropolitan Magazines, Inc.
"Horror House," Copyright © 1932, Metropolitan Magazines, Inc.
"Hollywood Ghost," Copyright © 1932, Metropolitan Magazines, Inc.
"Manhattan Monster," Copyright © 1933, Standard Magazines, Inc.
"Small Town Stuff," Copyright © 1933, Standard Magazines, Inc.

Cover design by John Locke

DOCTOR COFFIN: THE LIVING DEAD MAN
Copyright © 2007, Off-Trail Publications
ISBN-10: 0-9786836-3-3
ISBN-13: 978-0-9786836-3-4

OFF-TRAIL PUBLICATIONS
2036 Elkhorn Road
Castroville, CA 95012
offtrail@redshift.com

Printed in the United States of America
March 2007

CONTENTS

Perley Poore Sheehan
(1875 - 1943)

Inside Hollywood's Coffin
By John Wooley

> The junction of Wilcox and Cahuenga avenues forms the apex of a triangle—unconsciously phallic—of which Hollywood boulevard is the base. . . . The triangle is Hollywood boiled to its very essence. . . . Between these streets one can find actors, authors, artists, acrobats and astrologers, coon-shouters, chorus girls, confidence men, comedians, camera-crankers, Christian Scientists, and call-houses, directors, gagmen, song writers, sadists, psalm singers, soothsayers, and sycophants, press agents, pugilists, policemen, perverts, pickpockets, panhandlers, pimps, playwrights, prostitutes, and parsons and playgirls (both unfrocked), bootleggers, bandits, bookmakers, and Babbitts, remittance men, radio announcers and realtors, Jews, Gentiles, Mohammedans and Rosicrucians, all living like Mormons, manicurists, manikins, misanthropes, misogynists and masochists, women of all sexes and men of none.
> — From *Queer People* (Vanguard, 1930) by Carroll and Garrett Graham

WHAT MUST IT HAVE BEEN LIKE, that silent-into-sound Hollywood of the late '20s and early '30s, its denizens as variegated and wondrously strange as the teeming life in a California tide pool? Outside, the tipsy excesses of the Jazz Age ultimately evaporated into the long hangover of the Great Depression, but in that land of chiaroscuro, of eternal sunshine and endless nightlife swirling together like the wash of stars in a faraway galaxy, the beautiful actors and actresses still lived and loved like gods and goddesses, their Mount Olympus balanced on the massed shoulders of the extras, day players, technicians, costumers, producers, directors and writers, whose combined efforts gave those earthly deities new ways to be viewed by a worshipful public.

Hollywood in those days was a town where anyone could become a star—even someone who became famous for burying them.

As created by Perley Poore Sheehan, Doctor Mortimer Coffin was that guy—an unremarkable-looking old fellow with a neat little gray beard, who favored a black frock coat and string tie. In more than one story, his creator describes him as "looking like an old-time parson."

But despite his appearance, Coffin was a Hollywood luminary, famed for his string of Mortimer Funeral Parlors in and around Tinseltown. And what he was most famous for was, essentially, burying himself. He and his outfit had presided over the funeral of Del Manning, the silver screen's famed Man of 500 Faces. But Coffin was, in fact, Del Manning himself.

The reason Coffin had a bogus funeral for his alter-ego can be found in these pages, so I won't play spoiler here, except to say that Sheehan left it unclear as to when Del Manning added the ironically named Doctor Coffin to his list of portrayals, and just exactly how and why the doc rose to the top of his profession even as Del Manning was rising to the top of his. It's probably best to look at the two career arcs as happening more or less simultaneously. Maybe Manning just figured he needed something to fall back on in case the movie biz went south on him. (In the real world, '70s and '80s country-music hitmaker John Conlee, who'd worked in a funeral home early on, kept his mortician's license current even at the height of his fame—just in case.) Or maybe it was part of an elaborate revenge scheme, as hinted at in our lead story.

That tale, "The Living Dead Man" (from the June 1932 *Thrilling Detective*), is pretty much an origin story, giving us plenty of background on Del Manning. It also establishes an intriguing continuity that, unfortunately, runs through a couple more stories and then peters out. In the first couple of installments, we also meet a group of supporting characters who would've been right at home in director Tod Browning's infamous sideshow-revenge picture, *Freaks*, which made its debut a few months before Doc Coffin's first adventure came out. In fact, when the doc first hit *Thrilling Detective's* pages, movie horror was a happening thing. The original *Dracula* (another Browning picture) and *Frankenstein*, both released by Universal in 1931, had touched a nerve in Depression-era audiences, and lots more cinema scares were either on the way or already creeping across America's screens. In many ways, the Doctor Coffin tales can be seen as the print equivalent of early '30s horror pictures, with the added self-referential lick of being, at least in their first year, set in Hollywood itself. And, unlike the so-called weird-menace pulps—which would see their heyday a bit later in the '30s—any allegedly supernatural doings might not be explained neatly away at the end, something else the Coffin stories had in common with the fright films of the time.

Unfortunately, the man Sheehan modeled Del Manning after, the greatest horror star of the silent era, was long gone by the time the first Doctor Coffin story saw print. Like Del Manning, Lon Chaney had been a man of mystery, more often seen by the public in makeup than out of it, portraying a stunning variety of characters that ranged from blind beggars to the Hunchback of Notre Dame, Chinese ancients to the Phantom of the Opera. So popular during the '20s that a song was written about him ("Lon Chaney's Gonna Get You If You Don't Watch Out," from the film *The Hollywood Revue of 1929*), Chaney died of throat cancer in 1930, after completing his only talkie, a remake of *The Unholy Three*.

Then, along came Del Manning. His first and last names were one-syllable, two-syllable, like Chaney's, and Sheehan tagged him with the moniker of "The Man with Five Hundred Faces," a humbly depreciated play on Chaney's well-known "Man of a Thousand Faces."

Interestingly enough, in real life Sheehan had worked with Chaney on one of the latter's most famous features, the aforementioned *Hunchback of Notre Dame*, released by Universal Pictures in 1923. That plum assignment came during a time that Sheehan, a pulp scribe since 1910, found himself employed rather steadily by Hollywood. Granted, Sheehan was one of four writers on the picture, and his actual contact with Chaney may have been minimal, or even nonexistent. Still, it's intriguing to wonder if that's when Sheehan fastened on the idea of, basically, a Lon Chaney who used his makeup skills to combat crime and right wrongs.

Sheehan's days of employment in the movie capital ran largely from the late teens through the '20s, during which his pulp output dropped off drastically. He was involved with a number of productions during that time, first as a provider of source material (his "We Are French," from the August 8, 1914 *All-Story Cavalier Weekly*, for instance, became the 1916 feature *The Bugler of Algiers*), and then as a scripter. In 1924, he even took a shot at directing, with a bucolic Universal drama called *The Night Message* that he also co-wrote. As often happened with Hollywood veterans, he made his last filmic stand on Poverty Row, as one of six writers on the wild 12-chapter serial from low-rent producer Sherman S. Krellberg, *The Lost City* (1935). Sheehan died in Sierra Madre, California, in 1943.*

The Coffin stories were written after Sheehan's main tenure in the Tinseltown dream factories, and they reflect not only an understanding of how Hollywood worked back then but also of the unique topography of the place. They are detective tales, after a fashion, and while there's plenty of bloodshed, tough talking, and a couple of recurring cop characters, the Doctor Coffins can't really be lumped in with the hardboiled school of fiction writing. That's mostly because of Sheehan's prose style, which is far too filigreed to fit with the terse, staccato idiom that developed in the pages of *Black Mask* while he was knocking out scripts for the moving pictures.

These are, however, wonderfully evocative and often weird little Hollywood adventures (except for the last two, which find Coffin, now dubbed "Skullface" by the underworld, venturing beyond his Southern California haunts). Dealing with a slate of evils that run from cheating husbands to a crazy genius with a hand-held A-bomb, these eight entries in the Coffin canon also touch on such themes as euthanasia, the career-destroying effects of scandal, and the exploitation of the young and innocent by the old and corrupt. (As products of their times, they also, it should be noted, sometimes feature unfortunate racial stereotyping.)

Bemoaning the loss of pulp writers to the movies and using Sheehan as

---

* For a more detailed Sheehan biography, see *Thrilling Detective Heroes* (Adventure House, 2006), edited by John Locke and yours truly.

an example, the old pulpwood editor Harold Hersey once wrote that "the waters close over their heads and the literature of tomorrow will be judged without them." This first-ever book-length collection of Doctor Coffin tales, published almost 65 years after Sheehan's demise, may not make much of a ripple in the waters of today's literature, but it'll at least bring the writer bobbing back to the surface for a little time—proving that, like his Hollywood-crimefighter creation, Perley Poore Sheehan isn't quite as dead as one might think.

Doctor Coffin
The Living Dead Man

THE NUMBER OF THE ROOM was 3112. It was on the thirty-first floor of the newest and finest hotel in the city. And as the man from the East who'd been assigned to it took a close look out and down from one of the open windows, he jerked back with an involuntary shiver. There was practically no window-sill, no ledge; nothing but straight wall right on down, pierced by a diminishing line of windows like his own, to the pavement hundreds of feat below.

"Jeez!" he exclaimed. "I almost took a header."

He turned to his heavy traveling bag, that a bell hop had placed on a bench. From this he took a flask and fortified himself. From the bag he then brought out a bit of well-worn harness, limp but strong, supporting a holster. From the holster he extracted a short pistol—it looked like a block of blue steel. He handled this with fingers that were deft—tender, with a certain grace and affection.

But his face was hard. His eyes glittered.

You could see that he had the build of a rather undersized heavyweight, even with all his clothes on. When he stripped off his coat and vest and rolled up his sleeves, the impression that here was a fighter grew stronger. His hairy arms were quick and powerful. His shoulders bulged.

He worked his way into the harness so that the weapon was over his heart. He next put on his vest again. It was a special vest. It was not only good enough to stop a knife or deflect a bullet, it had a slit for the gun. After he'd put his coat on again, he practiced a few quick draws and feints at different angles. All his movements were quick. As he walked about the room he had the sliding grace of a panther.

The sun was going down. It was beginning to get a little dark in the room. He stood there brooding for a moment, feet apart, looking away through an open window—but not too close to it. He had the sensation of looking through the port of a plane. All he could see out there was blue air and distant mountains.

He looked at the watch on his hairy wrist and was about to help himself to another shot at the flask when there was a tap at the door.

Instead of speaking up, he slid over to the door with that panther-like step of his and silently opened it, meantime standing behind the door and keeping his right hand free.

"Who is it?" he asked.

"You're careful, Hootch," a man's voice answered. "This is Del."

"What's the idea?" growled the man addressed as "Hootch." But he laughed a little. A moment later he and his caller were facing each other. "I suppose," said the man who'd been called Hootch, "youse got to be an actor even when you come to see an old friend. Why didn't you give me a buzz, Del, to let me know you was coming up?"

The caller looked at him through the gathering dusk.

"I didn't come up," he answered. "I've got the room across the hall."

"You got the room across the hall!"

"Sure." The caller let out a curious cackling laugh. "That's how they happened to give you this room, Mr. Cooch."

Mr. Cooch appeared to be thinking hard. He was standing in the middle of the room with his back to the windows. There was still sufficient light to permit him a thorough study of his visitor's face. This face puzzled him considerably. It was a hard face and deeply lined—one that might have belonged to any gorilla of the underworld. At least, that was Mr. Cooch's judgment. And he knew gorillas enough, both in prison and out. He'd spent his life among them. He'd been a gorilla himself—he'd been Hootchy Cooch—before he'd become a big shot. Now he was Arnold—Mr. Arnold Cooch.

"You was expecting your brother, Petey, then, and not me?" said Mr. Cooch.

He wondered how much the man in front of him knew. Del Manning was tricky. They'd known each other as kids. And now Del was a big shot himself—in motion pictures. One of the biggest; if not *the* biggest.

"How could I be expecting Petey," Del Manning asked without change of expression, "when it was I myself who buried him?"

Cooch gave a start. His hand almost found his gun.

"What is this, a plant? Say, Del; what you tryin' to do, frame me? I suppose you think you got something on me!"

"I set a trap and you walked into it."

"I didn't even know Petey was dead. Petey used to talk to me about you. I knew you was in this burg. Like that I knew you must be when you said you was. And Petey told me when I last seen him that he was comin' here to see you. I even thought you and me might get together ourselves for old time's sake. Jeez! That's too bad about Petey bein' dead! What happened to him?"

Cooch was stalling—just talking wild.

Del Manning made no direct answer. He stood there with slouched shoulders, feet apart. His bony mask of a face, in the failing light, had somewhat the look of a skull. The resemblance to a skull increased as his naturally wide mouth became still wider in a mirthless grin. When he spoke his voice came in a hollow whisper.

"You dirty liar!"

Cooch, in a flash, presented his gun.

After that, for several seconds, nothing was said. Neither man moved. They'd been born in the same Kansas City tenement. They'd grown up as members of the same gang. Then their paths had sharply diverged. The "Law" had seen to this. A box car had been robbed. It was the future Del Manning who'd taken the rap for the rest of the gang.

"What's the idea?" Mr. Cooch inquired, still with his gun pointed from its nesting place against his breast.

"That you killed Petey yourself."

"Why should I have killed him?"

"You found out I was sending him money. You found out who I was. You wanted to shake me down, using him for the 'shill.' Oh, I haven't forgotten the old stuff. I'm rich, but I am not a sucker. Thought you could use Petey as a lure! That's all! When he threatened to squawk you let him have it."

"You can't pin no rap on me!"

"What you going to do with that gun?"

So far, the conversation, though tense enough, had been carried on in what might have been called easy conversational tones. Now, Mr. Cooch began to whisper.

"Del, listen! So help me God, if you got a mike in this room—if that's what you're talkin' to—if you got this room wired and the Law listenin' in—"

"Bah!" the actor scoffed. "I'm not advertising that way. Why do you suppose I've been playing freak parts ever since I came to the screen? Did you ever see my photograph so you'd recognize me? I'm the most photographed man in the world. Yet no one, except a few of you old-timers, know what I look like. The whole world knows Del Manning on the screen—the guy with five hundred faces. No one knows him off it. Stow the gat, I'm no more anxious for a crash than you are. A little scandal, nowadays, and I don't care how famous a screen star is, he's out."

"Nuts! You'll never be on the loose! Stick 'em up. I'm goin' to see, anyway, if you haven't got a little gat of your own. Then we'll look for any wires that don't belong. If you're on the up and up, why, we'll talk nice and friendly. If you ain't, well, you know, it'll be just too bad."

Del Manning had lifted his two hands without protest. While Mr. Cooch, still talking, frisked him lightly but thoroughly, the great screen star did not stir. Having satisfied himself that Manning was unarmed, Cooch took a guarded look up and down the hallway outside his door. There was no one near. Next, he switched on the lights and, still alert but with expert speed, made pretty sure that there was not a Dictaphone about the place.

Anyway, his own shrewd sense was convincing him that what the great Del Manning said was true. More than one famous screen star had been eclipsed practically overnight by a little unsought notoriety. Scandal was poison. Besides, what the actor had said strengthened his hand.

"Sit down," said Mr. Cooch, after completing his search.

The actor remained standing, still with his hands partly raised.

"I saw you at Petey's funeral," he said, "Do you remember the undertaker who was in charge?"

"Sure I remember him," said Mr. Cooch. "But where were you?"

"I was the undertaker."

"You?"

"Watch!"

Del Manning brought his hands to his face. His hands simulated a beard and a mustache. His face underwent a change of expression.

"My God!" said Cooch. "Old Doc Coffin himself!"

He was shaken.

"You see, I remembered my old man's trade. That's something else that might spoil my publicity. I'd be a wow on the screen as an undertaker's son and an escape from Copper John."

Again he cackled that mirthless laugh, while Cooch stared. Cooch was half stirred to admiration. At the same time he was pleased at the way the famous one kept handing him all the cards.

"Well, I'm your friend," he said without sincerity. "I'm not goin' to be a hog even if you are heavy."

"Suppose you show your good-will by opening that flask."

The actor's deep-set eyes had come to the open valise.

"Sure!"

Mr. Cooch's hands were free. He'd returned his gun to its holster. He lifted the heavy flask and started to unscrew the top.

"And forget all about Petey," he said. "Honest—"

"Sh!"

Looking up, Mr. Cooch saw that the actor had suddenly gone white, that there was terror in his eyes as he stared toward the nearest window.

"What—"

"I thought I saw Petey just now. Don't stir."

"Where?"

"Just outside the window."

"Are you goofy?"

"I thought I saw him pass, going down!"

"If anyone passed—going down—outside that window, they'll have to take him up with a mop."

"There!"

As Cooch turned, a little off his balance, the actor sprang. He caught Cooch in a flying tackle, with arms and legs, as a baboon might have caught him, and with more than a baboon's strength.

II

THE TWO WERE ALMOST EVENLY MATCHED. If Cooch might have had some advantage in weight and build, it was offset by the superb condition in which Del Manning had always kept himself.

Ever since Del Manning had come to Hollywood he'd been the man of mystery. He'd kept himself aloof from other actors. His private life had been kept as a sealed book. Later, when fame began to come his way because of his remarkable gifts, this very mystery had become a further asset. From becoming a man of mystery in Hollywood he had become a man of mystery throughout the world.

Was he a cripple? Was he a Chinaman? Was it true that he was some sort of monstrosity—half-man, half-ape?

The whole world had begun to ask these questions. Few in Hollywood itself, even in the studio where the great star worked, could have answered these questions and have been sure that the answer was correct. Del Manning had no intimates, few friends. Concerning his occupation "between pictures" or when off duty he made no confidences.

But this was known by those who'd watched him work. He used no "doubles." Nothing had ever seemed too painful, too hard, or too dangerous, for this strange man of mystery to undertake himself.

Cooch, caught off his guard, jolted out a whining curse. He'd been in a thousand battles. His reaction was swift. From the moment he and Manning were tangled, it became a battle for the gun.

"No," Del Manning glinted, "or I'll kill you. I didn't bring a gun myself—"

There were four hands on the holster. There was a muffled explosion. Cooch coughed and a spasm shook him.

Manning relaxed and drew back from him, bringing the gun along.

"You son of an ink-pot moll," Cooch gasped.

He was saying other things—or trying to say them—but much of what he said was incoherent. It was only when the stricken gangster muttered a certain name that Del Manning began to comprehend.

The name was Hennil—the name of Joseph Hennil, one of the largest producers in Hollywood.

Del Manning knew Hennil. None knew him better. Few knew him so well— a great movie magnate who'd risen from obscurity within a few years to become one of the czars of the industry.

"Hennil!" Manning whispered. "Was it Hennil who hired you to come out here and bump me off as you did the kid?"

There was no answer.

There were some curious encounters in Hollywood at times. Hollywood had become a crossroads of the world, a meeting-place of beggars on horseback, a place where it was often better to forget the past.

Del Manning could remember certain dark days in his own past when not only this man now lying before him on the floor but the great magnate, Joseph Hennil himself, were "outside the law." Only Hennil, shrewder than others, had always known how to keep out of prison, to hire his rough work done by those who were not so shrewd.

When Joseph Hennil discovered that Del Manning was a former tool of his who'd now grown rich and powerful on his own account, he'd been filled with angry fear. He hadn't shown this sentiment. That wasn't his way. But Del Manning had felt it—he'd known that Hennil was a man who sooner or later would try to destroy him as he'd destroyed so many others.

"Hootch," the actor whispered, using the old-time nickname, "you're going to croak."

From the fallen gangster there came a faint moan. The moan became words: "—yeah! You and Hennil—"

He was gasping for breath—going fast. He panted, but what he said was mere raving. There was a froth of blood on his lips.

"And—I hope—you'll both fry for this!"

They were the last words that Mr. Arnold Cooch ever uttered.

Manning had come to his feet. He had the gun in hand. He looked at it. He looked at the man on the floor. He hastily pocketed the weapon.

He knelt on the floor at the side of the late Mr. Cooch and made a swift examination. The man was unquestionably dead. He remained there for a couple of seconds, listening, expectant. There was no sign that either the struggle or the shot had attracted attention. These were soundproof rooms. Up from the distant street there came a murmur of traffic, an occasional shock of louder sound.

The corridor was still deserted when he looked. He locked the door and turned again to the dead man.

The thing that he had feared and wished to avoid had happened. That was why he'd come to the room unarmed. He had proof that Cooch was the slayer of his brother. He'd put this proof in a place where it could be found by others. He'd foreseen nothing worse than a trade—that commonest of all pacts in the underworld: silence for silence. At the same time he'd been ready, in case of accident, to disappear.

This was the accident he'd somehow foreseen.

Nor could there be an alibi. He was known at the desk of this hotel. He'd reserved this room opposite his own. He'd made the further arrangement that "his friend, K.R. Baxter" should be assigned to it on the latter's arrival from the East.

It would all look like a premeditated murder. It would look so much like a premeditated murder that that last wish of Arnold Cooch's would probably be realized. It was as if the words lingered in the silent room:

"I hope you fry—"

III

IT DIDN'T HELP MATTERS VERY MUCH when Manning made a discovery. It had to do with that special vest that the dead man wore. The bullet had not penetrated it. Cooch had died of a blow as a poorly conditioned boxer might die in the ring—from a blow over the heart. There'd been no open wound, no flow of blood.

The thing meant something to Manning.

Again he was thinking. It wasn't the first time in his life when his fate depended on a power to think. He remained there at the side of his dead enemy thinking. The presence of a dead man didn't disturb him. More than once he'd found it useful to recall the lessons of that obscure youth of his in a third-rate undertaking establishment.

"Doctor Coffin!"

It was a good alias, at that.

He remembered the macabre trick he'd played on one of the Hootchy Cooch mob following his brother's murder—making him believe that Petey had come back to life in the undertaking parlor. It was in that way he'd found out who the real killer was. The mokker himself—Arnold Cooch—the chief of the gang. Now here was Cooch himself. And Doctor Coffin had another job to do.

Manning got swiftly to his feet. Not more than a minute or two could have passed since the shot was fired.

His first move was to open the window. He leaned out and looked down. He felt no tremor at that dizzy height. His nerve was perfect. He could have stood on the window-sill itself without holding on, had he cared to, and have felt no more fear than he would have felt if he were standing on the pavement, so many hundreds of feet below.

There was hardly any traffic below at this hour. The pavement immediately below was that of a cul-de-sac at the side of the hotel. But less than fifty feet further on was the main street, running in front of the hotel. From this elevation, the people were ants, the streaming autos were beetles.

His first idea was that he would have to lam. He was thinking again in the language of his earlier days. He'd spent a lot of time "on the lam" in the old days. For a long time now he'd seen it coming—the crash, the wash-up. This was it.

But the free air of the mountains, blowing on his face, cleared his brain. If he did a run-out now, that would merely mean another victory for Joe Hennil—a chance for Joe to go on doing more dirty work. Joe had made his fortune in drugs. He'd begun by peddling. He'd become a smuggler. He'd become the head of the ring. Until there was a time when Joe Hennil was collecting profits on practically every poor "junkie" east of the Mississippi.

"No," Del Manning whispered, gritting his teeth. "I've got to get Joe Hennil himself!"

But how?

The mind works fast.

Manning let out a bit of laughter—the way he laughed when his mood was sad or dangerous.

There had come to him a breath of inspiration that tingled through his veins. He stood there at the open window staring at a sky-sign far below in the neighboring street. It was the huge electric sign of a moving-picture house. It blazed red, green, white.

He could read that sign:

DEL MANNING
In
The Living Dead Man

Again he let out a couple of notes of that dry and mirthless laugh of his.

"Del Manning—me—in—'The Living Dead Man!'"

Manning's inspection of the room was brief, but it confirmed the growing idea in his mind. He was beginning to move now like a man possessed, in the grip of inspiration. It was a state familiar to him. Only like this had he ever been able to work. Only like this would he ever permit himself to work—when he ceased to be himself altogether and became the character he was meant to portray.

He worked with the swift precision of an expert.

From his own room he'd brought a make-up box, such as he always carried with him. He'd thrown aside his clothing and wore nothing but his underclothes, slippers, and a silk dressing gown. He squatted on the floor at the side of Cooch and opened the box. Then, before the mirror that formed the underside of the lid of the box, he began to transform his face to resemble that of his dead enemy.

It was mostly a matter of darkening the hair and eyebrows, he saw; but he went about the business as carefully as if he were making up for a new rôle at the studio. First he lay on a thick coat of carefully selected grease-paint. This he built up cunningly to right tints and shadow lines. He was like an artist painting a portrait. His own face was the canvas. Cooch was the unconscious sitter.

When this was done, he stripped Cooch of his clothing. He put him into the dressing robe and slippers instead.

His nerve remained as perfect as it was a while ago when he was gazing down that dizzy void between the window and the street. There were many details. He forgot not one of them.

He wiped out his own fingerprints on his make-up box and substituted those of the late Arnold Cooch. For the make-up box was notoriously the one that the great Del Manning carried with him wherever he went—the box that contained the secret of the five hundred faces.

He took the cord of the dressing robe and twisted it about the dead man's neck.

There wasn't a detail neglected when he was ready for the final scene of this act that would never appear on the screen.

He was dressed in the late Arnold Cooch's clothing. It was a fair portrait of Arnold Cooch's face that looked back at him from the mirror. Back in his own room there was evidence that Arnold Cooch, after killing Del Manning, had made a hasty search for money and papers before taking to flight and deserting his own meager possessions.

All that remained was that final gesture that would baffle further identification forever. He snapped out the light.

Manning's nerve remained unshaken as he lifted the slayer of his brother from the floor. He carried the body to the luminous square of the open window. Again he looked down. There was no one below.

He toppled his burden into space.

IV

LATER, THE FLOOR MANAGER, with her desk in the foyer of the thirty-first floor, where she could see everyone who came and went from the elevators was able to swear that she'd seen the man assigned to Room No. 3112 rapidly leave not long after his arrival. As he carried no baggage, naturally there'd been no occasion to stop him. But she was positive of her identification. She'd noticed particularly a small mole on his cheek. Also she'd noticed his clothes and the way he walked.

The bell hop who'd accompanied "K.R. Baxter" to his room happened to be in the foyer on the street level when the same man crossed the hall from the elevators in the direction of a side exit. He was equally positive in his identification. He added the detail that the man now seemed to be in a hurry.

He might well have been in a hurry.

Even then a crowd was beginning to surge into the cul-de-sac at the side of the hotel to witness the horror that was lying there—a horror none the less vivid in that it left so much to the imagination.

The police were prompt, but, at that, by the time they began ardently to desire the presence of one K.R. Baxter, that gentleman was manifestly well on his way.

DEL MANNING MURDERED!

It was a headline scream that went around the world. The whole world, more or less, must have been howling it at once—across the Americas, across Europe and Asia, down through Africa and Australia, and through many an island of the Southern seas.

In many of these places there were pictures of Del Manning's that were running, or had been shown recently, or were about to be shown—as blind man, Chinaman, hunchback, cripple, clown. In these he spoke with different voices—he had a different face for every character and a different voice for every face. Yet he was always the same—the genius of the odd—the great Del Manning. There'd never be another.

Murdered! Yet, in a way, he still lived!

V

CAPTAIN JIM HUGHES, of the United States Secret Service, mulled over this phase of the situation, as he settled down in Hollywood to stay awhile. He'd come out to the coast in a little affair of some new counterfeit fives, and having settled this to the satisfaction of all concerned except that of the counterfeiters themselves, he'd been ready to start East again when he received a long and interesting telegram in code.

What it said was this:

> The International Association of Motion Picture Producers were in a blue funk following the murder of Del Manning. That murder alone stood to cost them several millions of dollars. There were indications that other stars of the screen were marked for slaughter. The local police, especially the detective branch, couldn't take care of the situation. They were, for the most part, capable and honest—no doubt about that—with Chief Costigan at their head—but they were too well known.
>
> The producers, therefore, had appealed to the Federal Government,

backing up their appeal with a million dollars—to which another million or two would be added, as the need arose. But what they wanted was to borrow the very best man in the Government's service, his identity to remain secret even to the producers themselves. He was to have a free hand, both in the spending of the money placed at his disposal and in his selection of aides—

Would the captain take over the assignment on the basis of an unlimited leave?

He would.

There was only one person in Hollywood so far, Captain Hughes decided, that he couldn't quite place. Crooks there were, aplenty—some of them big shots, too. You'll always find them where the big money is, and the "heavy money" of Hollywood had become a fable around the world. But the crooks were normal, so to speak.

So were the other hundred thousand or two that had so far passed under the captain's kindly but absorbent blue eyes—all sorts of people, all the nations of the world. It was a mob to remind the captain of certain old days of his in Paris.

But he was walking back to his modest hotel down a side street one night when a little ahead of him he saw a blind man. There was no one near and the street was comparatively dark. Arrived at the curb of a still darker cross-street the blind man halted and tapped with his cane.

"Want some help?"—and the captain took the blind man's arm.

The captain remembered the touch of that arm. Few blind men have highly developed muscles except when engaged in a special trade. This was the arm of a trained athlete.

Near the captain's hotel there was a large public market with a lunch-counter in one corner of it where the captain was accustomed to eat his breakfast.

He was sipping his coffee there a few mornings later when he saw a Chinaman come in with a basket on his arm—some one's servant, apparently, out for the day's marketing. Captain Hughes had a crazy idea that he'd seen this Chinaman before; but where—and why he should remember him—he couldn't immediately recall.

Presently he paid his bill and strolled over to the stall where the Chinaman was buying some grapefruit. The market was crowded and there was nothing conspicuous about his movements. The Chinaman didn't appear to notice it particularly even when the captain slipped on a bit of orange-peel and almost fell.

But, in the course of this near accident, the captain had touched the

Chinaman's arm. Then he knew where he'd seen the Chinaman before.

The Chinaman and the blind man were one.

Hollywood is surrounded by a curious tangle of hills and canyons, crooked, steep, and narrow, some of them still as brushy and wild as they were before motion pictures were even dreamed of.

Captain Hughes liked to take walks in the country. Old-timers in the Federal service are not very sociable. He was much alone. One of his favorite walks was up a hill-path that started almost from the heart of town and yet which soon brought him to a place of solitude. There he could lie on a ridge and look down on either side. The ridge was like a wall, steep, high, and narrow. It was, moreover, pretty thickly covered with sagebrush and cactus, which made it convenient for anyone who didn't care to be seen.

The canyons on each side of the ridge were deep. It was the only thing they had in common. One canyon was wide and well-developed, with numerous costly villas set in the midst of landscaped gardens. The other canyon, still wild, contained but a single small bungalow reached by a narrow winding road.

It was to this small bungalow that the captain had traced the Chinaman—the Chinaman who was also the blind man. And now, as the captain lay there comfortably on his stomach and looked down at the small bungalow it was another crazy thought that was obsessing him.

It seemed to him that both Chinaman and blind man were still someone else and that this was someone who, for some reason or other, ought to be well-known.

By and by he was rewarded—if you could call it that—by seeing an old man (white, like the blind man) come out of the back door of the bungalow with a coil of hose over his shoulder. The old man was a gardener, seemingly. He was dressed in an old blue shirt and patched overalls. He soon had a sprinkler at work and was pottering about a bit of lawn with a rake. . . . But the Chinaman didn't appear again.

That night the captain went to see a moving picture, one of the first he had seen in over a year.

This was a picture featuring the late Del Manning—a picture in which the famous character actor had played a dual rôle; that of a revered man of letters possessed of a Chinese devil. When the Chinese devil got possession of the good professor, he became as a Chinaman, he dressed as a Chinaman, he was a Chinaman—and not a very nice Chinaman at that.

Captain Hughes followed the story only vaguely, although his interest in the main character was not vague at all. He kept thinking of the blind man he had seen, then the Chinaman in the market. He was pretty sure they were one and the same. They might even be that old gardener, as well, three in one—a crazy idea!

Still, that little brown bungalow would be worth looking into—
He heard a whisper from someone at his side:
"Captain Hughes, would you like to feel my arm?"
The whisper was like a faint echo of the voice from the screen.

VI

"I SEE THAT YOU DON'T REMEMBER ME," said the stranger, after Captain Hughes had followed him out to the street.

Captain Hughes looked him over with interest.

The other was a middle-aged man. There was nothing about him to prevent one from thinking that he might even be a retired minister from Iowa. His chin and mouth were concealed by an old-fashioned beard and mustache, very straight-haired, going gray, and severely unornamental. He was dressed in a good but unfashionable suit of black.

"I might remember you better," Captain Hughes fenced, "if you took off that false hair."

It was just a shot in the dark. The whiskers of the middle-aged gentleman looked genuine. Even to the captain's trained eye—look hard as he would— there was no trace of the usual clumsy disguise. Yet—he had no doubt of it now—here was the blind man and here was the Chinaman.

And here was—but he checked himself, wondering if such and such a thing could be—Del Manning!

Was it possible that the great Del Manning wasn't dead, after all?

All this in a matter of seconds.

The two of them had strolled away from the more brilliant lights of the theatre as if by mutual consent. They turned into a side street where a row of black acacia trees cast heavy shadows. In the dark zone of one of these trees they paused again.

"You will excuse me for interrupting your pleasure in the theatre just now," the stranger said. "But I have certain news that would prove of interest to you. And life being as uncertain as it is I thought I'd better not wait any longer."

"Who are you?"

The other let out a dry cackling laugh. It was an entirely mirthless laugh.

"I'm Doctor Coffin."

"Do you practice medicine, Doctor Coffin?"

"Something else. My cures never fail—they last."

"I don't get you."

"I happen to be the proprietor of the leading funeral parlors in this part of the world," said the strange Doctor Coffin. "That's where I got a line on you, Captain Hughes."

"When was that?"

"The day they buried—the great Del Manning. Ordinarily, I don't appear at my place of business. But, naturally, for such an important occasion I wanted to be there."

Captain Hughes paused for thought, looking at his strange companion carefully. At the same time, the captain had an eye for the shadowy street where they were standing. It would have been a convenient place for getting rid of a bothersome enemy. But the street continued deserted.

"How did you know who I was?" the captain asked, in non-committal tones.

"I recognized you as an old friend of mine, Captain Hughes."

"An old friend?"

"Let us say—a friend of Del Manning's. He held you in high esteem."

"I'm sorry," the captain mused. "But you must be mistaken. I can't remember having ever met Mr. Del Manning."

"You met him thirteen years ago," said the strange Doctor Coffin. "It was at a time when Del Manning was barely twenty. At that time 'Del Manning' wasn't his name. He caused you some trouble. He always regretted this."

Again the captain took thought. Thirteen years ago the captain had been temporary warden of Auburn Prison—"Copper John," as the inmates call it. There'd been a jail break—an unpleasant affair.

"I remember a kid who caused me some trouble thirteen years ago," said Captain Hughes. "But I never blamed him. He escaped with a number of older men. They never got him, although they got the others. He disappeared. Personally, I was satisfied. Is this what you're talking about?"

"Yes. And do you remember that kid's name, Captain Hughes?"

"It wasn't Del Manning—"

"D-e-l-m-a-n—" Doctor Coffin began to spell.

"Delman! That's it—Jimmy Del-man! Del-man! Del Manning!"

"Does the old charge still hold, Captain Hughes, now that Del Manning— Jimmy Delman, that is—has been officially pronounced dead?"

Captain Hughes could feel the weight of longing that was back of the question. Again he was looking at Doctor Coffin curiously. The man gave no outer sign of emotion. To all appearances he was merely a respectable undertaker inquiring about a point at law.

"I suppose, Doctor Coffin, that you could furnish me with a certificate of Del Manning's death and burial?"

Doctor Coffin bleated his mirthless laugh. "I could do that," he said.

"And I suppose you could even furnish me with an affidavit that Jimmy

Delman and Del Manning were one and the same person."

"I certainly could, Captain Hughes—that is, if the information could be kept out of the newspapers."

"The newspapers would never know."

"You can have the affidavits at once. And, in that case, the old charge will be dropped?"

"It could be arranged," said Captain Hughes. "But there might remain another charge."

"Murder?"

"Yes."

"That will be explained to your satisfaction, Captain Hughes."

"How can you explain a murder? Someone was killed. Someone escaped. One of them was the killer. If the victim wasn't Del Manning, who was he? Who was K.R. Baxter? You?"

"I was Del Manning. I was also K.R. Baxter."

Captain Hughes stood silent for a while, his active brain at work on the problem that had been presented to it. He'd been up against some queer situations in his life, but never one so queer as this.

Del Manning was supposed to have been murdered—murdered and buried. Yet here was Del Manning standing before him now—talking to him—ready to explain. There could be no doubt about that.

"Aren't you taking a pretty long chance—Doctor Coffin?"

"It's a chance I wouldn't have taken, Captain Hughes, if I hadn't known who you were—if I hadn't wanted to square myself and pay off an old debt. Did you ever hear of a gangster known as Hootchy Cooch—Arnold Cooch?"

"Sure!"

"He was 'K.R. Baxter.' He was killed in a struggle for a gun—killed, perhaps, by Del Manning—but Del Manning is officially dead."

"What were they fighting about?"

"Cooch was brought out here to kill Del Manning—shake him down—or put him on the scram. Cooch died before he had a chance to clear things up. But he made it clear who brought him here."

"Who was that?"

"Someone who thinks Cooch—or Baxter—is still alive. I've talked to him over the telephone—pretending I was Cooch. I've arranged for him to see me. Would you like to be present?"

VII

"IT'S A NEAT HIDEAWAY," said Captain Hughes, as the two of them came to that small bungalow up the dark and wooded canyon.

"When you play the part of a living dead man, Captain Hughes," the late Del Manning answered softly, "you have to watch your step. That's the part I have been playing now for quite a number of years—and it's one that I may get on playing until I really am dead."

The captain was practically without nerves. Neither was he superstitious. And no one in the least acquainted with him would ever suggest that he was a victim of useless fears.

But he would have been the first to confess that his present situation might have been more pleasant. The walls of the deep and narrow valley, or canyon, rose steep and black. Since entering the canyon—perhaps a quarter of a mile back—they had met no one. If this was a trap, he was trapped all right.

The bungalow was dark and silent. A dark and silent dog—a Great Dane, the captain made out in the dark—appeared out of the deeper darkness. It was more like the black ghost of a dog than a live animal—the ghost dog of this living dead man. It sniffed them and made no demonstration.

Still, the captain had a hunch. It was the sort of a hunch that he'd followed before—at some personal risk, to be sure, but to the great profit of those who hired him. He would follow on.

"You say you've been playing the part of a living dead man for quite a long time," the captain prompted, as they entered the dark bungalow.

Doctor Coffin switched on a subdued light and faced him.

"Yes. It was the only way I could be free. Free!" He repeated the word in a whisper. "I learned that as a kid. Only the dead are free. I wanted to be free like the dead—but still be alive. As I doped it out there was a way—and that was—to be a living dead man. A millionaire, who could be a blind beggar when he wanted to. A famous actor, who could go to market as a Chinese cook. An undertaker, getting a bushel of fan mail every week. Now, pretty soon, even Del Manning will be forgotten. But me—old Doc Coffin!—will still be sneaking around the top of the earth and doing those things that he thinks ought to be done."

They were in the small hallway of the bungalow. While Doctor Coffin spoke another figure had appeared, as silently as the Great Dane had done out there in the dark garden. The newcomer was a dwarf hunchback. He might have been an ape dressed as a human being. He had enormous arms. In spite of his deformity there was a look of power about him. He had a monkey's shrewd eyes.

"This is 'Shorty,' " Doctor Coffin introduced. "Shorty, shake hands with Captain Hughes."

"I heard the buzz," said Shorty. "So I watched you coming."

"Shorty sees in the dark," Doctor Coffin explained. "And the canyon's wired. So nothing's ever going to get past him and the dog."

It has long been known about the Hollywood studios that the late Del Manning chose by preference his few companions from among the human misfits that occasionally came his way. Often enough these misfits disappeared, no one knew where. Shorty was one of these.

"Are you staying here, boss?" Shorty asked.

"We'll go over to the other place," his employer answered. "Is the box on hand?"

"The box is on hand and the stage is set," Shorty answered.

"How about Joe Grimm?"

"Sewed up."

Captain Hughes followed the conversation with both ears. The "box" referred to might have been a number of things, from a safe to a room; "Joe Grimm" means a victim; "sewed up" meant, in this case, probably that the victim was a sure thing.

In the meantime, the captain looked about the bungalow—as much as he could see of it. There was nothing elaborate about it. The furniture was poor. There was nothing about it to indicate the retreat of a famous star. But he hadn't overlooked that remark of Doctor Coffin's about "the other place."

Without delay Shorty produced a candle which he lit. Holding this high he led the way to what might have been the living room of the bungalow. There was a fireplace there. Shorty pulled this open as if it had been a door and revealed a narrow flight of steps. The steps led downward into darkness. From the opening there came a breath of stale earth such as might have come from a long abandoned tomb.

Doctor Coffin tittered.

"You are not nervous, Captain Hughes!"

"Not particularly," the captain answered cheerfully. But he was keeping his hand on his gun.

The steps brought them to a narrow tunnel. Originally this had been a bore through the narrow mountain ridge separating two canyons for the passage of a water-main. Since then the bore had been enlarged and fortified with concrete.

"Folks used to wonder what I did with my spare time," said the late Del Manning. "This is some of my work."

"Clever!" the captain commented.

"Not too clever! But it served me many a good time when this Joe Grimm was trying to take me along."

They'd come to the farther end of the tunnel. It couldn't have been more than two hundred yards in length. Here there was what appeared to be an ordinary manhole, with iron steps fastened into the cement that formed its walls.

"You haven't told me yet who this Joe Grimm is," said Captain Hughes.

Doctor Coffin turned and smiled. The light of the candle he was carrying flickered over his face.

"He's the head of the organization that brought you here."

"You mean Joseph Hennil?"

"Are you shocked?"

"He's a big man."

"Bigger in more ways than even you or Uncle Sam suspects."

"I'd have to have proof."

"My dear Captain Hughes, didn't I say you'd be permitted to listen while we talked?"

VIII

FROM THE MANHOLE THEY'D COME into a cement corridor, containing a number of iron doors. Here Doctor Coffin extinguished his candle and turned on an electric light. He then unlocked one of the doors and ushered his guest into a large basement. It was the basement of one of those fine villas in the larger canyon that Captain Hughes had previously seen while lying on top of the ridge.

In the basement a giant negro, who'd been sitting near the furnace, straightened up. His eyes were two white spots in a face that was black as coal.

"Hello, Jerry," said Doctor Coffin.

The man grinned and mumbled. He was blind and tongue-tied.

At the head of the stairs a woman stood waiting. Her hair and her figure were superb. So were her hands and wrists, as Captain Hughes observed with his practiced eyes. But he barely suppressed a start.

Her face was covered with a mask. Through the openings for her eyes Captain Hughes caught something equivalent to a flash of fire.

"Madame Jane!" Doctor Coffin presented.

The lady bowed. Her voice came warm and rich.

"You must hear her sing," said Doctor Coffin later.

He explained that she had been a famous star—one of the many who had been eclipsed forever. A bungling "beauty doctor" had botched his job.

"We're not all freaks," said Doctor Coffin with a touch of grim humor. "Take, for example, my butler, Ching."

Before him there in the lower hall Captain Hughes saw a powerful Chinaman—one of the largest Chinamen he'd ever seen. Most of the

Chinamen in the United States come from Canton, in the South. This man was a Manchu of the North—broad of face and shoulder. He was dressed in semi-Oriental costume—a well-fitted tail-coat over a tight-skirted robe of Chinese silk.

Ching smiled and bowed.

Doctor Coffin led his guest upstairs. There, in the upper hall, Captain Hughes had an overwhelming sense of illusion. Here was Ching again smiling and bowing—the same broad face, same costume, same expression.

"This isn't Ching; this is Lee," said Doctor Coffin. "They are twins."

He spoke to Lee in a Chinese dialect, giving him certain directions.

"I am about to assume another rôle," said Doctor Coffin. "It is one that will require considerable care—as I am always careful—with my make-up. As the wait is apt to be tedious for you unless you know more about what will happen, let us go up to the attic, which will be, as you might say, the theatre of this evening's entertainment."

They proceeded on their way slowly. The villa was fitted up like a palace.

"You see," said Doctor Coffin, "I knew that it was only a question of time when I'd have to retire anyway—and when I say 'retire' I mean that Del Manning would have to die and be buried, while Doctor Coffin should live on. It was with this end in view that I had laid all my plans, made all my investments, and gradually accumulated this club of other living dead people on whom I could depend."

"And our friend, Mr. Hennil, wished to block your plans?"

"Yes. Through his connections with the underworld—chiefly with the late Mr. Cooch—he found out who I was. But in the meantime I'd found out enough about him to keep him silent. I'm not sure yet, but I believe that it was he who lined up Cooch also to kill a kid brother of mine back East."

They'd reached the topmost landing. There they stopped, looking through a broad door at something that stood in the middle of a bare room just beyond.

"My namesake," whispered Doctor Coffin.

There was, in fact, a large gray coffin lying open in the middle of the floor.

Captain Hughes was about to speak when a faint buzzing seemed to fill the air. Then there came a multiple whisper, low but very distinct. It was a whisper that seemed to fill the house—to issue from a score of hidden mouthpieces. It said:

"*Police!*"

Instantly Doctor Coffin had become like a human tiger—a tiger at bay. He harkened to that whisper:

"Police! There's a policeman at the door! The house is surrounded!"

IX

THE WHISPERED WARNING was still incomplete when Doctor Coffin, crouching, turned and looked at Captain Hughes. The look must have been swift enough, but it seemed long while it lasted.

Captain Hughes hadn't moved. His own self-control was perfect.

"No!" said Doctor Coffin—and his hollow voice might have been a continuation of the multiple whisper from the microphones. "This is not your doing." He had a glint of realization. "This is Hennil's work. The double-crosser! Double-crossing a man already dead!"

Captain Hughes got the impression, as he looked at Doctor Coffin, of a laughing skull.

"You were to have met Hennil here?"

"Yes!"

"To kill him?"

"No!"

"Can I be sure?"

"I shouldn't have wanted you for a witness if that was what I intended."

"Then, why the coffin?"

There was no time for an explanation. From the lower hall came the suave voice of the big Chinese butler—Ching or Lee; it didn't matter, they were interchangeable. This was broken in upon by a gruff voice that was heavy and brusque. The voice carried.

". . . search-warrant . . . search the house."

Captain Hughes summoned his hunch.

"Hold it down there!" he shouted. He'd recognized the voice of the chief of local detectives. He and Chief Costigan had talked a number of times about professional matters. They'd been of mutual service. He announced himself. "This is Captain Hughes."

There was a murmur from the lower hall.

Hughes turned to his strange host.

"And God save you," he whispered, "Del Manning—dead or alive—"

"Del Manning's dead," the actor whispered. "I'm playing this straight. Will you see me through?"

There was just an instant of hesitation. The two shook hands. Doctor Coffin led the way down stairs.

It was he who did most of the talking in the interview that followed. He was suave. He was garrulous. He was flustered and amused. Of course, he knew Chief Costigan! And to think that the chief had made this silly mistake just when Captain James Hughes, of the United States Secret Service, should be in the house! Was the chief going to search the house for bootleg liquor?

"Something worse than that," said Chief Costigan, swelling up a little and feeling uncomfortable. "We got a tip that K.R. Baxter was in this house."

"Baxter? Baxter?" Doctor Coffin seemed to be making an effort to locate that name.

"The man who killed Del Manning!"

"Where in the world could you have got an idea like that?"

"It seemed to be a straight tip. I thought it might have come from Captain Hughes, here, himself."

"I'm out, Chief," said Captain Hughes. "Who gave you the tip?"

"I was warned not to say. But it's all right between just us. I got it from Joseph Hennil."

Doctor Coffin spoke up.

"That's odd. It's very odd," he said. "It's doubly odd in that I had planned for Mr. Hennil to meet Captain Hughes here tonight. He was to have been here at midnight. He was to discuss certain matters that I thought Captain Hughes ought to know about. But as a matter of fact, I happen to remember now that he was quite intimate with this so-called Mr. Baxter."

"Can you prove that?" Chief Costigan asked.

"I can prove it," said Doctor Coffin, "if you'll see that Mr. Hennil doesn't break his engagement. I've told Captain Hughes as much. We might even induce him to tell us something about the death of poor Mr. Manning . . ."

The two detectives interchanged a look.

"Worth while, Chief," said Captain Hughes. "Looks to me like Hennil was merely trying to double-cross a friend—or get rid of someone he was afraid might blab. As a matter of fact, our man Baxter was Arnold Cooch, and Arnold Cooch is dead. Hennil doesn't know this—"

Captain Hughes stopped talking. There'd come to his mind a recollection of that sinister thing he'd seen on the floor upstairs. He thought of other things he had seen and heard this night. He had a strange feeling that he'd somehow been let in on the ground floor of a mystery, so to speak, and yet that the mystery was more baffling than any he'd ever been up against before in all his long career.

Chief Costigan also was groping a little. But of one thing he was sure.

"I'll have Hennil here, if that's what you want," he said gruffly. "No one can make a monkey of me, even if he is a millionaire."

Without another word he stalked to the door. There he gave an order to someone who was waiting outside.

. . .

X

JOSEPH HENNIL WAS A MILLIONAIRE. There was no doubt about that. But there was always a good deal of speculation among even those who should have known him best where his money had come from—where it came from originally, that is. He was one of those who had bought his way into the movies. He was not a man to talk very much about himself. He was certainly not one whom people cared to question.

He was a large man, morose, known to be capable of a savage humor; a good deal of the rhinoceros about him—charging blind when aroused, no matter who or what got in the way.

He was one of those great ones of Hollywood who never went anywhere without a bodyguard specially delegated by the local police. Costigan's detectives had no trouble in locating the great man at a secluded mansion in Beverly Hills.

This mansion was the property of a rising young actress of whom great things were predicted—and by no one more than by the morose Joseph Hennil himself.

He growled when informed that the detectives wanted him to go with them. At first he said he wouldn't. They told him that their orders were to bring him along. At that, he went silent, meditating some fierce revenge. He'd teach a chief of detectives to send orders to him.

He was that sort of man and had the power.

"I'll be back in less than an hour," he told the young lady of the house.

As a matter of fact, she was never to see him again.

Very few of those who knew Joseph Hennil were ever to see him again. He disappeared. What happened to Joseph Hennil this night was to become another one of those Hollywood mysteries—today making a stir, tomorrow forgotten.

Not even the detectives who'd gone to get him could have cleared up this mystery. All they knew was that they had brought Mr. Hennil to a house in Hollywood where their chief had told them to bring him. There a Chinese butler had received the visitor and given them a note.

The note was from Chief Costigan, telling them to report back at headquarters. They lingered, curiously, just long enough to see that the house, except for the faint light in the hall, where Joseph Hennil had just disappeared, was dark—all dark; not a light in a single window.

Neither were they ever to see Joseph Hennil again.

For which they were grateful, in a way. The great man had been threatening to break them—and everyone else—when they left him.

Mr. Hennil, in the hall of this house had addressed the Chinese butler.

"Well," he growled, "where in the hell is Costigan?"

There was no answer.

The silence roused Mr. Hennil's ready suspicion.

"Is this a trick of Cooch?" he blustered.

At that moment the light went out. In the darkness, as he turned toward the entrance door, he was seized by each wrist in a grip that might have been the grip of iron tongs. He made a lurch to free himself. He was brought up short, panting, helpless, and knowing that he was helpless.

He was no fool. He'd noticed the size of the Chinese butler. Moreover, he'd been to China often enough in times past. He'd heard of something called pa-shih.

Pa-shih—that was the ancient Chinese style of fighting from which all Japanese jiu-jitsu was derived.

He saw a candle approaching. It was carried by a woman in white. He noticed that she was masked. But if they thought that would frighten him they were mistaken.

Only, he couldn't move.

His real fright began when he saw by the candlelight that not one Chinaman was holding him but two—both alike—so alike that they might have been one.

The woman with the candle looked him over in a leisurely way, holding the candle high.

"Hello, Joe," she said, in a voice that was barely more than a whisper.

"You've got a nerve!" he blustered.

"The last time we were together," she said softly, "you asked me to call you Joe."

Her voice was soft, ghostly even, without feeling.

"Who are you?" he asked.

"One of the dead," she replied.

"What do you want?"

"There is something upstairs that my master wishes you to see. I am merely here to show you the way."

"Who is this person you call your master?"

"He is called sometimes by one name and again, by another. But there is one name that he always keeps."

"What's that?"

"The living dead man!"

The woman's voice still soft, was as if multiplied. There had come a hundred whispers:

"The living dead man!"

Mr. Hennil gurgled an oath. "If you think this is a joke," he began—

"Ah, no," came the whisper; "this is no joke."

The multiplied whisper was repeating it:

"Ah, no! This is no joke!"

XI

"I'VE FOUND OUT ONE THING," the strange Doctor Coffin had told Captain Hughes and Chief Costigan a while back, when the three of them were still alone, "and that is, that it's better to work with the police than against them. So long as I break no law—except, perhaps, in the matter of law-breakers and with your knowledge—I can count on the discretion of you two gentlemen?"

The two detectives agreed. They were of an age. Both had grown old in the war on crime—Hughes in the Federal service, Costigan mostly in border towns where he'd often been brought into contact with Federal men.

"Then you will now excuse me," said their host. "I trust you will make yourselves at home and that later you will find out all that you care to know"—he broke off into his cackling laugh—"except about myself. I may wish to disappear for a time. But I shall not go far. When either of you need me, just broadcast a call for DCN over any station. I'll be pretty sure to hear of it."

"DCN?" Chief Costigan queried.

"Doctor Coffin to my friends," said the strange man. "And now, good-night."

He'd left them in a corner of the library—a sumptuous room—with coffee and a great variety of things to smoke. The two detectives had plenty to talk about during the half hour they were alone there together. With Doctor Coffin's permission, Captain Hughes was telling Chief Costigan the full story of a kid named Delman, who once got away from Copper John.

And the captain had just reached that part of the story that had to do with a room No. 3112 when a whisper filled the room:

"Gentlemen, Mr. Hennil is about to appear. Will you kindly take your places on the upper floor?"

XII

THEY HAD BEEN PLACED BEHIND a tall screen in that attic room of the villa. There were holes in the screen through which they could command every detail of the room, now and in the course of what was to follow.

They saw that the room had been dressed in black. There was no furniture in the room, other than the screen, except for a single chair and the long gray coffin. The coffin now had its lid on. The lid was closed.

Captain Hughes knew—this was that "box" to which his host of the night had previously referred.

There was no light except that of two tall candles. The chair was placed facing the coffin.

"What's this," whispered Costigan, "a funeral?"

There was no answer except for a long "Sh!"

It sounded like a sigh. It came from no one knew where.

After that, there was silence—a dead silence, a silence of death—until Joseph Hennil arrived.

They'd heard his altercation in the hall. They'd heard the thud of his feet as he unwillingly mounted the stairs. He came into the room flanked by the two stalwart Chinamen.

He was not a pretty figure as he appeared there in the flickering twilight of the candles. He was more like a human rhinoceros than ever—head down, his heavy face congested, an evil light twinkling in his small eyes.

At sight of what was before him his face was contorted with a sneer.

He made an effort. His voice came thick but there was no tremor in it.

"Someone is going to hang for this," he blurted.

It was a multiple whisper that answered him:

"See that it is not yourself."

Without any more effort than if they had been handling a child, the two Chinamen, with their pa-shih grip, brought Hennil forward to the chair and seated him there. Then they released him. He started to rise, to turn. Simultaneously, two heavy hands rested on his shoulders.

He sat there slouched and staring.

The wait seemed long.

Presently, a voice was heard. It might have been the voice of the masked woman. It said:

"You weren't at his funeral, Joseph." Hennil startled into speech:

"Whose?"

"Del Manning's. So we've brought him back."

"It's a lie!"

"Sh! He hears."

Hennil forced a laugh—there was a hint of hysteria in it.

"Hears, does he! Can a person hear who's dead and buried?"

"You—will—see!"

This time there was a long pause. The silence grew so intense that it seemed to those who watched and listened that they could hear the faint flicker of the candle-flames.

Through this silence there came a long-drawn sigh. Another pause, and the sigh was followed by another sort of sound. It was like the fragment of a mirthless laugh.

"Doctor Coffin decided," came a whisper, "that Del Manning was not dead."

Something was happening in the room.

The two Chinese giants stood like statues, half merged with the shadows that surrounded them. Hennil sat bow-backed in his chair, staring. There was a look of incredulity on his heavy features—the look of the sly man who has fooled others and who is fearful of being fooled himself.

But, gradually, this fear of being fooled was losing itself in a greater fear. His small eyes were becoming distended. There was sweat on his face. He was twisting his lips as if in an unsuccessful effort to speak. He half raised a hand, as if to unloosen his collar, then let his hand fall again, inert.

And all this time there was some other movement in the static room.

The lid of the coffin was beginning to shake. It was beginning to rise.

XIII

THIRTY-ONE FLOORS A HUMAN BODY HAD FALLEN. Was it this that was now trying to crawl from that long gray box?

It looked as if this were so.

Joseph Hennil had read that story of Del Manning's end. He had probably read it with a degree of satisfaction—one more enemy gone beyond recall— no bone left unbroken in his body. . . .

The lid of the long gray box was heavy. Yet it shook, it yielded. It might have been moved not so much by living muscle as by some blind but deathless will. It was a will that was taking on strength.

The struggle between that dumb weight of the coffin-lid and the thing beneath it became a sort of contest—something to be watched like any contest. Only, in this contest, the stakes were life—or death.

The lid rose. It yielded. It slid aside.

The thing that appeared brought a contraction to the throat of the man in the chair. He was no longer leaning forward. He was pressing back—against the back of his chair, every muscle straining.

Even before the thing in the box began to emerge, it could be seen that the movements of it were groping, broken, disarticulate. It was as if a clotted rag—a crushed and shapeless mass—were crawling into life.

Out of this moil and muck of what had once been a human being, a gaunt and bloody hand appeared at an inhuman angle, then a disheveled and misshapen head.

A strange feature of all this struggle was that the thing trying to emerge from its funereal prison seemed to work so entirely alone—with a sense of loneliness—asking no help—as silent and fateful in its struggle as something from another world.

Then with a quivering jerk, the swollen head came up and around, and Hennil, at any rate, could see the face of it.

It was a horror save to the two detectives.

The effect on Hennil was instantaneous. He visibly shrank in his chair—went lower, flatter. He was shaking. His voice came in a clicking breath:

"Del! Del!"

He spoke again:

"My God, Del! You're dead, dead!"

That which had been Del Manning appeared to hear. The sound of that familiar name seemed to give his crushed and shattered body strength.

He was pulling himself now from the coffin—limp, dislocated, stained almost beyond recognition of what he had been.

For moments he did not move. He gave no sign of breath. He was a mere unformed shape. He was tremulous.

As if some invisible force had caught him by the neck and was lifting him, he came up to his broken legs and stood there sagging. He took a sagging step and almost fell, then another, each step bringing him closer to where Joseph Hennil sat in a trance of horror.

"Stop!" Hennil chattered.

The thing in front of him stopped. There came from it a sound, very small and short, like a cackling laugh. It began to breathe—slowly, irregularly. It tried its voice.

"Dark!" it said. "I cannot see. Who called? Call me again!"

As there was no answer, it began to grope—arms like those of a broken scarecrow.

Now Hennil found his voice.

"Don't!" he screamed. "Stay back! Stay back!"

"Hennil!"

"Del, for God's sake!"

The great actor who'd become famous throughout the world as Del Manning—"the man with five hundred faces"—was now playing his greatest rôle. This was the masterpiece of all his make-ups.

He was playing the rôle of what he would have been, had it been himself, and not the late Arnold Cooch, who'd taken that plunge from the window of Room No. 3112.

Hennil began to babble.

"I didn't want Cooch to bump you off—"

"Hennil, don't lie."

"Forgive me!"

"Then speak the truth."

The frightful apparition was once more moving on Hennil—slowly, brokenly, blindly—as Hennil slumped to his knees. He began to confess—

crimes unrecorded except in the depths of his own dark soul.

Later, he was to sign a paper—a paper that contained a record of his confession. When he had signed this, he was allowed to go. He stumbled out into the early dawn.

Joseph Hennil had completed his career, either in Hollywood or elsewhere. . . .

Captain Hughes and Chief Costigan breakfasted together there in the villa. It was at the special request of their friend, Doctor Coffin.

But Doctor Coffin himself did not appear. Instead, he sent apologies by his personal cook and attendant—yet another Chinaman. It was this Chinaman who waited on the table.

In broken English, this Chinaman explained that he had been in the service of Doctor Coffin for many years.

Finally, Captain Hughes turned and gave the Chinaman a long look.

This was neither Ching nor Lee, the butler and his twin.

This, Captain Hughes saw, was that Chinaman he'd stumbled against in the market—the one with an arm like the blind man's—the one who'd turned out to be Doctor Coffin himself.

But, for the life of him, Captain Hughes could see no sign of make-up or disguise.

"What's your name?" Captain Hughes asked.

"Me, my name jus' 'Happy,' " the Chinaman grinned.

"All right, Happy, I hope you're happy," said Captain Hughes. "But Uncle Sam could use a man like you—if you ever need another job."

The Murdered Wife

THE HANDSOME BLACK LIMOUSINE, driven by a Japanese chauffeur in dark green livery, came to a stop near the cemetery gate, and two women got down. Both of them were soberly dressed, but they were not in mourning. There was sufficient about them to indicate that one was mistress and one was maid.

The maid was an elderly woman, large and bony. The mistress herself was no longer so young—but a small and delicate woman, something of an invalid; and still beautiful, with the beauty of a fading flower.

"I'm afraid," the big woman whispered, with a slight shiver of her gaunt frame.

"Don't be silly, Georgette," her mistress chided softly.

But an observer would have said that neither were her nerves any too solid.

"What if this here is but another trick of your husband, Mis' Lucy?"

The maid's form of address and a slight accent hinted of the South. As a matter of fact, there was a touch of Africa about her, as well—in her crinkly gray hair and her flashing dark eyes. But she was almost white. And she'd been caring for her "Mis' Lucy" since the latter's birth.

"Why should Mr. Mery waste his time?" the lady asked.

"Don't ask me!" Georgette droned. "But this here graveyard!—when it's almost dark! See, the gate's already shut! Nobody else around!"

"You're here, Georgette. And you said you'd bring—"

"The pistol? I got it here in my bag, Mis' Lucy. And if anyone—Mr. Mery or anyone else—"

"Sh! Koki will hear you."

The Japanese chauffeur, who hadn't left the car, sat at his place like a pale bronze image.

It wasn't for him to do a footman's work—opening and shutting doors—when another servant was on hand.

Georgette, supporting her frail mistress, gave the bronze image a look of distrust. The Oriental remained—the bronze image. The two women moved away.

As Georgette had intimated, it was already getting dark. The neighborhood was a lonely one, even as a site for a cemetery.

The cemetery was a new one and, except for a recent event, little known. It lay far back in the hills. The general melancholy of the situation was enhanced by a grove of ancient eucalyptus trees. The trunks of these, with their scaly bark, were a leprous white.

At every sough of the breeze the branches creaked, the leathery leaves found voice in a chattering whisper.

"I'm glad the gate is closed," Georgette muttered. "Suppose we go back home, Mis' Lucy."

"Home!" Mrs. Mery echoed with a note of bitterness.

"I mean our home—your home, back down South—since Mr. Mery—"

"See," Mrs. Mery interrupted. "Someone is waiting for us."

"A hunchback!" breathed Georgette.

Both women were shivering a little as they continued their way. The tall eucalyptus trees seemed to shiver with them. Through the shadows of that park of silence that lay ahead of them there were ghostly gleams of white marble. And that curious gatekeeper who now awaited them was not a figure to lighten their mood.

He was not only a hunchback. He appeared dwarfish, especially now by way of contrast as he opened wider one of the monumental gates. He was almost apelike, dressed in black. But the face he raised to them as they drew nearer was shrewd and friendly.

"Yes'm," he said. "You are the lady—the ladies—who've come to see the tomb of Del Manning?"

It was Mrs. Mery who answered.

She breathed an assent.

"I'll close the gate behind us because it's after hours," the hunchback said; "then show you the way. It's right near-by."

"Why couldn't madam have driven in?" Georgette began. More than usual she was assuming the air of an armed bodyguard.

But Mrs. Mery checked her. "You know, Georgette. He—"

The hunchback—"Shorty" to those who knew him—spoke up:

"That's right—he's—expecting you."

It was almost as if he'd meant that Del Manning—he whose tomb had been mentioned—was expecting them.

Del Manning's murder was still a subject of conjecture throughout the world. Del Manning's motion-pictures, in which that great actor—"the man with five hundred faces"—revealed his genius for striking characterizations, were still being run before crowded houses.

They followed a wide and winding avenue back into the cemetery for perhaps a hundred yards or so, no one speaking, while the silence seemed to deepen with the deepening dusk.

Then the hunchback, who'd been leading the way with his nimble apelike tread and his long arms swinging, stopped and pointed up a slope to the left.

"You'll find—him—there," he murmured.

As they looked, he was gone. They were alone. They peered ahead of them.

All they could see at first was what looked like a small Greek temple up there set against the almost jet blackness of a cypress hedge. Then they were seeing something else.

From this supposed temple of death a human figure appeared, the figure of a man which, even then, Mrs. Mery felt was vaguely familiar.

"Georgette," Mrs. Mery whispered through tightened lips; "it's my turn to be afraid."

Georgette glared in the direction of the apparition.

"We can't quit now, Mis' Lucy," she droned. "And ghost or no ghost, I got this pistol ready."

II

FOR AN INTERVAL the three of them were standing face to face.

The man from the tomb was a somber figure. Yet not repulsive. There was even something poetic about him.

His bearing was strong and graceful. On approaching the women he had removed a broad-brimmed, soft felt hat, showing a wealth of long, dark hair rolled and slightly curling. This, and the long, black cape he wore, made him appear like some Southern gentleman of a bygone century—a fact that both Georgette and her mistress found somehow reassuring.

But it was the man's face that compelled Mrs. Mery's closest attention— a strong face, she found it, with steady, deep-set eyes; a face in which the bony structure was so predominant that she could easily imagine it—in this deceptive light—to be the face of a skull.

In spite of this, her earlier fear was leaving her. It had almost left her—it had left her completely. She was asking herself where she had seen this face before.

"Are you—Doctor Coffin?" she asked.

"I am he who telephoned you as Doctor Coffin," the strange man replied.

Mrs. Mery was telling herself that even his voice was familiar. It was a voice that her feminine intuition found reassuring—low-pitched, warm, vibrant. Else—so she was telling herself—she wouldn't be here now.

His voice had inspired an equal confidence over the telephone.

"Why did you insist that our meeting take place here?" she asked.

"For a number of reasons," the man who called himself Doctor Coffin replied. "The principal reason was to test your courage."

"That wasn't such a test since you told me I might bring—Georgette."

"I knew Georgette—"

"*Me?*"

The gaunt maid, who'd kept her hand on the pistol in her sack, suddenly leaned forward.

"And she knows me!" Doctor Coffin declared in even tones.

His strong face gleaming whitely, he confronted the maid. His face was more like a skull than ever as he smiled.

"My God Almighty," gasped the woman. "Are you alive or dead?"

"Both!" He turned to Mrs. Mery. "Don't be frightened. But that's the simple truth. You see, Georgette does recognize me. Now, I am Doctor Coffin. But I am also he who was Del Manning, supposed to have been murdered, whose tomb is here. That brings me to another reason why I wished you to meet me here. I wished to show you that Del Manning's tomb is—unoccupied."

The famous actor, now playing the rôle of Doctor Coffin while all the world believed him, as Del Manning, to be dead, explained to the two women how he had made it appear that the body of a slain gangster was his own.

Doctor Coffin next produced a flashlight.

The small Greek temple—visited daily by hundreds of pilgrims, some of them merely morbid and some of them devout—as the last resting place of the great Del Manning was, as the late Del Manning himself now said, without a tenant.

As the light snapped off, Mrs. Mery stood for a moment in silent thought. Her slight form was tense. Her small hands were clenched. In the gathering dark her wide eyes searched the man in front of her.

"If I were in my tomb, Del Manning—"

"Doctor Coffin," he corrected her gently.

"If I were in my tomb, Doctor Coffin," she said with a catch in her voice that was almost a sob, "I shouldn't leave it."

"And that is the final reason why I wished to see you here," he told her. "You will understand, of course, the secrecy that was necessary for our meeting—on my own account, if not on yours. The late Del Manning lived for a world that wished to be amused. They paid him for it. He amassed a fortune. Now, in the person of Doctor Coffin, he's willing to pass this fortune back in the form of another sort of service."

"Meaning?"

"Justice! To protect the weak—make criminals confess and, perhaps, reform."

"And—you've included—me in your program?"

"Yes?"

"In what way?"

"Guess! Listen to your heart!"

Mrs. Mery's breast was beginning to rise and fall.

Gaunt Georgette, standing in the background like the shadow of a guardian angel, spoke up:

"You tell him, Mis' Lucy. Or shall I?"

"You, Georgette. I can't. Although—I feel it—he already knows."

"I do know," said Doctor Coffin, in his gentlest voice. "And shall I tell you how I know? For the past three weeks I have been a servant in your house. You took me as a servant because I came so highly recommended by the late Del Manning—"

"You? You were—but you couldn't have been!—the Chinese second man, Charlie Soong?"

"Yes, Missie," said Doctor Coffin, changing his voice to that of the Chinese servant. "Me Charlie—me all-same Happy Soong. Savvy, Happy? Only," he added swiftly and smoothly in his ordinary voice, "I wasn't happy. I already knew—"

Again the gaunt Georgette broke in.

"It's the truth, Miss Lucy. Now I understand. He knows all about Mr. Mery wanting you to die. He was there—I saw him—the day Mr. Mery was telling you to go and kill yourself—"

"Enough!" gasped Mrs. Mery, with a shudder.

She found support against the stronger frame of her faithful nurse. For a moment the three of them were standing there in the silence. They were like three dark ghosts standing there near the vacant tomb, debating the mystery of life and death.

The deserted cemetery was filled with a whispering murmur as the breeze stirred the livid trees.

"Since that day Georgette mentions it has been getting worse," said Mrs. Mery, controlling her emotions. She spoke with a forced calm. "Mr. Mery no longer hints that I ought to kill myself. I suppose he wouldn't trust me to make the deed final—or soon. He's been planning—to kill me himself!"

Doctor Coffin spoke:

"Of that also I have the proof. Your husband substituted poison tablets he brought back with him from Tahiti for your usual headache medicine."

"I need no proof," Mrs. Mery panted. "No woman lives with a man as long as I have lived with him—loved him as I have—and needs ask for proof when her husband is meditating murder. I should have obliged him and got rid of myself. I would have—if it hadn't been for her—this other woman! Oh, I could kill her!—kill her!"

"There, there!" Georgette soothed. "If it comes to that, I'll kill the hussy myself."

"There need be no killing," Doctor Coffin put in softly. "There is a better way. You have seen this empty tomb. It shows you that death need not always be what it seems."

He reflected a moment while that death's-head face of his shone whitely.

"I am Doctor Coffin," he spoke again. "I own not only the largest funeral parlors in Hollywood, but I also own this cemetery. When you ride back from here you may talk as if you had been here to see me about the purchase of a mausoleum. I have a number of them available. One of which will be placed at your disposition."

Georgette shuddered.

But little Mrs. Mery stood firm, her sober eyes wide and speculative with a certain horror.

"I merely tell you this," Doctor Coffin went on, "because Koki, your chauffeur, is a spy for your husband, telling him everything, repeating what you say. Tomorrow, I, your Chinese servant, Charlie Soong—we hope he'll be 'Happy' Soong again, before very long—may have a chance to give you details of my plan before—he—asks you for a paper of dismissal."

"Don't—don't leave me," panted little Mrs. Mery with her first accent of forthright terror. "Del—Mr. Manning!—Doctor Coffin—I'm almost afraid Mr. Mery will murder me—tonight—in my sleep!"

"He'll not murder you in your sleep. He thinks you—may die—without that! No! Leave me! It is time that we all should be getting away from here. Do as I say. Be brave—as you've shown yourself to be by coming here."

"Can't you ride back with us?"

Doctor Coffin smiled.

"You forget that Del Manning is dead. I'm going down to my private chapel now to change my make-up. In a little while not even Doctor Coffin will remain. But Charlie Soong will come to life. And—remember!—when you see Charlie Soong again he'll be none other than—Charlie Soong!"

III

THE AFFAIR OF MR. BASIL DUNWICH MERY, eminent motion-picture director, and Fausta Favo, the latest sensational beauty of the screen imported from abroad, had thus far been kept from the general public, even in Hollywood; but it had already reached a point where it was becoming a source of keen anxiety to those who knew.

And those who knew included some of the leading figures in the industry. For Mr. Mery was not only famous as a director; he was one of the great producers as well, with a studio of his own, an investment representing millions.

Send him down in the wreckage of a first-class scandal and the whole motion-picture industry would suffer. It might even lead to something in the nature of an international boycott.

Furthermore, Mr. Mery had allowed it to be understood, when certain friends and business associates ventured to hint at the danger of a scandal, that he didn't care a damn if it did come to a wreck; and if it did come to a wreck, he'd damn well see that there'd be plenty of others to share the disaster with him.

The threat had teeth. Apart from his great reputation and financial power, Mr. Mery also happened to know a lot of Hollywood's more intimate history—episodes in which several of these self-same friends and associates were themselves involved.

"Mad! Crazy!" they said of him. "The fellow's simply lost his head over Fausta Favo!"

In this respect Mr. Mery wasn't, as a matter of fact, so different from a number of others. Practically every man who saw her was ready to go crazy over Fausta Favo.

The girl was something of a mystery—brooding, slender, ivory-skinned, a Madonna in repose; but, when she moved—even so much as those strange eyes of hers—a sort of human serpent.

It was this particular quality of hers that had, in fact, given both the title and the theme to what was intended to be her first great starring feature. They were going to call the feature:

MADAME SERPENT

She looked the part more than ever as she lay there coiled—a few days later—in the special dressing-room that had been built for her at the Mery West Coast Studios. For two hours or more her personal squad of dressers and make-up specialists had been working over her with deft skill.

She now lay there—Madame Serpent—resting, biding her time.

Fixed and brilliant eyes that never seemed to close, a low forehead, a thin-lipped but wide and sensuous mouth; then that slender but powerful body of hers that so inevitably suggested the grace and lazy terror of a python's.

The effect had been heightened by the costume she wore—a spangled gauze of gold and black and nothing else.

The dressing-room itself was more like a human serpent's den than a lady's boudoir. It was dimly lit, heavy with strange perfumes, airless, cushioned like a divan.

There was a faint tap at the door.

Fausta Favo neither spoke nor moved. But her fixed eyes came to the door. She remained like that for seconds longer even when the door opened and Basil Dunwich Mery came in.

During the brief interval following his entrance he also stood silent, gazing. There was something about him to suggest the water-buffalo, a carabao, that has just happened on some giant python in a tropic jungle.

There was a good deal of the buffalo about Basil Dunwich Mery, anyway, not only in disposition, but in physique—a hulking man, massive about the shoulders, a big head on a short neck hung low and slightly thrust forward.

And dangerous as any buffalo, too, when it came to character—meditative, but ruthless, given to sudden rages, secretive, murderous when roused.

"I give in," he said, at last. "I came here to bawl you out, Fausta. But I can't. You're too beautiful, Fausta. Why do you keep us waiting?"

"Basil," she murmured. "Come here!"

He approached and remained standing. She uncoiled slightly and indicated her wish. He seated himself on the divan at her side.

"The stage has been set for an hour," he began to protest.

She coiled her arms about his massive head.

"Why do you keep us waiting?" he struggled on with breath that was beginning to labor.

"Why do you keep me waiting?" she parried.

"In what way?"

"Our marriage."

"When I'm divorced."

"T-s-s-s!"—it was like a hiss. "That woman you're married to will never grant you a divorce."

"Fausta, she may—die."

"Interesting, Basil!" she mocked caressingly. "What an impetuous lover you are!"

"More so than you think!" he stormed, softly, but with sudden fury. "What wouldn't I do for you! You know it! For you I'd go to hell. . . ."

There was a subdued tinkle from the small ornamental telephone that stood on a low table near the divan. The call was repeated—repeated again and again,

". . . One of your other lovers calling you up," said Mr. Mery, with a dash of savage amusement. "Go on, talk to him!"

"Very well," said Fausta Favo teasingly, and reached for the phone.

She was seated there with Basil Mery's arms about her as she listened. Mery was smiling—gloating. He could catch the murmur of a man's voice speaking, that was all. But he followed what Miss Favo said.

"Who?" she asked. "Doctor Coffin! What? What? Yes?"

Now she uncoiled herself—as suddenly, as swiftly, as an attacking snake. Like a snake she'd begun to vibrate—still clinging to the telephone, listening, drinking in the words of the message.

Then Mr. Director Mery interfered.

He seized the actress and held her tight against his breast, while with his free hand he listened in turn.

"Dead!" he whispered. "Are you sure it is she?"

The response that came over the telephone sounded like a cackling laugh—chilling, mirthless.

Then: "Murder . . . letters . . . proof!"

"My wife—is dead!" said Mr. Mery.

He was white.

"Your work was swift," breathed Fausta Favo.

By way of consolation, she again coiled her arms about his head.

"Wait!" he whispered, huskily; and he turned to the telephone again.

"Murder!— She left certain letters stating that you murdered her!— She left certain proof!"

The words buzzed through the brain of Mr. Basil Dunwich Mery.

What was this—a blackmailing scheme?

But he couldn't console himself that way. In the first place, his conscience wouldn't let him. In the next place, there was something about the way this Doctor Coffin talked.

No ordinary undertaker, Doctor Coffin—that was sure. An ordinary undertaker would have been more respectful. No ordinary undertaker would have dared to give him—the great Basil Dunwich Mery—orders.

Yet that was what Doctor Coffin had done.

Doctor Coffin had ordered the director to come to a certain obscure bungalow that night, where, it seemed, the late Mrs. Mery had gone to reside after their latest quarrel and where she now lay dead.

IV

IT WAS LATE THAT NIGHT when Mr. Mery and Doctor Coffin faced each other. It was at the entrance to a small wooded canyon not far from the center of Hollywood, but with an air of solitude and remoteness about it that suggested a country graveyard.

"You are—the undertaker?" Mr. Mery asked.

The other answered with that click of a dry laugh:

"We prefer to be called 'morticians,' Mr. Mery, especially when we rise to the top of our profession. Don't you remember me? I recall seeing you among the notables at the funeral of the late Del Manning, at which I had the honor to officiate. And now, to think that I should have such another client as the great director, Basil Dunwich Mery!"

"Who requested your services, Doctor Coffin?"

"The deceased herself! Her servant, Georgette, showed me a note your wife had written."

"Where is Georgette?"

"Disappeared, alas, Mr. Mery! She said she was afraid of you."

Mr. Mery stopped and looked about him. He had a buffalo's courage. Besides he was armed. He surveyed the man at his side.

Doctor Coffin appeared to be merely a middle-aged man, simple, not overly strong. With his old-fashioned black clothes and gray beard and mustache this Doctor Coffin might have been a backwoods preacher.

"Afraid of me!" the director echoed. "Now, listen, Doctor Coffin! Just what do you mean by these insinuations—now—and over the telephone?"

Doctor Coffin turned and faced the director. They were in the canyon by this time. The wooded slopes of this cleft in the Hollywood hills rose steep to either side. There was little light.

There came to the director a qualm of fear, almost his first. It was as if he had suddenly found himself not in the presence of a living man, but of a ghost. It was a curious illusion, there in the blue darkness, that he'd seen this man before somewhere and yet that man was dead.

It was, moreover, a ghostly whisper that came from Doctor Coffin:

"Would you rather, Mr. Mery, that I make these insinuations to the police?"

"No! But—"

"Eh, eh!"—again that dry laugh. "First let us see if the lady really was your wife, Mr. Mery. We can talk things over afterward."

They came to an obscure bungalow. There was a blue light burning over the door. A stunted, long-armed hunchback opened the door.

"Shorty!"

The director had recognized that grotesque figure from having seen him long ago about the studios.

"Good evening, Mr. Mery," Shorty greeted him.

"You must come to see me at the studio," said Mr. Mery.

It was a speech that would have turned the head of any star in Hollywood, let alone an obscure nobody such as Shorty had always been.

But Shorty merely grinned up at the great director, and Mr. Mery felt— again with some ghostly qualm—that he was in the presence of something greater than himself.

"She's in there," Shorty confided.

And he thumbed a direction toward a dark room at the side of the hall.

Into this dark room Doctor Coffin had gone. A strong white light was switched on.

Mr. Mery steeled himself.

"She asked"—Doctor Coffin's pitiful laugh sounded through the heavy silence—"that you see her again in her wedding-dress—the one she wore—you remember—when you and she were married."

Mr. Mery remembered that dress—old-fashioned now. He remembered every detail about it—the ruching about the neck, the brooch that he had given her.

He was seeing them again in the long gray casket with its lid drawn back. He was seeing again the face of his wife—lifeless, composed, beautiful in a faded way. He stood there looking at it for a long, long time.

On his own face there was no emotion visible—unless it was a trace of satisfaction.

"I'm willing to meet all ordinary expenses, of course," he said, at last. "I'm willing to meet even certain extraordinary expenses—such as keeping the funeral quiet—avoiding unpleasant publicity. My lawyer, Mr. Stone, will see to that."

Doctor Coffin watched him in silence without dissent.

"But, touching on those insinuations of yours—"

The director paused.

"Not mine!" said Doctor Coffin. "Hers! She left certain letters—"

"Yes? So has my lawyer certain letters of hers—threatening suicide! I turned them over to Mr. Stone this afternoon."

Doctor Coffin let out his cackling laugh, but there was no trace of joy in his face.

"Well!" he said. "I guess that settles that, Mr. Mery. But isn't there one thing you've overlooked?"

The voice of Doctor Coffin as he said this was that of a doddering and disappointed old man. Was the old fossil—Mery wondered—again hinting at blackmail?

"What have I forgotten?" he blurted.

The scorn and threat in his voice was such as had often made those about him in his studio run to cover.

But Doctor Coffin eyed him now without confusion.

"You've forgotten," said Doctor Coffin in a voice suddenly gone rich and deep, "that the dead—the martyred dead—sometimes have strange ways of coming back!"

• • •

V

NOT LONG AFTER THIS MACABRE and in some ways unsatisfactory interview of Doctor Coffin and Mr. Mery had ended, he who had been Del Manning— otherwise, "the man with five hundred faces," and now, by his own preference, "the living dead man"—came back alone to that obscure bungalow in the dark canyon where the blue light burned.

He'd acted the host. He'd accompanied the hard-hearted Mr. Basil D. Mery back to the director's limousine at the mouth of the canyon—had watched him drive away with the bronze-faced chauffeur, the Japanese, Koki, at the wheel.

A silent Great Dane and the apelike Shorty were there to meet the master of the place.

"He offered me a job, boss," Shorty cackled. "I'd like the job of bustin' his snoot!"

Doctor Coffin smiled faintly.

"Take him up, Shorty," he recommended.

"Me! Go to that bird for a job?"

"Yes!"

"Ah, gee! What's the idea? Are you throwin' me out?"

"Less than ever, you bum," said Doctor Coffin, and he made a playful pass at Shorty just to reassure him. "But I happen to know what he has in mind for you. It's a job that you may not like, but it's your first big chance at some real detective work."

"Boss," said Shorty with a gust of awe, "lead me to it!"

"I'll send someone else to relieve you here," said Doctor Coffin. "When you're through, come over to Number One and talk with the real detectives."

Without further speech, the two of them entered the dark bungalow. There, Shorty lit a candle and passed it to his strange employer. Not even to Shorty himself was this employer of his ever free of mystery—the mystery which, perhaps, a dog feels when it looks at its master.

There was certainly that feeling of doglike and unshakable devotion in Shorty's heart as he remained in the dark hallway of the bungalow and looked at his master now.

Doctor Coffin, holding the candle aloft, had come again to the side of the casket. He stood there looking down at that serene face of the woman who'd loved and served the man who'd repaid her devotion at last with thoughts of murder.

"Poor girl!" said Doctor Coffin.

His expressive voice was freighted with grief. But the grief was gone—gone also from his deep-set eyes as well—a moment later when he added:

"So he thinks he'll replace you with Madame Serpent, does he! Ha! Ha! We'll see!"

He abruptly turned aside and, as if by magic, the fireplace of the little parlor had opened like a door.

Slowly, muttering to himself, Doctor Coffin descended through an open trap to the tunnel that would bring him to the villa he had just referred to as "Number One."

VI

IT WAS IN NUMBER ONE—that large and luxurious villa in the neighboring canyon—where the late Del Manning, having ceased to be Doctor Coffin for the occasion, sat long at table that night with Captain Hughes, of the Federal Secret Service, now on special assignment, and Chief Costigan, of the local detective force.

Shorty also was there.

But the powerful little hunchback was keeping himself as inconspicuous as possible. Wasn't he learning to be a detective?

"Suppose," said Captain Hughes, "this lawyer whom Mery mentioned tries to mix in?"

"He won't," Chief Costigan came back with assurance. "He knows that Mery's record won't stand investigation."

Both detectives, Hughes and Costigan, had been hidden in the little bungalow while Doctor Coffin talked to Mery across the open casket.

"I've seen some hard-boiled gents in my time," said Captain Hughes, "but never one as hard-boiled as this one. He practically had a murder charge hanging over him, and he knew it. Yet, he never batted a lash. He saw his wife lying dead in her coffin, and himself as good as having murdered her— murdered her as surely as if he'd used a hatchet on her. Was he moved? No more than a man of granite."

"We'll move him," said the erstwhile Doctor Coffin.

"I think you fazed him a bit, at that," Chief Costigan commented, "when you pulled that line about—how'd you put it?—'the dead—the martyred dead—' "

The late Del Manning, his bony face devoid of make-up, sat staring in thought.

"It's true," he said. "The dead do sometimes have strange ways of coming back. I wonder when Mr. Basil Mery will arrange his marriage to this woman-snake who's got him poisoned."

"Not long after the funeral," Chief Costigan ventured.

"I'll see to the funeral, Chief," said the volunteer undertaker; "and I'll see that it's the finest that Doctor Coffin's funeral parlors can provide. Tomorrow, there'll be the usual notice in the papers under 'Deaths': 'Mery, Lucille R—wife of Basil D. Mery—' "

"Was that Mrs. Mery's suggestion?"

"Yes. She has no family and few real friends, except back at her old home in the South. She's there now—with Georgette. If anyone there sees the notice it will be—well, just another mistake."

"And her acquaintances here?"

"They'll forget her within a week. They always do—in Hollywood— unless there's been a first-class scandal or something."

"Won't a lot of them want to come to the funeral—have a last look?"

"Sure! Let them come! That hard-boiled husband looked at her for half an hour and didn't see that what he saw was merely a mannikin and a wax mask."

"A wax mask?"

"One of the finest—made from a cast of Mrs. Mery's face before she left for the South—garnished with her own hair—tinted, made up, by Doctor Coffin himself. . . ."

It was Captain Hughes who was asking these questions. He'd been absent for a number of days on another case and was just now catching up on the swift developments in the Mery case.

". . . And the clothes were real enough," said Doctor Coffin. "Her wedding dress—the gown and the ornaments she wore when she married Mery— when both of them were poor. Those are the details that not even a man like Mery is apt to forget. . . ."

The woman whom Doctor Coffin sometimes referred to as Madame Jane came in—masked, because of her face, which a clumsy beauty doctor had marred—but her fine and slender figure revealing the former beauty that had made her famous during one brief hour of glory on the screen.

"I've arranged—the wedding clothes to fit me," she announced.

Doctor Coffin expressed himself with that unholy laugh of his.

"This is still another angle," said Captain Hughes. "What's up next?"

"Help us to put on the last act," said Doctor Coffin. "And, trust me!— you'll be there for that final curtain."

VII

THERE WAS PLENTY OF EVIDENCE in the following days that this last act in the affair of "The Murdered Wife," as Doctor Coffin and his friends came to refer to it, would not be long delayed.

It was evidence relayed to them mostly through the detective efforts of one entered on the payroll of the Mery West Coast Studios as R. Boggs, but better known to all concerned as "Shorty."

There was, it seemed, some added twist of infamy in the character of Fausta Favo that had made her long desire the services of a hunchback dwarf as a personal attendant. It was a want that she'd often communicated to Basil D. Mery. Now, even, in this respect, Basil D. Mery had been able to give her what she wanted.

Moreover, to Mery's amazed satisfaction, Shorty had shown himself capable of meeting the requirements of the job.

And these requirements were of the hardest.

They involved, for example, wearing the most outlandish of costumes—mostly early Arabic, in the style of the Arabian Nights.

They involved the performance of various degrading monkey shines for the amusement of Fausta Favo's guests.

Worst of all—but not so much worse than those other requirements, perhaps—was a willingness to accept, with doglike humility, the lady's temperamental outbursts.

For Fausta Favo had these outbursts. She could always be cruel. Shorty learned that. But she wasn't always the brooding serpent. There were times when she was more like a mad jungle-cat—spitting, clawing, slapping, gurgling incoherent hate while she inflicted pain. . . .

It was in a rage like this that Shorty heard her, one day, hiss at Basil Mery certain words that he repeated later to his friends in "Number One."

"*Yes-s-s! You pois-s-soned your Luc-e-e-e, you s-s-snake, but you won't pois-s-son me!*"

But Shorty felt that his troubles were over only when he was able to announce that Basil D. Mery and Fausta Favo had agreed at last to delay their secret wedding no longer.

Not only this, but Shorty was able to name the time and the appointed place.

VIII

THERE WAS NOTHING SO VERY SURPRISING in the sudden disappearance of Fausta Favo from the Mery West Coast Studios in Hollywood. Famous stars were in the habit of doing that—for shorter or longer periods—especially when they stood high in the favor of those in power.

Besides, it was generally understood that her marriage to Mr. Mery, now that the first Mrs. Mery was out of the way, would be but a question of days.

The publicity department of the studio soft-pedaled the news. As for the general public—that screen-fan public that extended around the world—they'd got hardened long ago to the way stars came and went, however famous these stars might be.

A Chaplin, yes! A Del Manning, sure!

Not even the easy-going patrons of the motion-picture trade would ever forget such singular geniuses as these. But, after all, a Fausta Favo! Merely another vamp! Tonight, the most brilliant star in the movie skies! Tomorrow, gone like a meteor!

Sometimes the meteors came back to be stars again. Sometimes they didn't. The astronomer-fans of the movie public could list a dozen cases like that. . . .

Fausta Favo had decided that the proper setting for her wedding to Mr. Mery should be a ruined mission she'd seen while "on location" across the border in Mexico. If the wedding had to be secret it could at least be picturesque. Then, in order to carry out this picturesque effect, she spent considerable time and money trying to find a mission padre who'd perform the ceremony in the ruined mission.

Having found that this was absolutely impossible, she did the next best thing. She found a civilian who would perform the ceremony disguised as a mission padre.

You could never tell. Perhaps, at that, there'd be a few newsreel photographers on hand to grind the screen-report of the great event when Fausta Favo and Basil Dunwich Mery consummated their romance. For all her mystery and temperament, Fausta Favo—as the publicity men themselves expressed it—"knew her onions."

Having arranged these details to her satisfaction, Fausta Favo sent word to Mery that all was ready. He had merely to drive—or fly—down to a certain well-known Mexican resort where she'd be waiting for him.

The resort, much frequented by Hollywood's rich and famous gentry, had a casino that made Monte Carlo look like a honky-tonk. It had a race-course rivaling any. Its one hotel, catering almost wholly to Americans, was superb. And here, for one day at least, Fausta Favo had been feted like a queen. They'd let her win at the casino. The horse she picked in the big event was an easy first. She had the royal suite at the big hotel.

It was in this royal suite, though, that she was visited that night by a couple of substantial but entirely unpicturesque Americans. They looked like ordinary small-town business men.

But one of them introduced himself as Captain Hughes, of the Federal Secret Service, now on special assignment. The other remained unintroduced except vaguely as Doctor Coffin and he also, it appeared, had a Federal commission of sorts.

Captain Hughes did the talking. Such as there was. There wasn't very much.

The gist of it was this:

Fausta Favo would do certain things or she'd be arrested for murder.

"Murder!"

Captain Hughes repeated her little poison speech—the one Shorty had overheard—and added details; and, after that, Fausta Favo sat tight.

She would agree to anything, now that her own safety was involved. Anyway, she'd been assured, her passport had been taken up. If nothing worse happened to her, she'd be deported as an undesirable alien. Wouldn't it be better for her to go back quietly to where she came from and—no more said?

It would!

There were a number of Mexican ports from which she could sail. It might even be arranged that she leave for Europe by way of Panama.

In any case, there were two things settled:

One was, she couldn't re-enter the United States.

Another was, that she'd sent her last message for the present to Mr. "Poisoner" Mery—unless, of course, she wanted to take a chance.

She didn't. . . .

Unaware of what happened to the lady he was going to take as his second wife, Mr. Mery drove south with the Japanese chauffeur, Koki, at the wheel.

The border officials made a good deal of trouble on Koki's account. Considerable time was lost before they could be assured that Koki's papers were in order. As a result it was almost night before the expectant bridegroom arrived at the Mexican resort where he was to join his bride.

There, to his consternation—expressed in terms that no bridegroom should use—he learned that Fausta Favo had expressed the wish that the wedding be performed this same evening and that all was in readiness—and waiting—at the ruined mission, still some twenty miles further on.

To make matters worse, Koki was now reporting trouble with the car. Koki didn't know the road to the mission anyway. It was reported to be pretty bad—like all Mexican roads off the main highways—and easy to lose at that.

It was at this juncture that the situation was saved for Mr. Mery by the appearance of a gentleman who introduced himself as Señor Nitos—"Meester Nitos," as he preferred to be called, for he explained that he was more than half American.

He looked it. But he also showed a mixture of Indian or some other blood—a broad strong face, bony but pleasant; swarthy, but not too swarthy.

He spoke English with only a slight accent and had the easy bearing of a man of culture.

Meester Nitos, it appeared, was driving past the mission in question. His hacienda lay in that direction. Would not *el caballero americano* do him the honor of sharing his limousine?

There was nothing else to do.

The telephone also, it seemed, had broken down.

IX

LONG, LONG AFTERWARD, Mr. Basil Dunwich Mery was to remember that night-ride of his with the mysterious Meester Nitos in the latter's limousine—Meester Nitos at his side, two giant Chinamen, who appeared to be twins, acting as chauffeur and footman.

The car sped on through the dark. It seemed that all that Señor Nitos could talk about was murder—especially of men who murdered their wives.

Then, at last, their arrival at the crumbling ruins of the old mission, where, for a time, Mr. Mery had found himself deserted and alone.

Nitos—the man who had been so obliging with his limousine—had suddenly driven away with his Chinamen. There was no sign of anyone else. No sign of light, nor life, nor anything. Nothing but crumbling walls, a broken arch against the sky, a sense of death.

Then, Mery was recalling not only things that Señor Nitos had said—he was recalling Señor Nitos himself. It seemed to him now that he had seen that man somewhere. But where?

His mind groped back.

There was something about Nitos that recalled—but that was absurd!—the undertaker who'd officiated at the burial of his wife. Could the two be one? Absurd, of course! But why, then, should Señor Nitos have insisted on talking so much of murder—the murder of a wife!

"All right, boss!"

Mery started as an ape-like figure appeared through the gloom.

"Shorty!"

"Yes, sir! She's waiting! Everybody's waiting!"

"Everybody?"

"Well, the bride—and the man who's doublin' for the padre—"

"All right! Lead the way!"

"—and, of course, there had to be a couple of cameramen," Shorty completed. "They're waitin', too, ready to grind the scene."

They followed a weed-grown trail back through a ruined garden. For a while they were following the broken arches of an ancient cloister.

"They say this place is haunted," Shorty whispered.

Mery didn't reply. It was haunted for him, all right. He was wishing now that he'd brought Koki along. He was wishing he had a gun. He was wishing—a lot of things that he wouldn't express in the haunted dark of his own ruined heart and brain.

Then, as they crossed the cloister and came into a little patio, an abandoned chapel reared ahead of them, revealed by the first gleam of light they had thus far seen.

A moment later, Mery had come stumbling to the chapel door. He had then, at least, one moment of self-forgetfulness. What he saw, he was telling himself, would make a pretty effect on the screen. It was something he might use, even, in his current production—the one that his publicity department was already touting as Basil D. Mery's greatest masterpiece:

MADAME SERPENT

At this moment, he thought he saw her—Fausta Favo—standing there at the other end of the chapel, waiting for him. She was standing near the figure of the man who was to act the part of the padre in this romantic wedding—a man garbed in the surplice and cowl of one old Franciscan such as they who had built this mission centuries ago.

Then it may have been a phonograph—or it may have been a portable radio—that began to drub out a moan of music. By some satanic coincidence it was no wedding music, though. It was something sad, something wailing, something with the click of coffin hammers in it and a rattle of bones.

Mery recognized it: That—

Danse Macabre!

It may have been only then that he knew that he'd been caught in some infernal mesh of misery and guilt. His heart failed him.

He was looking at that new bride of his who was coming toward him. Something was the matter with her. There had been some change. It was a change that was making him sick.

He recognized the wedding gown. It was the gown in which his wife had asked to be buried. He'd seen her in it when she lay dead—gray silk, ruching, brooch.

Paralyzed with a growing sickness of remorse and horror, he brought up his reluctant eyes to the bride's face.

"Lucille!" he gasped in a choking voice.

He saw the face of his murdered wife look back at him—recognizable still, but the face of one who had long been buried.

He heard the whisper:

"Come to me! Come to me! Basil! I love you still!"

Now the cowled figure of the padre was coming forward, and as the cowl slipped back Mery saw another ghostly face. Was it Del Manning's—he who also was back from the tomb? Or was it the face of that weird undertaker, Doctor Coffin?

Mery never knew.

At that moment there was a blinding flash of light and several hidden cameras had recorded the scene.

It was reported in Hollywood that Basil Dunwich Mery had suffered a slight paralytic stroke. Among his intimate friends—or those who had been such—it was also whispered that his mind was affected. He looked that way, when anyone happened to see again—in the sanatorium where he'd gone to live. He looked like a living dead man himself, they said.

As for Fausta Favo—pouf! Already there were a score of favorites to take her place.

Down at her old home in the South "the murdered wife" received a package containing a faded wedding dress. With it there came a letter from her friend, Doctor Coffin.

"If you wish," he wrote, "I'll get word to Mr. Mery that your part in 'the second wedding' was played by an old actress friend of mine. He's finished, forever, so far as Hollywood is concerned."

She wired back simply: ". . . blessed are the dead. . ."

It was just as well. Basil Dunwich Mery, in his sanatorium, had become interested in a pretty nurse.

Dead Man Blues

IT WASN'T VERY OFTEN that Doctor Coffin himself put in an appearance at the Mortimer Funeral Parlors on Hollywood Boulevard, of which he was the nominal owner. But he was there this evening. And he'd dismissed his other employees.

This was all the more exceptional in that there was a "case" in the morgue of the establishment.

But Doctor Coffin, as his employees well knew, was an old gentleman of eccentric habits. Nor was he a man to start an argument with. Under that dull and homely exterior of his, there was a hint of power—a hint of power and something else, something mysterious—that always kept the staff of the funeral parlors a little afraid of him, although they liked him and respected him.

The funeral parlors had large plate-glass windows. Practically everyone who passed along outside looked in. Some mentioned the fact that it was from this place that the funeral of the late Del Manning had taken place, The murder of that great screen star was still very much in the public imagination. So was the funeral that followed—streets blocked for a mile in each direction, all the great and the would-be-great of the screen-world there on review.

All that the passing crowds on the boulevard now saw as they glanced through the broad plate-glass windows was the spacious and dimly lighted office. It was very orderly. It had even an air of somber and chilly luxury about it—a heavy dark carpet over an expanse of floor, a few chairs of shining mahogany ranged neatly along the walls.

Then, seated in a shadowy corner of the big room, they saw—very respectable, silent, and unmoving—that elderly man with a grim-set face and a small gray beard. He looked like an old-time parson in his black frock-coat and white string tie.

But most of the passers-by knew this to be no less a celebrity than Dr. Mortimer Coffin in person. They recognized him generally from having seen him in charge the day of the Del Manning funeral.

They'd have thrown one universal fit if they'd known that the quiet old gentleman seated there was Del Manning himself.

The late Del Manning, now made up in his favorite rôle of Doctor Coffin—"the living dead man," as he sometimes referred to himself—sat very still. He had taken a chair quite close to the big plate-glass windows. He neither smoked nor read.

Anyway, there wasn't enough light to read by. The only light in the office was the shaded globe over the polished mahogany desk far in the rear of the big room. Most of the light, here where he sat, came in from the street—the boulevard.

The street was brightly illuminated. A few blocks farther along there was a premiere tonight at one of the big motion-picture houses. They were touting it as the last feature made by the great Del Manning—"the man of five hundred faces."

Doctor Coffin, sitting there very still and watching the crowds go by, remembered the making of that picture. Most of the scenes had been "shot" to the refrains of a theme-song that he'd written himself.

The song was already popular along the boulevard. It had been jazzed and the orchestras were playing it as their most popular waltz. It was one of those things that might better have served as a funeral march. It was a wailing bit of melody with a paralytic jerk.

They called it the "Dead Man Blues."

Doctor Coffin, without appearing to do so, kept a sharp eye on everyone who passed. As for that, watching people had been his principal occupation when he was alive and at work as Del Manning. It was like that he'd built up his stock in trade.

But all the time that he was doing this—sitting as still and grim as one of his own "cases"—there softly played in some part of his brain the slow lilt and beat of that theme song he himself had written—the funeral dirge that had become a dance—a dance of death.

It made him think of that "case" of his in the morgue of his establishment and how "it" happened to be there.

II

TWO DAYS BEFORE, at a certain Mexican resort just over the border and much patronized by Americans, the man who now lay dead in the back room himself had held the center of the stage for a few dramatic moments.

Doctor Coffin had seen the whole affair.

At the time he was not Doctor Coffin. Certain business had caused him to become, for the time being, a rich Mexican planter who'd allowed himself to be known as Señor Nitos.

And as Señor Nitos he'd been seated at a table of the Mexican casino with certain American friends of his. One of these friends was Captain Hughes, of the United States Secret Service, now on special assignment. The other was Chief Costigan, of the Hollywood detective force.

The thing had happened so swiftly that not even these able officers had had the time to interfere.

They'd seen a young man enter. He was of the sporting type common to the resort—well-dressed, muscular, light on his feet. He had a good enough face, so far as the features went, but his expression was not altogether pleasant.

"I know that bird," breathed Captain Hughes.

"Worth a pinch?" asked Costigan.

Costigan, like most of the higher officers in Southern California, was on intimate terms with the higher police officials in northern Mexico. They worked hand in glove. They had to. Otherwise, they'd never get anywhere, with the border wide open as it is and the crooks slipping back and forth.

"Not worth it," said Hughes. "But a shifty hide. Used to be in the fight game until he double-crossed his crooked backers."

"What's his moniker?"

"Last one he had was Lionel Lorraine. That's him! Wants to charm the women. I bet some goof of a girl—"

He got no further.

Lionel Lorraine had walked up to where a striking blonde sat drinking at the bar. Without a word he drew a gun and fired.

The blonde, it turned out later, hadn't been touched. But she screeched and went over backward. Then, before Lionel Lorraine could fire again, even if this had been his intention, the bartender had seized a gun and pumped it twice—just like that!—and Lorraine had taken both bullets through the chest.

It was at an hour when there'd been few other patrons in the casino. And, as usual on such occasions, the dead man was hastily removed and the affair hushed up.

When the blonde was revived and questioned, it was clear that she had no idea who the dead man really was. She thought he was a rich American who'd just made a fortune in Mexican mines. When he didn't shell out, she'd spotted him for a Fritz and tried to lose him, that was all.

She was a sweet filly and sharp as a razor, so some of the racing gentlemen testified in her behalf. But the Mexican chief of police—a polite man and anxious to maintain the high standard of his town—decided to ship her back to Panama where she'd come from. That was all—for her.

"And as for the victim, *amigo*," said the chief of police as he smiled on Costigan, "you can have him, if you want him. No one else knows him. Certainly no one here will pay for his funeral."

Costigan spoke softly to the disguised Doctor Coffin.

"Will he do?"

"We'll never get a better."

Costigan exchanged whispers with Captain Hughes. They were professional whispers that the Mexican chief of police also was free to hear.

"It will take some time to make out the identification," said Captain Hughes. "But he might, at that, turn out to be the man who killed Del Manning."

"*Por Dios!*"

The Mexican chief was now all excitement.

"Control yourself, *jefe*," Costigan grinned. "There wouldn't be much glory in it if this *hombre* does turn out to be—Arnold Cooch."

"You mean no glory for me!" exclaimed the Mexican chief. "It is you who will have all the glory."

"In any case," said Costigan, amiably, "you'd better keep it out of the papers."

It was honest advice and the Mexican official may have meant to follow it. But, whatever his intentions, the news got out. It was nothing but a rumor. Yet the rumor spread. It took on dimensions.

Almost before the smoke had cleared from the neighborhood of the casino bar, the report was out that Arnold Cooch, the man who'd long been sought for the murder of Del Manning, had himself been killed.

But even before that report was abroad, the body of the supposed Arnold Cooch was already being rushed over the border in a special car.

The special car didn't travel alone.

It was preceded by a black limousine in which were Captain Hughes, Chief Costigan, and he who had been Señor Nitos, but was now, once again, the elderly and dignified Doctor Coffin.

They made a trio who could expedite things both at the border and again when they were back on the California side, bound for Hollywood.

"A queer situation, this," droned Captain Hughes, as the speeding limousine lurched him lightly against Doctor Coffin. "You buried the real Arnold Cooch once—"

"That was as—Del Manning!"

"And now you're burying someone else as Arnold Cooch."

Doctor Coffin made no comment to this except to let out a cackle of his mirthless laugh.

"Do you think you'll have any trouble, Del, making him up so the friends of Arnold Cooch will recognize him?" Chief Costigan asked. He added: "That is, if they do show up!"

"They'll show up, all right," said Doctor Coffin. "And as for making up this bird, he was almost a ringer for Hootchy Cooch as he was—or just as he is. Just give me the last best 'mug' of the real Hootch out of the Rogues' Gallery and I'll turn out a double to fool the devil himself."

The job had, in fact, turned out well.

This was not surprising. It was generally conceded that the late Del Manning had been the world's greatest master of make-up. And not only had he now that latest official portrait of Arnold Cooch to work by, he'd had his own very clear recollection of Cooch.

And this recollection was very clear indeed.

What wasn't surprising, seeing that it was Arnold Cooch who'd tried to kill him and that it was he himself who had killed Arnold Cooch instead.

As he made over the face of that dead man now lying in the back room of the funeral parlor—the room they called the morgue—the most intimate friends of the late Arnold Cooch would have sworn that it was he.

At least, so Doctor Coffin hoped, as he sat there sedately with the refrain of the "Dead Man Blues" running through his mind.

He was expecting those friends now.

III

As might have been expected, the killing of Arnold Cooch had made an even greater stir in the underworld than it had among the general public.

In the first place, Cooch had been the chief of a well-organized gang. Most of the members of this gang had followed him to the coast and were in and about Hollywood now.

In the second place, what had become of him? So far, the gang had been unable to place him.

But, most important of all, how much had he cleaned up on the murder of Del Manning? That was the big question. He must have been paid "heavy money" for the job itself. Then, it was currently believed that he'd cleaned the victim for another worth-while sum before making his getaway.

Was Arnold Cooch trying to double-cross his old friends?

"It's the chance of the century," said Captain Hughes, as he and Chief Costigan discussed this phase of the question. "If we can clean up the rest of the Hootchy Cooch mob, we'll be well on our way to the end of that present assignment of mine."

"You know them better than I do, Cappy," said Costigan modestly.

"I'll see that you're introduced," smiled the Federal man. "First of all, there's Chicago Minnie Gay, a beautiful doll, and good for any racket from kidnaping to murder."

"Next?"

"Next I'd put Big Benny the Deal. He's also dabbled in kidnaping and a killing or two, but, as his moniker implies, he prefers a little synthetic scandal and the old-fashioned pay-off. Now that Arnold Cooch is out of the way, he'll probably be playing around to add Minnie to his string."

"Who's Number Three?"

"Number Three, as the mob now stands, might be one of several. But I have my suspicions that it might be our old friend, Ducks Mallard."

"I know that bird," smiled Chief Costigan. "Only white man who ever worked for the chink murder tongs up north."

"That's him! But, like a lot of other crooks, now up in the world and traveling with the millionaires."

"Who else?"

"We've got to find out. That's where Doc Coffin's idea comes in so fine. All we'll have to do is to promote this layout of his and make the pinch."

The plan that Doctor Coffin and his detective friends worked out, and at once began to put into execution, was extremely simple. Yet it was not devoid of those picturesque details usually present in the former Del Manning's work.

An important detail of this plan was to let the Mexican chief of police have all the glory he wanted. As a result of this, the generally accepted story was that Arnold Cooch, the slayer of Del Manning, had been traced to Mexico long ago. There, as a result of careful detective work, the dangerous assassin had been located in a fortified hideout. From this hideout he had been lured by a clever ruse and then shot down in a duel with the Mexican chief of police himself.

Neither Costigan nor Hughes would have anything to do with the deception so far as the newspapers were concerned, but they were willing to push the tale to the limit in other quarters.

Chicago Minnie Gay, Benny the Deal, and Ducks Mallard, and even other members of the band whom Captain Hughes was able to locate without delay, were tipped off through underworld channels that the dead gangster had left a personal estate of about one hundred thousand dollars.

The tip also went out in two delayed telegrams from Mexico and one special delivery letter from San Diego, all of which were supposed to have been written by Arnold Cooch himself, shortly before his death. It was made to appear from these messages that he'd foreseen his impending end. He was in a jam. He was in a spot where he could no longer buy protection. Anyway, he wanted to square himself with his former pals.

This part of the story as well, was played up through those various underground channels open to Chief Costigan. He had a wide and valuable acquaintance among the touts and grifters who carried most of the news throughout the haunts of the underworld.

The chief item, however, in the story of Arnold Cooch's fortune was conveyed to the ears of a firm of shyster lawyers. It was to the effect that around Arnold Cooch's neck at the time he was fatally wounded he carried a small bag containing a key and a scrap of paper. And Arnold Cooch had—so it was said—made a dying request. It was that this bit of property, unless claimed by some member of his family, should go with him to the grave.

The lawyers had promptly done their part in getting into touch with "the family." Some member—or members—of the family would soon arrive.

In the back room of the Mortimer Funeral Parlors, Doctor Coffin showed the two detectives his completed masterpiece.

"Arnold Cooch to the life!" said Hughes, as he looked at the face of the late Lionel Lorraine.

"How about the phony key and number of the fake safety-deposit box?" asked Costigan. "Will you plant that on him here?"

"That comes later," said Doctor Coffin. His dry laugh cackled. "We will give at least one of these gorillas the scare of his life."

And he revealed that one final detail of the plan that, thus far, he'd been keeping to himself. It was a detail in keeping with the genius of the late Del Manning.

IV

ON THIS PARTICULAR EVENING when Doctor Coffin sat in his vast front office alone, the two detectives were seated in a darkened limousine parked across the broad street.

"There's the first of the mob now," said Captain Hughes softly.

A taxi had drawn up in front of the funeral parlors and a woman had got down—petite, fair, dressed in mourning. It was Chicago Minnie Gay.

"She's on time," said Costigan. "I hope the rest of the mob shows."

"They will. But she's the front in the present game. She used to travel as Arnold Cooch's sister."

"There's the next booster."

A second taxi had drawn up and delivered a fare in front of the Mortimer Funeral Parlors. The new arrival was a large man wearing an expensive pelisse over his evening clothes. His silk hat cast bright reflections. So did his gold-mounted cane.

"Him I get, all right," said Costigan. "That's Benny the Deal. He's been out here a month posing as an English lord. I'd have picked him up, but I couldn't get anything on him."

"We'll get something on him this time, all right," Captain Hughes predicted. "They're rising to that bait of a hundred grand like a bunch of suckers."

"There go two others," said Costigan. "Strangers to me!"

"Members of Cooch's old mob, anyway," Hughes surmised softly.

"I guess they don't trust each other. They're all pretty closely locked and they haven't picked a new head-end yet. Each of them's out to garner the purse."

"Shall we move in, Cap?"

"Might as well," the veteran Federal man agreed.

The limousine lazied on down through the crowded traffic of the boulevard to the first side street. There it turned off and after a detour of several blocks deposited Chief Costigan and Captain Hughes before the unfenced garden of a vacant house.

Without haste, but with an eye out anyway for prying eyes the two men strolled back into the darkness of the garden.

"All clear, Chief," someone spoke.

"Okay, Andy," Chief Costigan said. "Follow us back and watch the alley—just in case. But keep under cover unless something makes up."

"Yes, sir!"

Costigan and Hughes went on their dark way. There was an alley back of the garden. They crossed this into an unlighted garage. There were a number of cars in the garage that Costigan, in passing, scanned with a pocket-flash. One of the cars was a hearse.

But neither of the men made audible comment. They walked softly.

It was Hughes who slipped a key into the door leading from the garage into some other part of the establishment to which it belonged, The room in which they now found themselves was cold and dark.

They stood there listening. Then Costigan flashed his torch again.

Near at hand there was a double glass partition. As the light played over the dark space beyond this partition there lay revealed for a moment a sheeted figure on a marble slab.

"Everything set," said Costigan, in a careful undertone. "Doc's still holding them out front as he said he would until we gave him the office."

Hughes moved over to a telephone that hung against the wall and dialed a number.

He stood there waiting while Costigan gave a final look at a tall closet standing near. It was one of a long series of such closets that lined the wall opposite the glass partition. This particular closet was empty. In the door of it were two small holes through either of which anyone in the closet could command a view of the room.

Captain Hughes, at the telephone, had not long to wait. It was Doctor Coffin himself who answered the call:

"This is Joseph, sir," said Captain Hughes in a husky whisper.

"Yes, yes, Joseph!"

"The minister is here at the house, sir, and wishes to see you."

"Dear! Dear! Well, tell him I'll be at the church tomorrow morning."

This brief and innocent conversation would have meant a lot to Chi Minnie Gay and her friends out front had they been able to understand it. But by this time they'd become so convinced that Doctor Coffin was what they sometimes called a hayseed and sometimes a rube that they'd scarcely listened.

That first "yes, yes," that Doctor Coffin had spoken, supposedly to some man-servant at his home, meant that the gang was now assembled in the front office. The second double affirmative meant that the gang would be coming back to identify the supposed Arnold Cooch.

As for the good Doctor Coffin himself, he'd been informed that his detective friends were on hand. They would be waiting in that tall closet of the morgue in case of trouble.

It didn't look like trouble. There was no occasion for trouble—yet! But you could never tell with a mob like this.

It was a mob that had been coming to a huddle in Hollywood for some time past. They were big shots, all of them—in for the heavy money, each one of them, and willing to frame in on any sort of a layout.

The late Arnold Cooch had been one of them, and it had been Doctor Coffin's idea that, sooner or later, he could use that eminent gangster's death as bait for a good old-fashioned funeral which would bring the whole mob together again.

The time had at last arrived.

The two detectives were waiting and listening. They waited until they heard the approach of muffled footfalls and voices through the hallway that connected the morgue with the front of the building. They then quietly slipped into the tall closet that had been made ready for them.

A key rasped. A door opened.

The watchers heard that cackle of a laugh that wasn't a laugh and knew that Doctor Coffin was leading the way. A light flashed on and the room was revealed in all its stark ghastliness.

V

IT WAS DOCTOR COFFIN who was in the lead, all right. He was apologetic.

"If I'd only been sure," he said, "or if I'd known that his dear sister would be here tonight—"

"That's all right, sir," said Benny the Deal, "maybe it wasn't our poor dear friend, after all. We can't be sure until we've had a look at him."

Benny had spoken with a deeply sanctimonious voice. He turned and winked at those who followed over the head of Chicago Minnie Gay who walked beside him, clinging to his arm for support.

"Oh, Arthur," she said, "my heart tells me not to hope!"

"Be brave, Gertrude!" he counseled her.

None of them were using their right names.

Gertrude, alias Chicago Minnie Gay, who had just made that reference to her heart, raised a pair of hard bright eyes to Benny the Deal. There could be no doubt in the minds of those who saw her as to whom Minnie had picked as the dead man's successor. She made that clear—by the way she clung to big Benny's arm—although her pretty face remained as hard as painted marble.

Just back of her, and as close to her as he dared crowd in, was a short thick man—also in evening clothes—with the face of a French bulldog.

Captain Hughes, from the closet, recognized him as Ducks Mallard. The captain had long been interested in Ducks, as one of a gang who'd specialized on the shakedown of Congressmen and Senators—until the government, meaning largely the captain himself, had made it too hot for them.

Now, evidently, Ducks turned his attention to that equally rich field which was Hollywood.

Ducks kept his French bulldog eyes rolling up at Chicago Minnie Gay.

There was a lead in that, Captain Hughes opined; and he tucked the observation aside for future use.

The other two men who completed the party were unknown to Captain Hughes, but Chief Costigan knew them—two of the big local take-a-chance boys, each of them good looking enough to take a flyer in the movies when the opportunity came their way, but with the morals of cobras—and about as dangerous.

The detectives still waited. Two of those they had seen enter the funeral parlors before coming here to take up their post in the closet had failed to appear. Had they gone away again?

Doctor Coffin seemed to sense that question of the unseen watchers.

"I'll remove the sheet," he said, "then join your friends out front. You may follow me there at your leisure."

On tip-toes, as if afraid to awaken the sleeper there, he opened a door and entered the glass enclosure. There came from the compartment a gust of added chill.

The five watched him in silence.

They were silent until Doctor Coffin, having turned back the sheet, had left them there alone.

Then there was a running whisper:

"It's him, all right!"

"It's Cooch!"

"My God!"

"*Pst!*"

The warning had come from Benny the Deal. He'd turned to one of the Hollywood boys and nodded toward the door through which Doctor Coffin had disappeared. The young man stepped swiftly to the door and made sure that Doctor Coffin was well away. He signaled all clear.

"You want to watch that old croak," said Benny. "Some of these yaps get awful bright with a smash like this in sight."

He shook the hand of Chicago Minnie Gay roughly from his arm and ran to the door of the glass partition. In an instant he was standing there at the side of the sheeted figure. While the others still watched him, he flung the sheet further back. It was as if at the sight of that bare breast he'd gone black with rage.

Two bullet-holes were there—and nothing else.

For a number of seconds there was perfect silence, and then the beginning of a muttered riot.

"The double-crossing—"

"Gypped!"

"He never had it!"

"Sure he had it. He had it hangin' around his neck—"

"He wired me just before he died," said Minnie Gay in a voice of thin ice. "He said he kept the key and the number of the box in a little sack like a—"

Benny the Deal came from the glass enclosure with his hat jammed down and rage still in his face.

"It's the croak," he said hoarsely. "I told you these punks get hard when the stake's a hundred grand—"

There was a nervous, mirthless laugh from the door. Doctor Coffin was standing there.

"Is there anything wrong?" he inquired.

VI

THERE FOR SEVERAL SECONDS it looked as if there'd be murder on the spot— Doctor Coffin facing Benny the Deal, Benny the Deal caught off his guard and unable to conceal his rage.

It was the girl who smoothed things over. She had the nerve, at least, to have made a good actress. The only trouble with her was that she lacked the feeling. But she'd managed to make a pretty good bluff at it.

"Oh, Arthur!" she cried. "What is money in the presence of death! Doctor Coffin may be able to help us!"

Benny the Deal forced a calm expression. Besides, he must have seen that if there was any killing to be done it could wait.

"You're right," he murmured to the girl. "You see, sir," he growled, with a semblance of grief, "my emotions got the better of me because of my life-long interest not only in this poor boy"—he indicated the dead man—"but in his sister. His last wish, as we happen to know, was that Gertrude here have a little keepsake that he always carried about his neck—"

"Quite so! Quite so!" said Doctor Coffin.

He noticed that the two remaining members of the gang had now pressed into the room from the front office and were interested spectators to what was going on. They were not only spectators. They were willing to become actors if called on.

That made seven in all—the five who'd already been in the morgue, then these two who'd been waiting out front.

The detectives, watching all that passed from their place in the closet—and ready for action if it came to that—recognized the two new arrivals. They were, as Captain Hughes had previously surmised, a couple of members of the original Arnold Cooch mob—important only as potential killers.

"A couple of junkies!" Captain Hughes communed with himself.

"A pair of hopheads!" Chief Costigan expressed his silent opinion.

The two would bear watching. At the slightest signal from Benny the Deal, either one of this pair would be as ready to pump lead as to open a door.

Yet, so far as appearances went, there was nothing especially wrong about them. They were dressed in dinner clothes. They were correctly groomed. Just a little pale, a little nervous in their movements—that was all. They stood in the background taking in all that passed.

The two Hollywood young men who'd been in the original party had separated—one to one side of Doctor Coffin and one to the other. In front of Doctor Coffin stood Big Benny the Deal—with the hard-eyed Minnie shrinking against him. Ducks Mallard stood aside, tense.

If it came to a smash, Doctor Coffin wouldn't have a chance.

Doctor Coffin, taking his time about it, turning slightly, had a glance for each member of that menacing party. As he turned there was something about that dignified old head of his to suggest a hairy and bearded skull.

"There's a very strange thing about the dead," he cackled dryly, like an old man who has lost the thread of a conversation. "I could tell you some very strange stories of people who were buried alive—or who continued to live on after they were supposed to be dead."

The remark, coming when it did and in such strange surroundings, struck the crowd to silence.

"Oh," Doctor Coffin wavered, "I hope that none of you dear souls will ever have such an experience! It is almost impossible to tell which is the more dreadful—either to be buried alive yourself, to wake up and find that your friends thought you were dead and so disposed of you, or to find yourself embraced by one whom you yourself believed to be dead."

One of the "junkies" shivered and muttered: "Jeez! Let's get out of this dump!"

"Eh! Eh!" cackled Doctor Coffin. "I wouldn't like to offend the dead. I wouldn't advise anyone to offend the dead."

"Say, listen!" Benny the Deal broke in. "We were talking about something else."

"That's right!" whispered Chicago Minnie Gay. "My God! Ain't I suffered enough already?"

"You were about to inquire?" Doctor Coffin recalled.

"Listen!" said Benny. "This is Arnold Cooch's sister. That's Arnold Cooch. This is his sister. He wore a keepsake of hers around his neck. The lawyers tell us you got it. We want it—for her!—now!"

"Oh, yes! Quite so! Quite so!"

"How do you mean, 'Quite so'?" asked Benny. "Do you mean that you have this memento yourself, or haven't you?"

"Was it a little sack on a piece of tape that Brother Cooch wore about his neck? Is that what you are referring to?" asked Doctor Coffin.

"Yes!"

"Could you tell me what was in it?"

"No matter what was in it."

"Oh, but it does."

"Then you've got it. You know what's in it."

"Let us go out to the front office," Doctor Coffin suggested with his nervous laugh. "We'll be more comfortable there."

"Wait a minute!" said Benny, as his chin ground forward.

He was measuring chances. But he was doing this swiftly. It would be easy to "plant" the old man here, search him, search the place. But what would that get him? Even if he found the thing he was after it would be no good. Even with the number of a safety-deposit box and the key to the box you couldn't walk into a bank and simply take what the box contained.

Doctor Coffin laughed again. It was an effect more like clearing his throat.

"As a matter of fact," he said, "Brother Cooch left instructions that this little memento you speak about should be buried with him."

"Buried with him! You can't do that!"

"Oh, but I must! Such demands are sacred. Would you—and Brother Cooch's dear sister—like to go in now and arrange the details of the funeral?"

As Doctor Coffin turned away there was a sharp interchange of glances among "Brother Cooch's" friends. They'd reached an understanding.

VII

THE FUNERAL OF THE MAN supposed to be Arnold Cooch, that leader of the underworld whose chief fame rested on the fact that he was believed to have killed Del Manning, the famous actor, was held the following afternoon. It was a funeral carried out in the best gangster tradition—at least six carriages filled with flowers, a casket supposed to be of solid silver, and the streets in front of the Mortimer Funeral Parlors once more blocked by a throng of morbid sightseers.

Only, this time, there was no great evidence of mourning.

There was only one member of the dead gangster's family present, it seemed—a sort of Madame X, described as both beautiful and mysterious, said to be the gangster's sister.

It was five o'clock—the end of a perfect day—when this lady returned to the expensive flat she occupied in a fashionable part of town.

A grinning mulatto maid had opened the door for her.

"You sure look grand, Miss Minnie," said the maid. "I'd wear black all the time if I was you!"

"Like hell you would!" said Chicago Minnie Gay. "Gimme a cigarette and rush me a rye!"

She'd begun to peel off the things she wore before she'd reached the room where she usually carried out the elaborate rites of her wardrobe.

"Are the boys here?" she asked, when the maid returned.

"Yes'm! Mos' of 'em's asleep but Benny, he's been waitin' fur yuh."

"It's him I want to see. Tell him."

The lady had finished her rye and was just slipping into a peignoir of pink satin when Benny the Deal strolled in. He was about to salute her affectionately but she shrugged him away.

"Wait till I rub some perfume on me," she urged. "Jeez! I feel like I been buried alive myself."

"Well?" he inquired.

The mulatto girl was a good servant. She came in with a bottle and an extra glass. Benny helped himself and poured out another drink for the lady. They waited until the mulatto was gone before they talked again.

"All sewed up so far as it goes," the lady declared, coming to rest on a divan.

Benny seated himself beside her with a bright-eyed smile.

"Did he have it around his neck?"

"I'll say so. The old croak—Doc Coffin! my God, what a name!—even give me a look at it—a little bag, just like the tip-off said—with a flat key in it and a paper with writing on it. A little more and I'd been able to read what was written on the paper."

"The number of the safety-deposit box and the name of the bank."

"I tried to palm it," said Minnie, "but the croak kept buttin' in. Anyway, I could make sure that it was still there when they closed the lid on poor Arnold."

"Poor Arnold, my eye!" said Benny. "This is his idea of a joke—first, getting us all hepped up, then playin' us for a bunch of gimpers. Anyway, he won't be there for the pay-off."

"Have you talked to the shysters?"

"Sure. They've fixed the law-end of it so's all you'll have to do to open the box is to show with the key and the correct number. How about the graveyard?"

"Just like the old man said. Not a house within two miles of it. The mossy-lee—or whatever it is they call those granite huts like the one we arranged for—is right on the main road. I made a lay-out as we rode in. I got it in my sack. And that ain't the only thing I brought back."

"What else did you bring back, sweetums?" Benny the Deal asked, getting tender.

"A key!"

"Not the key Hootchy had on his neck!"

"No, but the next best thing. The key to the mossy-lee! I pinched it off the old croak when I was leaning on him for support coming back to where the auto was waiting to bring us home."

"At-a-girl!" cried Benny. "How about another little one?"

Minnie held her glass while he poured. The drinks she'd already had were giving her some display of feeling.

"But, my God, Benny," she said, "I hate to think of you going into that graveyard after dark. Ain't you afraid? And opening that coffin, and fishing around, and everything!"

"Don't be nuts! Drink up!"

"All right! But I can't forget what the old croak said last night about dead people comin' back to life—"

"Cut it!" Benny replied, with a sudden gust of temper.

And they finished their drink in silence.

VIII

AS A MATTER OF FACT, Benny the Deal was none too fond of this graveyard stuff himself. But it was a job that he could entrust to no one else. He'd done a little housebreaking as a youth. And if he'd been able to get away with that, he ought to be able to get away with this. He wasn't particularly superstitious.

All that was necessary was to make his way into a secluded and not very carefully guarded cemetery, there open the mausoleum to which he now possessed the key, open a coffin with which he was already familiar—he'd been the one who'd selected it—and remove that small "memento" which the gentleman in the coffin unquestionably had about his neck.

Still, anyone would have said that there was proof of some unusual nervousness on his part, in the fact that he was taking the whole gang along to support him on this easy raid.

There were to be three cars. In one, there would be one of the Hollywood boys and a junkie. The other junkie would be in a second car with the other Hollywood boy. You couldn't trust the junkies together. They might get too much hop and then there was no telling what foolishness they might pull. Nor did Benny like to trust the two Hollywood boys together too much. The first thing you know they'd be pulling some dirty deal to cop out Chi Minnie or even turn law—that is, blab.

The two cars had their particular routes clearly indicated, to two different points where it would be easy for one man from each car to cross the cemetery fence.

The third car, conveying Benny himself and his more or less faithful "sparring partner," Ducks Mallard, was to approach the cemetery by yet a third route, where Ducks would wait while Benny crossed the fence for the inside work.

The meeting-place there, of course, would be the mausoleum where the supposed Arnold Cooch had this day been deposited for his last repose. Everything was perfectly precise, perfectly timed. This was no amateur job, and there wasn't an amateur on the job.

The night was all the more favorable, in that it was almost perfectly dark—just a waning moon showing itself now and then through a rift of heavy clouds.

But something went wrong.

It went wrong at the critical moment—just after Benny the Deal had unlocked the door of the mausoleum and entered that grim place of darkness and silence.

Benny was heard to scream:

"He's alive! He's come to life!"

This was followed by a dry cackling laugh.

As this happened, the cemetery and the roads around it suddenly swarmed with police. So it must have seemed.

Not a shot was fired, as the police took charge of those who had taken their instructions from Benny the Deal this night.

As for Benny himself, still in the grip of powerful hands which he ardently believed were the hands of a dead man but which were really the hands of Doctor Coffin, Benny poured out the full tale of all that he had been doing lately and had planned to do in the immediate future.

Doctor Coffin—that is to say, the late Del Manning—was entertaining his two friends, Captain Hughes and Chief Costigan at breakfast a few hours later.

"And they say that gangsters won't talk!" said Captain Hughes.

"It's all in the way you handle them!" Chief Hughes smiled.

Doctor Coffin made no other comment than his peculiar laugh.

Seven Seconds to Die

THE YELLOW TAXI made labor of the steep, winding street, even in low. Besides, the chauffeur had trouble spotting the numbers. The numbers, as often as not, were partially concealed by the roses and other ornamental planting that overhung the high walls. The walls shut in the street on both sides. At irregular intervals, there were ornamental gates and tunnel-like doorways. These invariably revealed stone or concrete steps leading up to mysterious gardens.

It was a very quiet neighborhood, one of the richest and most reserved in Hollywood.

The houses were not visible from the street. They were all large houses, and set far back—luxurious in a rather old-fashioned way. Each was surrounded by a garden so densely planted that it resembled a bit of forest. Each also had its own winding driveway, leading down and out by the rear where there was an easier and wider public road.

But the taxi-driver didn't know this and his fare hadn't seen fit to advise him of the fact.

The chauffeur cramped his machine against the curb in front of No. 1717, and the fare stepped out nimbly.

The fare was a musician. You could see that, not only by the violin-case he carried, but the general looks of him. He was graceful and well set-up— as a violinist is apt to be. There's a lot of exercise in wielding a bow. His face was expressive, with a certain touch of poetry about it, especially the eyes. He could have posed for a portrait of Edgar Allan Poe. He wore a flat-brimmed black felt hat of a foreign make and his clothing—also black—had a sort of foreign and romantic look.

"Wait for you, boss?" the chauffeur asked.

"Please!" said the poetic stranger, with only a slight hint of some foreign accent. "Maybe, they do not invite me to stay. But I pay you now. If they invite me to stay, I send you word—"

"Sure, by the cook!" the chauffeur grinned.

He was pleased with the tip. Generally, he didn't like foreigners, but this bird was okay. And it wasn't merely because his tip was right, either. There was something about this guy the chauffeur liked.

The stranger saluted, as if bidding farewell to a friend, and disappeared into the vine-hung portal of No. 1717.

Two Japanese gardeners were at work about the flower-beds and shrubbery as the man with the violin-case mounted the stone steps from the level of the street. The garden was rich and abundant, but it had an air of having been deserted for a time. The house, a large one, and bearing the unmistakable stamp of wealth, still would have impressed most persons who saw it—if they were in the least bit sensitive—as somehow gloomy.

Children, dogs, birds, might have changed the atmosphere of it. Instead, there were only those secretive, silent gardeners. The whole place was silent. The view, from one part of the winding path leading to the house where the view lay open, was magnificent. In one direction it overlooked all Hollywood and Los Angeles, and the mountains beyond. In the other, it commanded a stretch of the blue Pacific.

The stranger paused to admire this view, as any ordinary stranger would. First he turned and gazed away toward the distant mountains. The sun had risen above them not so very long ago. They were pale blue except for the crest of them, which was a dazzling drift of white.

Then the stranger peered down through a rift in the heavy foliage where a bit of Hollywood lay—almost at his feet. He seemed to be charmed by all he saw. He even spoke a word of enthusiastic appreciation to the two Japanese. Neither of them answered him. Perhaps they did not understand.

"You no savvy English talkee?" he asked.

This time one of the Japanese answered him. Manifestly he was the smarter of the two. If it hadn't been for the worn and dirty American clothes he wore, he might have passed for an educated man—proud, straight, with something bold and defiant in his immobile face.

"No savvy!" he pronounced, with a certain blank brusqueness.

"You savvy who live here?"

"No savvy?"

"No savvy, big boss?"

The Japanese simply turned his back with busy concern as he began to thin a rambler.

The visitor showed no resentment. He had a poetic soul. That was evident in the way he still lagged on his way to the house to admire the patch of blue Pacific.

It was strange that people with a view like this should keep their shades down—strange that the two Japanese, who'd been too busy just now, should have paused in their work to gaze after him furtively, then move closer to the house—strange that the house itself should have such an air of veiled tragedy about it.

The man with the violin-case noted all this as he made his way meditatively, without haste, toward the imposing front door.

A stout, elderly woman, in clean blue gingham, opened the door. She regarded the caller without favor and waited without a word for him to state the purpose of his call.

"I've come to see Chief Costigan, please."

"You've made a mistake."

"This is 1717 Oriole Terrace?"

"It is."

"Mr. Theron Saro's residence?"

Again the woman merely waited, unwilling to commit herself.

"There now," said the caller gently; "go tell Chief Costigan that someone is here—on the part of—Doctor Coffin."

"Come in," said the woman.

The caller entered, and the front door closed. A few minutes later the ample shape of the woman in clean blue gingham appeared again. She was going down to the front gate to dismiss the taxi. But on her way, she stopped and called the smarter-looking of the two Japanese.

"Fred!"

She didn't trust these Japanese. Fred came toward her without question or change of expression.

"You two boys go away now and come back Monday."

Without question or change of expression, the man turned and spoke a quick soft word or two to the other gardener. While the woman watched them, they silently gathered their tools together and went away.

Meantime, in the spacious and rather gloomy hall of the big house, Chief Costigan had stood for several perplexed seconds looking at the man who waited before him.

"What's the matter, Chief," the caller asked at last, "don't you recognize me?"

"Good God, Doc," Costigan cried softly, "I would have passed you anywhere and not suspected."

The former Del Manning—"the man of five hundred faces," as he'd become world-famous on the screen—accepted this compliment to his genius for characterization without unnecessary comment. He and the head of the Hollywood detective force had known each other too long for idle talk on important occasions.

That this was an important occasion Del Manning knew, else the chief would never have called him by their private radio signal from a vacation he'd been taking in the mountains.

"I didn't dare to come as Doctor Coffin in person," the former genius of the screen said guardedly. "He's too well-known as Hollywood's leading undertaker."

"Right! But you'll be needed as Doctor Coffin also. I had to be careful. I couldn't tip you off. Mr. Saro's dead."

Theron Saro was one of the richest men in Southern California and also one of the best known. Not the least of his fame had come to him less than a year ago when he'd married a celebrated beauty of the screen.

The late Del Manning—he often referred to himself as "the living dead man" when he was with the very few who knew that he was still alive—breathed the name of the lady the millionaire had married.

"Irene?"

He and the lady who'd become Mrs. Irene Saro had known each other well in the days when both of them were still at work in the studios. In a number of Del Manning's starring features the present Irene Saro had been his leading lady. He had admired her. He respected her greatly. But also he knew—none better—her tempestuous nature.

Also, the marriage had been one of those which appear to everyone—except, perhaps, the bride and groom themselves—as inevitably slated for tragedy. Theron Saro was already old when he married the young and beautiful heroine of the screen. Both had been married before. The careers of both had been marked by violent contrasts of light and shade.

Saro, the millionaire, had begun life as an immigrant pick-and-shovel man. It was current gossip that he had never learned to write more than his name—even when the writing of that name could make and break careers. The pick-and-shovel man had become a contractor. The contractor had become the owner of a small playhouse—a nickelodeon and dance-hall—in a slum neighborhood of Chicago.

From such a beginning had grown the great string of Saro Theatres, the Saro Vaudeville Circuit, the Saro "interests" in some of the greatest picture-producing studios of both Hollywood and Europe.

No man could have had a career like that and remained immune from the attacks of enemies—nor, perhaps, very delicate in his handling of such enemies. There'd been women among them—many women.

The new—and latest Mrs. Saro—also had an adventurous career. The first time she'd married was when she was sixteen, the next time two years later. Both former husbands were dead—the second of them six years ago. But the newspapers had recalled his passing.

It had happened in New York—in the dressing room of a vaudeville house where the present Irene Saro and her actor-husband were booked for a popular act—"the d'Amours," they'd called themselves: "Jack and Irene d'Amour, Rhapsodists"—great hoofers, both of them.

They'd heard Irene d'Amour scream.

She was standing at the door of her dressing-room. In the room was Jacques d'Amour. Someone had shot him. It was murder, all right—one of those mysteries that were never solved, though Irene herself was cleared.

There was both sympathy and dread implied in that questioning way the former Del Manning had pronounced her name just now. "Is Irene—in trouble?"

Chief Costigan understood. He also had known the lady well in her professional days. That's how he happened to be here now. The chief spoke softly:

"She's in a bad spot. Mr. Saro died of poison! She says he took it himself."

"When?"

"Less than two hours ago. She called me. I called you. None of us lost any time."

"I was in this get-up when I got your signal," said he who was now generally known as Doctor Coffin. "I'm now Raoul Deplanche, if that will help."

"She'll need all the help she can get. So will I."

"What does the doctor say?"

"That's the point. Dr. Vestorius! Ever hear of him?"

"I know him well."

"He wants a hundred thousand dollars or he'll accuse her of murder."

"Where does he get that stuff!"

Before the detective could explain further, the stout old lady in the clean blue gingham returned. She cleared her throat loudly and closed the door back of her with sufficient firmness to make sure that they'd know she was there.

"Mrs. Doyle," said Costigan, "I want you to meet a friend of mine and a friend of the Missus. This is Mr. —— Smith."

"He ain't the gentleman Mrs. Saro and you were waitin' for to see?"

"The same, Mary, dear; and will you ask Mrs. Saro shall I bring him up?"

Mary hovered for a moment before proceeding on her way.

"It's funny," she said, with her eyes on "Mr. Smith," "but the minute I saw you at the door it seemed to me that I'd seen you somewhere before."

"It was probably at the studio," alias Mr. Smith reminded her. "I—also was an actor."

II

IRENE SARO HAD LOST NONE OF THAT BEAUTY that had made her famous on the screen. If anything, the stamp of grief and tragedy that now marked her fragile and expressive face made her more beautiful than ever. She looked— as Sarah Bernhardt might have looked, when that great actress was young and all Paris trailing at her feet.

She'd risen from the chaise-longue on which she'd been resting. She wore a peignoir of flame-colored velvet that draped her slender figure like a Roman toga. Her naturally blond hair—carelessly arranged—fitted her small head like a helmet of woven gold.

The room—evidently one used as a private sitting-room or boudoir—was spacious and luxurious. But it also showed certain signs of disorder as the lady did herself. Both had been struck by some sudden gust of storm.

"Irene—Mrs. Saro," said Costigan, "this is the gentleman—"

The lady also looked at the newcomer for a lingering moment as if she'd seen him before and was trying to remember where.

"Be seated," she said, quietly. "You are kind—Doctor Coffin."

Costigan had already told her something about the man for whom he'd sent out a hurry-call. She'd expected to see an older man. She'd certainly not expected to see a musician, obviously a foreigner. Her expressive blue eyes—shadowed by trouble—continued to study Doctor Coffin.

The newcomer had placed his violin-case on the floor. He was busied for a moment drawing up a chair. The lady also was seated as they faced each other.

"Yes, I am Doctor Coffin," he told her quietly. "As such, you do not know me, Mrs. Saro. But we know each other better than you think. I'm your friend. You can trust me."

"I'm sure I can," she answered impulsively. "Your voice reminds me strangely—strangely of a friend whom I did trust."

The scrutiny lasted a moment longer.

"Did he ever betray your trust?"

"Never!"

"You speak of—"

"Del Manning! You knew him?"

"Better than anyone else in the world. We had—the same mother. We were brought up together. I lived with him."

Irene Saro listened with a rapt expression. There were tears in her eyes.

"It's strange," she said, in hushed tones. "Just now—just now when you were speaking—I could have sworn that you were Del Manning himself. It's foolish, I know." She blinked her tears away. "He's dead. You—are his brother."

"More than that. I was—I am—Del Manning's other self. He made me his heir. Had I wished it he would have made me even heir to his name."

"To me—you'll be—Del!"

"Call me that, if you wish, Mrs. Saro—"

"Not Mrs. Saro," the actress shuddered. She brushed a hand across her face with the gesture of one who would free herself of certain memories. "Call me Irene, as Del Manning did. It will steady me. And I'll call you Del. You're Del to me—even when I look at you. And if anyone ever needed the strength and the genius of a Del Manning to save her from damnation, I do now. . . ."

Without further preliminary or prompting, the young Mrs. Saro began to sketch in rapidly the essential details of her story that had culminated in her present tragic situation.

As for that, the affair had been tragic from its beginning—the old husband, the young wife, poles apart in temperament and training, yet both of them strong-willed, emotional, violent. The tragedy was merely heightened by the fact that they'd loved each other.

It was at one of the Saro theatres that Jacques d'Amour, the lady's former husband and dancing-partner had been killed. Saro had, at that, employed his immense influence to see that she'd get a square deal. It was thanks largely to him that she'd been absolved even of suspicion. Again, it was thanks to him that she'd been given her start in pictures.

All that part of it was straight enough. Thereon Saro had done as much for others.

Irene d'Amour had written to thank him. There was no reply. He never answered letters. She'd seen Saro now and then. But she'd never dared speak to him. He wasn't a man easy to approach.

But he'd made a strong appeal—without knowing it, apparently—to both her heart and her imagination. A sad man. A lonely man. All the money in the world. All the power a man could hope for—power over thousands of talented and gifted men—writers, musicians, actors—power over thousands of gifted and beautiful women.

At a crook of Theron Saro's finger the least of these could, literally, become rich and famous overnight.

Yet himself forever shut out of their lives. Ignorant. Unable to write. Ugly. Growing old. Lonely. Sad.

"I don't know whether or not you get what I'm trying to tell," said Irene Saro.

"We get it," both Doctor Coffin and Chief Costigan agreed.

"They say I married Saro for his money," the lady said. "I didn't give a damn for his money. He'd been a friend to me. I wanted to be a friend to him, that's all; and when he said that he thought we'd better get married—why, I agreed."

"You remained friends?"

"Yes—although we fought. Both of us had been fighting all our lives. But friends—a sort of love—a great love! It's one of those things you either understand or you don't. You can't explain it."

"Where does Dr. Vestorius come in?" the former Del Manning asked. "Chief Costigan mentioned Dr. Vestorius."

The actress hardened. Her shadowed eyes went round and bright.

"Did you ever hear of a poison called 'thanacene'?" she asked. "A poison that kills in seven seconds?"

"No."

"Vestorius invented it—or discovered it. He has used it before—here in Hollywood. It leaves no trace. It simply—stops the heart—I heard him say so himself—in seven seconds."

III

NO ONE HAD FOLLOWED THOSE TWO Japanese gardeners whom Mary Doyle sent away so abruptly from the Saro home with the word that they might come back Monday. A peculiar proceeding, because this was only Thursday and quite early in the day at that. The smarter of the two Japanese pulled out a nickel watch and consulted it as he and his companion were making their way down through the rear garden of the Saro place.

"Nine-ten!" he announced shortly in the language of Nippon.

The other grunted.

"You drop me quickly at the home place. You come back with Iyado twice quick and work next door."

The other grunted. They entered a rusty Ford and drove away.

The home-place referred to was a small Japanese nursery on Santa Monica Boulevard. The nursery comprised perhaps an acre of land under an open-work roof of lath, intensively cultivated, and a number of shacks, which served as living quarters for the master of the place and his workers.

Over the entrance to this place was a sign:

George Washington Gardens
Fred Onoe, Prop.

Fred Onoe was the man with the nickel watch.

There were several Japanese women and children on their hands and knees working among the plants as he entered his establishment. They did not look up. A lean Japanese youth in old army clothes was working at a potting bench. Neither had he looked up or turned.

"You go do garden work," said the boss walking past him. "Ford outside."

The boy went off briskly.

The proprietor of the George Washington Gardens then went to a lath compartment of his shadow-house, the door of which was fastened with a padlock. He produced a key-ring, selected the right key and entered.

It was a small compartment, seven or eight feet long and about three feet wide. Against a lath wall of this a number of frail vines grew with pale green leaves and clusters of star-like flowers. Several of the plants had also fruited—the fruit resembling wrinkled, purple cherries.

Mr. Onoe looked these over with an appraising eye. He then brought down a pair of heavy cotton gloves suspended from a nail. Having put these on, he very carefully—very, very carefully—plucked a number of these fruits and put them with equal care into an empty tobacco-tin.

After that, with the tin in his pocket and the gloves rather gingerly returned to their nail, he left the compartment and snapped the padlock into place, jerking it to see that the link was solid. He then went into one of the shacks and spent a few minutes of quiet conversation at the telephone.

Still without speaking to any of the other workers about the place—without a glance in their direction or a glance from them—he walked out to the sun-drenched street. He was just in time to catch a passing street-car.

The next time he was looking at his nickel watch was when he entered the broad driveway of an estate in Beverly Hills. There was a polished brass plate on one of the monumental gateposts of the driveway. The name was that of Reynold Vestorius.

The name itself was followed by an inconspicuous "M.D." It was clear that Reynold Vestorius was not one of those doctors who had to advertise.

Onoe had barely entered the grounds when he heard the light pad of a horse's hoofs on the sanded driveway. He was apparently intent in his search for signs of aphis on a rose bush as he heard the horse come to a sliding stop just back of him. He cast a glance over his shoulder.

It was Dr. Vestorius himself. He'd been out for his morning canter. He was what some people would have called a handsome man—but with rather too much color, beefy, going on fifty. Yet groomed and tailored to the best traditions of a British squire.

He'd also acquired somewhere what he took to be an English habit of speech. But it was certainly no English hand that had jerked the quivering horse to a stop.

Dr. Vestorius swung down rather heavily from the saddle.

"Now, then, get back to the stable, you swine!" he addressed his mount. And before the horse could get away he gave it a parting cut with his whip.

Onoe had turned back to the rose bush. He only half-turned as the big white man bent over him.

"Hu-m-m!" droned Vestorius. "After aphis, eh?" More softly still he queried: "What are you doing here?"

"Police-mister come to the Saro house early this morning," Onoe replied without turning. "He still there when I go."

"What in the hell did you leave for?"

"Mary send me and my man away. Said come back Monday."

"Why?"

"It puzzle me greatly. Maybe music-mister give her tip—fella with violin—come in taxi—ask for police-mister—Mary let him in—her come out—"

"Damn it, and you leave just when you should have stuck around!"

Onoe flinched slightly and looked around. His yellow mask of a face was very close for a while to the beefy face of Dr. Vestorius. There was a dangerous gleam in the Asiatic's small black eyes, but his lips were smiling.

"No like? You damn it me? You want me carry killem-cherry to police-mister, eh?"

The big man's face went from black to red and black again before he could master himself sufficiently to speak as he felt he should.

"You blighter! Go ahead, if you want me to cable Tokio!"

It was Onoe's turn to change color. Vestorius pressed his advantage.

"Now cheer up and cut the nonsense!" he pursued. "There's no imperial family here—"

"No! No!" urged Onoe with a touch of frenzy.

"Wot-o!" the doctor chortled softly. "We've barely begun. Only three so far! Saro's our first big game!"

The Japanese whispered: "We have not got him yet."

"You are sure?"

"I telephone to the house before I come here—Saro house. It was Mr. Saro himself who answer me!"

IV

NOTHING HAD BEEN SIMPLER than for Doctor Coffin to imitate the voice of Theron Saro over the telephone. As Del Manning he'd had more than one long conversation with the great producer who now lay dead in an adjoining room of the house on Oriole Terrace. It had been as simple for him to adopt the voice and mannerisms of the dead millionaire as it had been for Fred Onoe, that wily Japanese, to explain that he was a Number One house-boy who'd been asked to telephone by Mr. Saro himself. . . .

Irene Saro and Chief Costigan had been present at the telephone conversation. There was a telephone extension in that up-stairs sitting-room where they sat in conference.

"So far, then," said Doctor Coffin, "no one but us four—the four of us now here in the house—know of your husband's death."

"Only us four," said Mrs. Saro. "You and Chief Costigan, Mary and myself. Mary, of course, I count on as one of us. She's been a mother to me."

Doctor Coffin nodded. So had he known Mary Doyle for years.

"She ought to be sitting in with us now."

Costigan went for her. Mary was in the distant kitchen.

"Where is he—your husband?" Doctor Coffin asked Irene Saro gently. "May I see him? You need not come."

"I wish to. He's—here!"

She rose and opened the door of an adjoining room. It was a large room, darkened by drawn blinds. Mrs. Saro moved to open the blinds, but the former Del Manning stopped her. There was a portable electric lamp on the table beside the large old-fashioned bed where the still figure lay. Doctor Coffin went over to this and switched on the light.

The face was older than it had appeared in life, less fleshy. Under the quiet mask of death, it seemed that even now the skull appeared.

Doctor Coffin finally lifted the light and held it close to the dead face. He studied it long.

"Within the hour," he murmured, "I could put on a make-up that—not even you, Irene—could—"

"Del!"

Irene Saro had whispered his name. Doctor Coffin hesitated. He slowly turned and looked at her, his face still in the shadow of the lamp.

"You're Del Manning himself," she said, with a catch in her vibrant voice. "No one but Del Manning would speak like that."

Doctor Coffin slowly raised the lamp until the light shined on his face.

"Don't be frightened, Irene. Yes, I'm still—Del Manning!"

"My friend—that was dead!"

He shook his head and smiled.

"Alive—and still your friend."

It took but a few hurried questions and answers to explain how he'd been forced to kill a gangster in self-defense, and how he'd afterward made it appear that the gangster's body was his own.

"You say, Irene, that you overheard Dr. Vestorius describing this poison to your husband?"

"Mary heard him first."

"There were no other servants?"

"No. You see, the house—this house—had been closed. He was building me a new home in Beverly Hills. While it was building, we went to Japan. In

Japan he heard of this Dr. Vestorius who'd been expelled from the country for supplying poison to those who wished a quick and easy death. There were too many clients—not all of them, perhaps, getting the stuff for themselves. Tasteless, painless, speedy! The Japanese had a name for it that meant 'seven seconds to die.' "

"Seven Seconds to Die! An attractive name! No wonder there was such a demand for it!"

"There was a book about it published in Japanese, by the Imperial Medical Research Society in Tokio. It had been suppressed after a cousin of the Emperor himself had died, too swiftly and too mysteriously, and a number of the Emperor's friends.

"But Mr. Saro managed to get a copy of the book and he had a special translation made. It told how the new poison was the essence of a plant developed by a Japanese gardener—a plant so deadly that even the fruit of it had to be picked by special tongs or hands protected by gloves."

"A pretty thing to escape and run wild in the country!"

"That's what happened over there."

"What became of the gifted gardener?"

"He escaped with some sort of an enormous price on his head. They found out later that he'd been connected with a plot against the Imperial family."

"And Vestorius was simply expelled!"

"His interest in the affair was believed to be merely scientific. Besides, he was in a position to help the government run down a number of the native conspirators."

"And your husband located him of his own volition?"

"Even before we'd left Japan. It was why we left Japan and hurried back. We'd intended to tour the Orient. But Mr. Saro had cabled his agents here. You know something about the resourcefulness that was his when he'd set his heart on anything. He received a code within a month telling him that Dr. Vestorius had been located."

"He told you about it?"

"No. All that I'm telling you now I found out only after I'd discovered the poison-book on the steamer, coming home. Mr. Saro got me to find a passage in it telling how easily and simply the victims died."

"Why should that have interested—Mr. Saro, Irene?"

He again turned and flashed the light over the face of the dead man.

"The light tells you partly," she faltered. "He was old. He was tired. He'd never guessed how old and how tired—he'd always been so used to commanding the world he lived in! Del! Del! I feel as if—before God, I feel as if I'd killed him myself!"

For the first time since entering the house Doctor Coffin uttered a faint cackle of his mirthless laughter. But there was a gleam of sympathy in his own broad and skull-like face as he looked down at the dead face on the pillow.

He addressed the dead man in a murmur of sympathy:

"But you'd give your soul to live again—wouldn't you, old boss?—if you knew what Vestorius was up to!"

"Perhaps—he does!" Irene Saro whispered.

They heard Chief Costigan and Mary Doyle entering the adjoining room.

He who'd become Del Manning again switched off the light after another long and lingering glance at the dead face of the magnate he'd known so well.

V

WITHIN A VERY FEW MINUTES a plan had been agreed upon. Before the regular afternoon editions of the evening papers went to press the announcement would reach them that Theron Saro had died—quietly, in his sleep—of a heart attack.

There could be no mention of poison—no slightest hint of scandal—that was certain. If there should be, it was doubly certain that the previous tragedy in the life of Irene Saro would be recalled.

She'd murdered one husband by shooting him—so the story would run; from the consequences of that crime Saro had saved her, for ends of his own, only to be murdered in turn after having made his will naming her as his sole legatee.

It had been with the threat of an "exposure" like this that Dr. Vestorius had threatened the actress on the eve of the tragedy—last night when she pleaded with him, tried to force him with threats of her own to take back the poison she then knew he'd sold to her husband at some fantastic price.

"What was it—the name of the poison you mentioned?" Doctor Coffin asked.

"The Japanese called it 'The Seven Seconds to Die.' "

"There was another name."

"Yes—the name Dr. Vestorius invented for use here. He called it 'thanacene'—"

"That's it!"

"—from a Greek word—he said—meaning 'to die.' "

Irene Saro had sat up through most of the night watching at the side of her husband. Saro had assured her over and over again that he had no poison. She'd left him only toward dawn. When she returned, a short time afterward, it was just in time to see him pouring the contents of a small phial into a glass of water. Before she could stop him he'd swallowed the poison.

Even then he'd clung to her, sought to reassure her that he'd done nothing wrong.

It was—she said—as if a nightmare gong were sounding in her brain. Each time the gong struck, a second was gone. At the seventh stroke of the gong—Theron Saro was dead. . . .

"Rest, Irene," Doctor Coffin told her. "You'll need your strength. You'll have to be the same good trouper you've always been."

"But when this beast, Vestorius, telephones?"

"I'll answer."

"Won't he suspect?"

"I'll be Del Manning again. It's been a long time, Irene, since I've been able to do either you or him such a service. Theron Saro never cheated me. I'll not cheat him—or you."

"I know that, Del. But—but what you propose to do seems so grotesque, so horrible!"

"The grotesque and horrible made poor Del Manning—the late Del Manning—rich and famous."

"And God bless you now, sir, for coming back!" said Mary Doyle, as she put a motherly arm about Irene Saro and led her away.

"I followed your tip," said Costigan, when he and Doctor Coffin were alone. "I've got word to my men. They'll be looking up those Jap gardeners you spoke about. 'Twas Mary Doyle herself who gave me a good lead on where to look for them."

Doctor Coffin gave a start.

"And tip them off quick that if they find a certain kind of vine—"

"Not to touch the fruit with their bare hands! They've got that. I relayed that to them out of the poison book. I've also tipped off Captain Hughes. He'll see to getting a couple of your men from the funeral parlors here without advertising to the neighbors who they are. But how will you work, Doc, without your make-up box?"

"That's something I always try to have with me, Chief," said Doctor Coffin as he picked up the violin-case he'd carried with him as he entered the house.

He poised the case carefully on his knees and opened the lid with a pressure on a couple of secret springs.

Chief Costigan came around back of him and peered over his shoulder.

"Perfect!" he said.

Inside the top was a large bright mirror. The body of the case was fitted out with various compartments containing an outfit of make-up materials more elaborate than most actors ever see.

Carefully, methodically, the great technician of the screen began to transform his face into a living semblance of the owner of this house who now lay dead. The work was only about half-completed when there was another ring at the telephone.

Carefully, noiselessly, Doctor Coffin—now a sort of living combination of Del Manning and Theron Saro—lifted the implement from its rest. This was the call they'd been expecting, and Mary Doyle had received her instructions as to how she should answer it.

Doctor Coffin heard Mary's voice on the extension below:

"Who do you say it is?"

"Oh, it's you, Doctor. . . . Sure, now, and Mr. Saro's been wantin' to see you. He's been complainin' all night. But I think he's—"

Doctor Coffin, after making a faint clicking movement with the hook of the instrument, growled into the microphone and cleared his throat.

"Well! Well! Didn't I 'ear a ring? Wot? So it's you, Vestorius! Augh!"— and again he was clearing his throat with stifled emotion. "You fool me, eh? Listen! Quiet! You come here! I tell you the medicine did not work! I want it!"

There was a panting, snoring pause.

"My wife call the police!"—and Doctor Coffin, the supposed Theron Saro—dropped his voice to a gasping whisper: "She's downstairs now playin' the piano for—some damn fiddler. I will take care of her and her friends! But—listen, Vestorius! You try to make a monkey of me—listen!— a double dose—and if—you know—under my pillow—ten thousand dollars. . . . Hurry!"

Doctor Coffin hung up—a final touch! with a clumsy and shaking hand.

"Action!" he breathed. "We have less than half an hour!"

VI

"WELL, HOW IS OUR PATIENT?" Dr. Vestorius asked in his best professional manner as he stepped into the front door of the Saro home.

It was Mary, the familiar servant, who'd opened the door for him. She gave him simply her usual hard look.

"I'll leave Mr. Saro tell you himself," she said. "He's been swearin' at you all night!"

Dr. Vestorius laughed his cheery professional laugh. He'd glimpsed the mistress of the house standing in a door leading into the hall. She looked more beautiful than ever—more desirable and frail.

Like all large and "handsome" men of a certain type, Dr. Vestorius regarded any pretty woman as his natural prey. As usual, he was faultlessly dressed and groomed, as sleek and well-fed as a rajah's pet tiger. He paused with a softened look as Irene Saro glided toward him. She was wearing pajamas and a mandarin coat—shell-pink, black and gold.

"Oh, Doctor!" she breathed, lifting her stricken blue eyes to his.

He took the small smooth hand she offered and held it to his lips.

"Heiress to the Saro millions!" he was telling himself, while his head was bowed. "Delicate, alluring, exotic—and the kind of a woman who loved you best when you treated her rough!"

He straightened up his fine figure and looked at her.

"There, there!" he told her fondly. "You see that your quarrel with me was unfounded! But I fear that you have been overtaxing yourself."

"Mr. Saro's so anxious to see you!"

"He'll be all right! And I think that afterward you'd better let me give your own charming self a thorough examination."

The shadowed blue eyes held his for a moment longer with an expression that was mysterious, questioning, deep.

"You frighten me," the lady breathed. "I'll go up with you."

"You are—unoccupied?"

Irene Saro appeared to be faintly disturbed.

"I have a confession to make," she confided. "I called a detective I used to know at the studio—after our talk last night." Her wide eyes never left the doctor's face. "He came to see me this morning—drunk. He's even asked a musician from the studio. It—it—was a nightmare—and Mr. Saro— No wonder I'm ill!"

Vestorius would have consoled her with a kiss—Mary was gone, the hallway dusky, the house was still; but the lady drew sharply back with sudden alarm.

"I hear Mr. Saro calling," she announced.

And, this time, there was no acting in her sudden agitation.

From somewhere on an upper floor of the house there came the throaty, petulant voice of the living Theron Saro, snarling and swearing and asking the Almighty why that cursed doctor didn't come.

VII

VESTORIUS WAS FAMILIAR WITH THAT GRIM BEDROOM on the upper floor and even he felt a touch of eeriness as he entered it, he'd been so certain that last time he'd come here that the room would swiftly become a room of death.

He looked at the big bed now, half-expecting to see a dead man lying there. He was greeted by that rough, familiar voice.

"Well, well!" in a petulant, growling inquiry. "Go on! Excuse yourself!"

The voice fell off into a choking, grumbling murmur.

"How's our patient?" Vestorius asked, with professional cheer. "Let's have a little light!"—and he moved toward one of the darkened windows.

Mrs. Saro put out a soft detaining hand.

"He says that the sunlight hurts his eyes," she said softly. "He prefers his lamp." She raised her voice and addressed the figure on the bed: "Theron, darling, shall I light the lamp for you?"

"Is that you, Irene? Get out! What are you doing here? Get out, I tell you!"

The voice from the bed had risen to a raucous scream, then broken into a gasp and a throaty cough. Then a shadowy hand had reached for the bed-lamp and turned it on with a fumbling effort. In the light of the lamp the hand was veined and yellow, shrunken, feeble.

In that sudden flood of brilliant light the face also of Theron Saro himself was brilliantly illuminated, a spectacle of living decay. The eyes were still fierce and dominant, under their beetling gray brows. They still had the look in them that had dominated Theron Saro's world.

But the once powerful jaw now hung open, the ponderous lips disclosed broken and discolored teeth, the grizzled cheeks were flabby.

The quivering lips formed a shaking and desperate whisper:

"Is she gone?"

"Yes, sir!"

"Damn her—damn all women!"—and the spectral image on the bed had sunk back to the shadows of the pillow again. "Damn her!" the gasping voice repeated. "It was she, Doctor, who double-crossed us. Have you brought me another dose—a double dose? Gimme!"

Dr. Vestorius was cheerful as he drew up a chair to the bedside and seated himself.

"She's gone," he announced in silken tones. "I suspected as much. Her work! There's no such thing as failure with—thanacene!"

From his vest pocket he brought out a small bottle filled with a white, transparent liquid. He played it before the light and the liquid in the bottle took on a sort of added glow.

"No failure!" gasped the old man's voice. "Are you sure?"

"Sure! Over a thousand tests in Japan alone—controlled cases! No pain! No suspicion! Just seven seconds—to die!"

"But the Japs—they are not white!"

"That makes no difference."

"How do you mean—that makes no difference?"

Dr. Vestorius laughed softly.

"It's been tried—successfully—on several of your own motion-picture luminaries here in Hollywood—both with—and without—their knowledge."

"Who?"

Dr. Vestorius, in a whisper that had become purring, droning, and yet with a snarl of pride in it that couldn't quite be suppressed, named one, and another, and yet another.

"Are you ready?" he concluded, softly.

"Yes."

"You said something about a small packet under your pillow."

"Give me the bottle. Ah! Now, under the pillow—on the other side—reach across!"

As Dr. Vestorius, suave, powerful, thinking again of those twin goals of so many a man's ambition, more gold yet and one more fair victim, leaned over the stricken creature on the bed, a fist like the head of a sledge-hammer caught him under the jaw.

His head snapped up. His brain had become a swift jangle of pain and shooting stars.

He sagged over slightly, trying to recover himself. But before he could do this something still more horrible had happened to him and he'd been flung over onto the bed, back down and helpless, with two terrific hands clasped about his throat.

Strangely enough, the mere physical shock and the strangulation were not the principal elements of his horror. The horror came from the unearthliness of this attack. There was a quality of nightmare in it.

It was as if he'd been attacked and was now being throttled by a ghost.

For, over him, closer and closer, came the old, old face of Theron Saro—fierce-eyed, loose-lipped demoniac with joy and hate.

And now, with all that Vestorius still had of brain-power, he was convinced that Theron Saro had actually died after all and that this could be nothing else than his living, his galvanized corpse. . . .

By and by Vestorius got some of his breath and senses back.

He found that he had been handcuffed and that the bedroom was filled with a dazzle of sunlight. He lay there for seconds longer wondering what had happened to him—wondering if he was alive or dead. Then he heard voices and he struggled up.

One of the first persons he saw was Mrs. Irene Saro.

She was beautiful. She was composed. She was looking at him again with wide eyes filled with mystery.

Then, he saw Mary Doyle, whom he'd always hated and who—with perfect frankness—had always hated him. She was crying.

"What is this damned outrage?" he began to bluster.

He heard the cackle of a mirthless laugh, and he turned his aching neck to see what was still a spectacle of horror to him.

He was seeing Theron Saro and yet he was not seeing him. The Theron Saro who stood before him now had the same old face. Yet his figure was lithe and powerful, graceful, unmistakably young.

"Who are you?" Vestorius gasped.

"I'm Doctor Coffin, the undertaker," the specter replied. Again he let out that chilling laugh of his. "You and I should be working together."

Suddenly the room seemed to fill with detectives. As a matter of fact, there were only two of them, Chief Costigan, of Hollywood force, and Captain Hughes, of the Federal Secret Service, now on special assignment.

"We got a wagon for you down below with your Jap friends in it," Costigan told the prisoner with a smile.

"And Japan'll be wanting them all again if California doesn't," said Captain Hughes.

"When California's through with them, Japan can have them," Costigan made cryptic reply.

On his way out Vestorius took a last look at that mysterious Doctor Coffin. He saw the human enigma helping poor old Mary Doyle dry her tears.

Horror House

DOCTOR COFFIN LOOKED LONG AT THE STRANGE NOTE that had been handed him just as he was leaving the darkened theatre. He'd taken it mechanically. He hadn't noticed who'd handed it to him—an usher he'd supposed, as a matter of course. The ushers in this particular motion-picture house were always passing out advance notices. Only now, here in the lobby, had he seen that it was an envelope he held and that his name was printed on it:

DR. MORTIMER COFFIN

These letters were in ink and had been neatly done. But under them was the word "Private" awkwardly scrawled in pencil.

The deduction was clear. The letter, whatever it was, had been prepared in advance, evidently with a certain amount of care. The word "Private" had been an afterthought, probably written in the darkness of the theatre.

There were other deductions to be drawn, of course. The person who'd handed him the letter had manifestly not wished to be seen. This meant fear. Whoever had handed him the envelope just now must have known him, by sight, at least, and followed him into the theatre from the street.

But why the hesitation? Why the disguised handwriting? Why the delivery of the message in the dark? Why—the fear?

The processes of Doctor Coffin's thinking were always of an unusual rapidity. So far, but a couple of seconds had slipped by since his first glance at the envelope.

Another thought occurred to him.

The mysterious messenger would certainly follow him to see what he did with the communication. He might toss it aside.

Hollywood was infested by advertising rackets. The messenger had had a misgiving that Doctor Coffin might think that this communication was such a fake.

Not that Doctor Coffin, the well-known "mortician," proprietor of The Mortimer Funeral Parlors, looked hard-boiled or worldly-wise. Nothing like that. He looked more like a country parson—kindly, calm, and a little stupid—as he stood there now in the lobby of the picture palace with the odd message in his hand.

Hollywood was full of types like him, mostly from Iowa—getting a little old, dressed in black. As a matter of fact his chief claim to fame was that the late Del Manning, the greatest character actor the screen had ever known—"the man with five hundred faces"—had been buried from his establishment.

No one but a very few knew that that funeral itself had been a fake. There would have been a riot had it become known that this innocent "old" gentleman standing here now was none other than Del Manning himself.

Doctor Coffin was slow in his movements and also, apparently, in his thought.

Anyone watching him would have seen his shock of surprised perplexity when he saw his name on the envelope. Evidently he didn't see very well without his glasses. Anyway, the light was poor where he stood.

In a confused and doddering way he advanced to one of the ornamental lights bracketed against the wall of the theatre's lobby and took another look, holding the letter away from him and twisting his head to get a better focus. He then, very deliberately, brought out his steel-rimmed glasses. He held the envelope in his teeth as he used both hands to polish the glasses and adjust them.

At least part of the mystery was cleared up for him as he was doing this. He'd already suspected that the scrawled word in pencil on the envelope had been put there by a woman. He saw her, unmistakably, during his by-play with the glasses.

He was a little shocked when he saw her. She was a young actress he'd known well when he was still working in the studios. He'd known her well although she'd never known him well. That had been his chief occupation, even in his acting days—knowing people well, studying them. But no one had ever known Del Manning well.

And in those days—only a few months ago—she had been beautiful, robust, full of vitality and what the French call the joy of living. Now, she looked—like a ghost of herself.

There was a crowd drifting back and forth through the lobby. She was watching him but keeping as much as possible out of sight.

"Arlene Perin!" the girl's name came back to him.

By this time he'd gotten his glasses adjusted. With hands that looked a little nervous and awkward he tore the envelope open and pulled out the sheet of paper within.

The message also had been printed by hand. He was not surprised to see that there was no signature. While he was apparently reading the communications with an air of bewildered interest he saw Arlene Perin saunter toward an exit and disappear.

He started to follow her.

As for the message, it was already photographed in his receptive mind. As a camera might, he'd caught it at a glance. Anyway, it was brief enough:

DOCTOR COFFIN PLEASE COME PERSONALLY AT ONCE TO 11-S

ECHO CANYON. OH PLEASE FOR GOD'S SAKE. FORGIVE THIS
SECRECY. WILL EXPLAIN.

II

ON LEAVING THE THEATRE, Arlene Perin had paused in front of a shop-window.
It was a large bright window attractively dressed with artificial orchids, the
portraits of several of the reigning queens of Hollywood, and a display of
the latest in Paris fashions. But while Miss Perin pretended to look at a hat,
Doctor Coffin could see that her chief interest was still concentrated in his
own not very attractive self.

The girl, in spite of her haunted look, was still beautiful. Her clothes,
while not expensive or new, had that touch of "chic" about them that most
girls coming to Hollywood rapidly acquire and never lose.

Doctor Coffin himself had come to a pause on the sidewalk—apparently
an old man who had difficulty in making up his mind. He allowed the good-
natured crowd of strollers to jostle him a bit. He was getting in people's way
but neither they nor he minded this very much.

The movement had brought him closer to where Arlene Perin stood.

She was near enough to hear him when he stopped a young man and
inquired the whereabouts of Echo Canyon.

"Goin' to walk or ride?" the young man asked.

"Eh?" asked Doctor Coffin, cupping a hand behind his ear.

"Ride or walk?" the young man raised his voice.

"Why," Doctor Coffin replied, "I'm a little late and I've got a friend from
back home—"

"Take a taxi," the young man advised. . . .

Even during this brief interchange, designed especially by Doctor Coffin
to let Arlene Perin know that he was on his way, he saw that he wasn't the
only one who had his veiled attention fixed on the girl.

From the crowd of strollers a man had brushed close to her and also was
making pretense of looking at the window-display. He was heavy, powerful,
swarthy, and overdressed. That the girl recognized him or, in any case,
divined his intention of speaking to her, was clear. It was equally clear that
she regarded him with loathing.

She'd started to move away. "Hold on!"—the newcomer commanded in
a sharp undertone.

She stopped.

"Where you been?"

"Home!"

"Give him a ring."

"I—"

"You'd better. Godoy wants to see you."

Arlene Perin gasped.

Just then her wide and startled eyes met the eyes of Doctor Coffin. In them she saw a look of such intensity that she was vaguely, fleetingly reminded of the way Del Manning, the great character actor, had once looked at her when they were playing a scene together. And just as the great Del Manning might have given her a cue with those compelling eyes of his, so was this elderly undertaker now giving her a cue.

"All right," she said—and it was a message to both the swarthy man at her side and to the elderly gentleman who looked like a retired preacher.

And a moment later the little group of three had dissolved in the drift of the crowd as three bits of flotsam, brought together by accident, might separate again in the drift of a river.

But the girl was waiting for him as Doctor Coffin turned the corner into the nearest side-street. He knew she would be. She was standing a little back in the shadows of an unfenced garden.

"Scram!" he warned her in a whisper as he walked slowly past. "He's watching."

The girl was intelligent. She said nothing. She faded into the darkness of the garden in the direction of the house.

He himself disappeared, a little farther on, behind the double concealment of a parked car and the swaying shadows of an ancient pepper-tree. After a minute or so he was rewarded by seeing the stout and swarthy individual who'd addressed the girl stroll back in the direction of the boulevard, satisfied, apparently, that he'd discovered Arlene Perin's home.

Doctor Coffin slowly retraced his steps. This time he paused as he saw the figure of the girl in the shadows of the garden. Her face was more ghostly than ever as she peered at him through the shadows with a questioning look.

"All right, Miss Perin," he told her.

"You know me?"

"And I also know you gave me that note just now. Meet me in half an hour at the address in Echo Canyon and see—that you are not followed—by Malibu Mex."

III

Echo Canyon was a narrow valley, steep and twisting, back in the Hollywood hills. It was about the nearest thing to a motion-picture "colony" that Hollywood possessed. It was much patronized by the poorer class of studio-workers—exceedingly numerous just now—because it was cheap. It was patronized by the comparatively rich and famous because of its seclusion.

A free and easy neighborhood. One where no questions were asked. One where no kicks were registered unless things got too noisy—and not even then, if the party-throwers happened to be good neighbors. Autos came and went all night—everything from cut-down jits to imperial limousines.

Doctor Coffin knew the canyon well. He'd lived there himself when he was Del Manning and Del Manning was not yet famous. He'd come up to the canyon by taxi considerably before the allotted half-hour had elapsed. But he'd given the taxi driver a false address and still had some way to walk.

"Eleven-S," the address that Arlene Perin had given him in her anonymous note, was off the main highway. It would be one of the tiny shacks stuck high up against the wooded hillside above the place where he stood.

As soon as the taxi was gone he struck into a dark footpath that made a short-cut to the upper roads. Nothing had changed since he'd been here years ago. Dogs barked. Pianos jangled. Radios crooned and orated.

The shacks and bungalows were like a town of playhouses built for children. So they were, Doctor Coffin opined, as he nimbly mounted the steep and winding path. This was one of those places where the children of Hollywood grew up. Not the kid-actors, like the Coogans. But the boys and girls who came sailing into Hollywood—every month, and every day of the month, of every year—as to a port of dreams, only to find shipwreck there.

It wasn't like Doctor Coffin to let himself go very far in sentimental imaginings. Not when he had business ahead of him. His business was of a nature to forestall such broodings. But he'd sort of fallen under the influence of the old neighborhood, he guessed.

Without difficulty he found No. 11-S on one of the upper levels. It was a shabby little place, not much larger than a one-car garage, in which respect it differed none from a hundred others in the neighborhood. But an effort had been made to embellish it to some extent with flowers—geraniums mostly, as Doctor Coffin could tell by the aroma of them although it was too dark to see. There were no lights at all on these upper roads, except such as shone from an occasional window.

The windows of No. 11-S were still dark. Evidently, Arlene Perin had not yet returned.

Doctor Coffin seated himself to wait.

Again he'd let himself go in his brooding, with the familiar scents and sounds of Echo Canyon keeping him company there in the darkness, when he saw two dark and silent shapes advancing along the dim track of the road. Doctor Coffin, dressed in his habitual black and invisible in the darkness, drew himself silently behind a clump of sage.

The two figures—men, he could see, and that was all—had come to a furtive halt in front of the dark little building.

"Arlene's not here," one of them said softly.

"So much the better!"

"Would she have left the kid alone?"

"We got to see."

"Suppose she comes back while—"

"Stall her! I thought you had some guts!"

"All right. You go in. I'll stall."

"And don't let her squawk."

"She won't have a chance."

The shadows separated, one of them remaining in front and the other going around to the back of the dark bungalow.

Doctor Coffin had been creeping steadily forward through the darkness. The sand and disintegrated granite over which he crept were friendly to silence. The scattered brush and darkness were helping him.

He waited until a faint sound from the back told him that the man who'd passed to the rear was occupied with a jimmy.

He didn't even speak as he reared up in the darkness and shoved the muzzle of a pistol against the back of the lookout's neck.

The lookout had uttered a gasp, almost a cry—a cry with a shudder in it—a cry that was almost instantly hushed by a warning hiss and also the feel of that bit of steel against his neck.

"Up!" came an all but breathless whisper, and the lookout put up his hands.

He didn't have to be told the rest of it, just then. He had a good idea of what would happen if he made a noise. He felt himself swiftly and thoroughly gone over. In a few seconds he'd lost a pistol of his own, a coil of picture-wire and a roll of heavy adhesive tape.

Next a hand that felt like a hand of steel had taken a grip in his hair, and it was more in response to the compulsion of it than to the faintly whispered command that reached him that he sagged to the earth and lay there flat, face-down.

One thing he was sure of. He was in the hands of an expert—a super-expert. No ordinary crook he'd ever met or officer either—whether harness-bull or dick, Burns or Pink, or the dreaded "snakes"—the SS's, the Secret Service men of Washington—could have been more expert than this man he'd never seen but who'd taken such complete charge of him now.

The lookout was being gagged and "sewed up" with his own tape and wire—not roughly, nor gently either; but with the swift and merciless efficiency of a steel machine.

The man on the ground was as silent and as helpless as a mummy. He'd been left there like that, still without a word.

At least he could still hear.

He heard a taxi climbing the hill-road, sputtering and back-firing now and then as it came.

He heard a—shot! Or was it just another backfire?

IV

DOCTOR COFFIN HAD HAD A NARROW ESCAPE. The approach of the taxi had evidently worried the man with the jimmy and started him back the way he'd come. He'd collided with someone at the door. It was a split-second before he discovered that the man he'd run into was a stranger. Just as he fired, one of the stranger's hands had gripped his pistol-wrist and the other, in a fist like a rock, had jolted his solar-plexus.

With a final back-fire explosion the balky taxi had come to a halt in front of the bungalow. Doctor Coffin was there waiting for her as Arlene Perin got down.

"Let me pay," he commanded her softly.

She protested, but there was something strangely masterful about this elderly man. Here in the faint light of the taxi she caught a momentary flash of his face—sober, broad, with deep-set eyes. There was nothing that frightened her about that face but it reminded her somewhat of a living skull—a skull that was thoughtful, slightly luminous. She wondered where she had seen a face like that before.

"I have money," she started to protest.

Doctor Coffin cackled a note or two of dry laughter. Where Arlene Perin wondered—had she heard a laugh like that before?

The taxi rolled on its way and they faced each other.

"I'm sorry," she apologized, "that I let you get here first."

"It's just as well," said Doctor Coffin. "You had a couple of visitors?"

He told her what had happened and she listened to him with horror. It was an exaggerated horror—almost a theatrical horror—he was inclined to think at first.

He'd barely completed his brief account of the two intruders when he heard a scrambling in the brush at the back of the little house.

"That's one of them now," he cried swiftly, and he rushed away.

He was too late. The man who'd fired at him and who'd been knocked out hadn't been properly tied up. To search for him now in this dark maze of a thousand hiding-places would be a waste of time. At least one of the pair was still safe and—he could be made to talk.

He collared his captive on the way back to join Miss Perin.

She'd been waiting for him on the dark little porch.

"If you don't mind," Doctor Coffin suggested, "I'll bring him in when you've turned on the light. Maybe you'll recognize him."

For the first time since his capture, the fellow began to struggle. It was evidently a struggle of protest more than an effort to escape. Escape was impossible. He must have been satisfied of that. He was working his jaws in their plaster of tape and there was a strangled sound in his throat as he tried to speak.

"Wait!" whispered Miss Perin.

And from her sack she brought out a box of matches. She lit a match and held it toward the prisoner's face with a trembling hand.

The prisoner shrank from her scrutiny.

She'd recognized him, all right, and he'd recognized her. Both faces were outlined as if with fire for a few seconds in the flickering light of the match. The man's face was that of a blood-sucking weasel surprised at its work and rendered still more savage by fear. The girl's face was a mask of mingled rage and grief.

"You!"

She'd put such fury in this exclamation that it was equivalent to a curse. And she'd have thrust the half-burnt match into his face if Doctor Coffin hadn't restrained her.

Again he'd thought that her grief, her rage, whatever the emotions that were moving her, were a trifle exaggerated, a trifle theatrical.

"Who is he?" he asked.

"One of the creatures from Godoy's place," she panted. Her voice was almost a sob. She'd spoken with an effort. If she was acting, her acting was superb.

"What's his name?"

"Mikhal! We called him that."

"Shall I bring him in?"

"No! No!" she cried softly. "Oh, for God's sake!"

"Steady, Arlene! You don't want him to get away. That friend of his might be coming back."

"You're right," she said, fighting for self-control. "But the back way! The back way! I'll help you!"

It wasn't until they'd disposed of Mikhal in a tiny combination kitchen and laundry at the rear—and in such a fashion as would hold him safe whatever happened for a while—that Doctor Coffin discovered at least one sufficient cause for what he'd believed to be the girl's excess of emotion.

He'd followed her into the front room of the little house—the only real room that the place could boast. There Arlene Perin had switched on a shaded light. And Doctor Coffin saw the body of a girl—just the white shadow of what had been a girl—lying on a narrow white bed.

It had taken him but a glance to see that she was dead. She had that same look of ghostliness about her—of sapped and exhausted youth and beauty that he'd remarked in Arlene Perin herself. And someone—Arlene herself, he guessed—had surrounded the girl on the bed with geraniums and branches of wild sage.

"My little sister," Arlene whispered.

"Olga? I remember her!" said Doctor Coffin. "How did she die?"

"Murdered! By—Vampires!"

V

LATER THAT NIGHT—not much later—Doctor Coffin, the former Del Manning, was holding a council of war with his two trusted friends, Captain Hughes, of the Federal service, now on special assignment in Hollywood, and Chief Costigan of the Hollywood detective force.

They'd assembled in Doctor Coffin's luxurious residence in Oakwood Canyon, the place he generally referred to as Villa Number One.

Neither Captain Hughes nor Chief Costigan had arrived there in a way to attract the attention of neighbors—or, for that matter, of either enemies or friends that might have been interested in their whereabouts. Both had arrived by way of a tunnel connecting "Number One" with "Number Two"— the obscure little bungalow beyond the steep but narrow mountain ridge just back of Number One.

"Why did Miss Perin think of you in the first place, Doc?" asked Captain Hughes.

"She wanted an undertaker—the best there was."

"When she had no money!"

"That part's easy," Chief Costigan put in. "All the actors in Hollywood— even the extras—know the Doc will take care of them, rich or poor."

"Did she explain why she slipped you the anonymous letter in the dark?"

"Yes. There'd been a crime. A crime that couldn't be explained in just a few words. Nor one that she'd like to see tied up with her dead sister's name. Besides, she was scared stiff. She felt that she was surrounded by enemies—which was pretty near the truth."

"She wanted to keep the crime part of it dark?"

"On the contrary. That was another angle. She'd seen me talking in a friendly way with the Chief, here, on the boulevard one day. She wanted my advice on getting the matter to the cops."

"Where does Malibu Mex come in—the big bird that spoke to her on the boulevard while she was waiting to see what you were going to do? I've had him on my list for a long time—tout, crooked gambler, dope-ringer."

"Mex, she says, was one of the customers at Godoy's combination sanitarium and roadhouse. And not one of the biggest of them, either. He may have a cut in the take of the joint, at that. He used to have a rep for muscling in."

"He still has," said Chief Costigan. "I'm having him brought in, anyway. Let's see what the boys are doing." He reached over to a convenient telephone and spoke into it softly. His wait was brief. "They have him," he announced, returning the instrument to its place. "And he won't be slipping out on us this time, either. We've got him on a short affidavit—murder—in the first degree."

"Godoy!" mused Captain Hughes aloud. "Dr. Godoy! Running a combination sanitarium and roadhouse! There's something about all this that sounds familiar, especially in connection with what Miss Perin said about Vampires. I'll get it in a minute. Could the girl tell you anything definite?"

"There's Ming with a bit of supper," Doctor Coffin announced, as his huge Chinese butler appeared at the door of the library where the three friends sat.

Ming, smiling but dignified, dressed in the best old Chinese style, but all in white—long white coat, white trousers tied neatly at the ankles with satin ribbons—carried a wide brass tray heaped with sandwiches and various tasty knick-knacks dear to masculine palates. He was immediately followed by his counterpart, his twin brother Ling, bearing a similar tray on which were refreshments of another order, from coffee to cigars.

The trays were placed on convenient teakwood stands, and the two giants deftly performed their office of an initial serving before they withdrew. They'd been as unobtrusive as friendly twin spirits summoned by magic.

There was often a hint of magic in that which concerned the former Del Manning, as there always had been when he appeared on the screen. He sat there now, the master magician, as few had ever seen him. He'd put aside his favorite make-up. He was no longer Doctor Coffin, the elderly undertaker. He was just himself—deep-eyed, poetic, but strong—as strong and lithe as a lion at the zenith of its powers.

"The Vampire part of it has me rattled," Del Manning (or Doctor Coffin) announced, as he poured himself a cup of coffee.

"What did Arlene say about that?"

"She said Godoy's scouts were offering work to—entertainers. And he wanted only the best. They had to be not only there with the looks and the talent. They had to be young—and strong! Strength! Vitality! If anything, so far as I can gather, vitality—pep! vim and vigor!—came first. But the others were requisite, too! Youth! Brains! Genius, when he could get it! And as he was offering big money and his game seemed perfectly respectable, he had his pick. You know how Hollywood is—overstocked with talent of that sort—especially now."

"Greatest city in the world for that," his friends agreed.

"Then what?" Captain Hughes questioned, still pursuing some inner line of thought.

"They went up to Godoy's place in the Sierra Madre and entertained his guests—bridge, music, everything decent."

"Who were his guests?"

"For the most part, heavy respectables. Old, rich, heavy—mostly men, but a few scarecrow dowagers among them. Arlene said that it was the way these old people sat about looking at her and the other girls and boys—there were a few sheiks among the entertainers, too; the way these ogres would sit around just staring at them was what gave her the Vampire thought.

"Still, nothing wrong. There was a rule of silence and all lights out at ten and the rule was enforced. It was part of the Godoy system. And the funny part of it was it worked without enforcement. Arlene said that from the first night they reached Godoy's place they were crazy for sleep even before the set time. By ten, they were asleep. They compared notes. It was that way with all of them. They slept eight solid hours, at least.

"But here's where the catch comes in.

"Living as they did—sleep, exercise, mountain air, the best of food—they should have been adding to that pep of theirs every day. Instead, there wasn't one of them who didn't feel like a rag in the morning. And each morning worse! Washed out! Drained!

"They tried to stick it out, of course. They needed the money. No go! Most of them could stand it only for two days at the most. Some longer. Godoy would come around and look them over. He was gentle, smooth as oil. He would ooze them out—and most of them damn' glad to go—money or no money; and fresh ones coming up from Hollywood almost every day.

"Another queer thing about it that Arlene noticed—a clever girl, that, and deserving a break—"

"We'll see that she gets it," said Costigan.

"I'll say so!" muttered Captain Hughes.

"About the queerest thing Arlene noticed before she got wise," Doctor Coffin pursued, "was that bad as this mountain air, or whatever it was, seemed to be for the youngsters, it was having just the opposite effect on the old ones. The old ones would show up in the morning frisky as goats—young goats. Those old birds would even make a stab at tennis and dancing. They'd eat liver and bacon for breakfast and a couple of tumblers of raw eggs and orange juice, things like that.

"The spurt would last the old birds along until about luncheon, when they'd gorge again, this time on some sort of pre-digested food; after which the ogres would all turn in and sleep until dinner time, when they were bathed and massaged and turned out fresh for the evening. And evenings, it was the same thing all over again—the young ones trying to keep their end up and the pie-eyed ogres staring at them with that funny look of wanting to eat them alive."

"How did Arlene come to get wise?" asked Captain Hughes.

"First of all, because she was watching that kid sister of hers."

"Olga! The one who died?"

"Yes! They were both trying to stick it out for a week—at least a week. You can't blame them. They'd both been starving more or less for a year. And they'd been lying to their mother about how great they were getting on—like all kids will. But each had been noticing how they were on the skids. Then—"

"Do you guys follow all this?" Doctor Coffin paused to ask.

"Sure!"

"Then, last night, something went wrong—so far as Arlene was concerned. She prayed, or something. I don't know. Or spoke a charm or just made up her mind. Anyway, her suspicions were aroused, and she refused to go to sleep at the regular time. As a matter of fact, she didn't sleep all night. When she passed me that note tonight she hadn't been to sleep for upward of forty hours. That's why I had her brought here and put to sleep with a nurse in charge.

"Last night as she lay there in her room, holding the thought to stay awake, she heard a stir in the hall. She looked out and saw Godoy and two of his men—that Mikhal I caught tonight was one of them. They were all dressed like internes and Mikhal and his mate were pushing a wheeled operating-table.

"Arlene saw them go into her sister's room, just opposite her own. And God knows how she was able to do it and keep her mouth shut, but she saw Godoy make a few moves that she didn't understand and then wrap the sheet around the poor kid and put her on the table. Arlene tagged along, keeping out of sight."

"She's a wonder!"

"Some nerve!"

"She says that she knew that if she opened her trap they'd both be killed.

She said she could see that in Godoy's face, and I believe her. They rolled the sleeping girl on into a big room Arlene had never seen before. Not an operating room. But a room like a big conservatory filled with palms and a fountain or two, dimly lighted and a radio going, or a phonograph, very soft. But the thing that struck her most was the number of other operating tables here.

"There must have been a score of them scattered about, but always in pairs, two-by-twos, one beside the other. She hid. There was plenty of place to hide. She saw them place Olga's table at the side of another and arrange some sort of an apparatus between the two. It wasn't until then that she saw that on each pair of tables, one of the sleepers was young and the other one old.

"You know the rest. She was half-crazy by this time, but she watched her chance. She snatched Olga from the apparatus with which Godoy had harnessed her to the old man at her side. Arlene believes the old man died right then from shock. But she got Olga, somehow, out of the house and out of the grounds—both of them in nothing but their night-clothes, and Olga dazed with sleep.

"A God-blessed old tourist and his wife brought them into Hollywood and up to Echo Canyon. They were from Iowa. They didn't ask many questions. I suppose they thought that this was part of the regular thing in Hollywood— and—maybe they weren't so far wrong, at that. And then, Olga woke up and seemed to be all right—almost all right—all day and getting better. Until tonight. Last night, now. When—at the regular time to go to sleep, Godoy's time—she did go to sleep—and died."

Captain Hughes, listening intensely, suddenly broke from an even greater intensity of thought.

"The Baron d'Yoog!" he exclaimed softly with a smothered oath. "The girl was right. Moldavian! Turn the letters around—Godoy, d'Yoog!—last of the Vampires! There are at least six governments looking for him right now."

VI

A NEW BOOTBLACK SHOWED UP at the executive offices of one of the largest motion-picture studios in Hollywood a few hours later this same morning. He was new, but no one noticed the fact particularly. He was as silent, smooth, efficient, and as dirty as the regular Tony. He was a dark man, well set-up, dressed in a blue flannel shirt that looked as if it had never been off of his back, blue serge trousers, black shoes, a black porter's cap pushed down on his black greasy hair.

He knew his way about perfectly. He made his way from office to office with his whisk-broom under his arm and his black box of his trade dangling from a hairy hand.

Now and then he muttered: "Shine?"

But generally he didn't have to say that much. People merely stuck out a foot at him from where they sat. Whereupon, they'd forget him until a tap on the sole indicated that the job was done. Or they merely shook their heads and he melted away.

The last office of all that he visited was the big private office of Mr. Grindel, the old man of the great establishment.

The new Tony entered the place without even knocking.

Without so much as saying "Shine!" the bootblack went over to the huge shining desk at which the magnate sat and lifted one of the old man's feet to the shine-box and began to brush it.

Getting his shoes shined was one of the ways Mr. Grindel had of killing the day. He'd done no work about the studio for years. The other executives wouldn't let him. It was getting so that they wouldn't even let him ball up other people's work any more. And the bankers in New York were beginning to inquire why he should go on drawing a salary of one hundred thousand dollars a year.

A flabby little old man. All except his face and—so some said—his heart, which were of a proven hardness.

"What? What?" said Mr. Grindel, starting awake.

He always dozed when the bootblack was brushing his feet. He found it soothing, like a gentle massage. But now he was awake, yet he had the sensation of dreaming.

The bootblack, still kneeling in front of him, had raised his face and was staring at him with a curious smile. The bootblack had just said something and was now saying it again—in perfect English, in the remembered accents of an unforgettable voice:

"Look into my face, Mr. Grindel! Don't you recognize me?"

"Thou God in Heaven!" the old man gasped. "No! What? What?"

And he was fumbling for the telephone.

"Sit still! Don't be frightened!"

The former Del Manning, without haste, giving the old man time to recover from his shock, came to his feet. As a matter of fact, he needed a little time to control his own emotions. There had always been a whole lot about Mr. Grindel that had filled him with loathing—not just on hearsay, either; things that had turned him sick with loathing.

He'd even threatened once or twice to paste the old gentleman in the eye. Privately he had made this threat, to Mr. Grindel's face—and the great magnate, scared and apologetic, begged him, pleaded with him, not to lose his temper.

"Grindel," the spectral bootblack now said, "I'm not a ghost, but I'm as dangerous as one."

He let out a few notes of his cackling laugh.

"Manning! Mr. Manning!"

"I've some friends who want to talk to you, Grindel."

"Where?"

"At my home."

"You have a home, Mr. Manning?"

"Forget all that, Grindel! I'm in a hurry! Listen! We go out by your private entrance—the one you use when you have visitors here you don't want anyone else to see—so there'll be no supporting witnesses against you. Come on! From my house you can telephone your family that you've gone—"

"Where?"

"Out to Godoy's sanitarium for another course of treatments."

Mr. Grindel, still in the grip of fright and amazement, was almost stunned by his first clear thought:

"Godoy's!" he exclaimed. "Why, I'm the one who set Godoy up in business! Why he never told me you was a customer of his?"

VII

SO FAR AS THE ABSENCE of old Mr. Grindel was concerned, no one about the studio ever did notice that he was absent—that day or subsequent days—except that the executive offices were unusually peaceful and the work got on better. Tony the bootblack, alias the late Del Manning, alias Doctor Coffin, conducted the old man down and out from the studio so smoothly that the old man forgot he was a prisoner, forgot that the late Del Manning never was and never could be his friend. Later, he was going to talk a lot about Del Manning being still alive. For a while he was going to talk about it. But gradually he noticed that people merely thought he was crazy, and he wound up by believing that what had happened to him this day was nothing more than some sort of queer and terrible dream.

First of all, the phantom-bootblack had conducted him down through that tunnel-like private passage that Mr. Grindel had devised as a private entrance and exit to his own private office. The secret passage ended in an alley, and here an automobile waited.

The car was a large black limousine, curtained like a funeral car, and driven by two stalwart Chinamen. It brought Mr. Grindel and his escort to Villa

No. 1, where, under exceedingly acute but amiable questioning, Mr. Grindel came across with much information—not only about Dr. Vigo Godoy's sanitarium and roadhouse, but a lot of other things.

Then Mr. Grindel was invited to telephone to Dr. Godoy and warmly recommend to his attention a brother of his, Mr. Eben Grindel, who would come out to see him along toward the dinner-hour.

"And that," Captain Hughes told Chief Costigan and Doctor Coffin, "is the only part I don't like about it. It's too great a risk for Doc. This Godoy— or Yoog, to give him his right name—is a killer. He's not only a killer but he's got ways of killing that have been handed down in his family since God knows when. He comes from Vampire stock—Vampire blood. He proved that in the way he killed poor little Olga Perin—killed her at a distance, probably by hypnotism, then sent a couple of his men to bring her back to him dead or alive. What he wanted with her poor wasted body the devil himself only knows. Doc—Del—don't go! Let's make just a regulation raid on his joint!"

Doctor Coffin—the late Del Manning—was seated in front of his make-up table. He was already far along in the work of transforming himself into a characterization of Eben Grindel, that fictitious brother about whom the real Mr. Grindel had telephoned to Doctor Godoy. The great character actor paused in his work to let out a cackle of mirthless laughter.

He paused a little longer to examine a patch of collodion that was hardening into a wrinkle under his left eye.

"I'm not overlooking anything," he said. "But I'm thinking of all those other kids of Hollywood—girls and boys—who come out here to have their blood and vitality drained—by Godoy and his kind. I get Godoy! If he kills me, anyway, I kill him!"

VIII

IT WAS LATE AFTERNOON when a large black limousine, driven by a stalwart Chinese chauffeur in purple livery, turned into the grounds of the Godoy Sanitarium up in the Sierra Madres. In the back of the car was a senile old man—or what was supposed to be a senile old man—lolling against another stalwart Chinaman in purple livery, evidently the old man's attendant.

The entire estate of the sanitarium was surrounded by a strong mesh fence and there was a watchman at the gate who looked as if he might have once been a crooked policeman. The watchman took the old man's name.

It was all right; "Mr. Eben Grindel" was expected.

The car rolled up and around a curving driveway out of sight, and a few minutes later Dr. Godoy in person was greeting the new arrival.

Godoy was a man about six feet tall. But a lot of this height seemed lost by a sort of way he had of shrinking himself together—stooping, drawing in his shoulders. And hairless, so Doctor Coffin—the imaginary Eben Grindel—observed; bringing to the new arrival the whiff of a thought that here was a man of unguessed age, supernaturally old—centuries old, perhaps—who had lengthened his own life by shortening that of others.

The imaginary Mr. Eben Grindel, tottering on his feet and glad to cling to Doctor Godoy's arm, now that he didn't have his Chinaman's arm to cling to, was directly and brutally frank in his questions. Also he was very stupid. While the doctor steered him over the place, Mr. Grindel made the expert tell him over and over again about his system of making worn-out old people young and strong.

"Was it like"—Mr. Eben Grindel inquired—"like what they now call blood transfusions?"

Doctor Godoy laughed.

"No! No! No!" he explained again. "But the principle is somewhat similar. Only, it is not a transfusion of blood. It's a transfusion of life itself. Blood is merely the cart, so to speak. Life is the stuff it carries."

"And what do you call life?"

"Ah! Look out of this window! See those beautiful young people on the lawn—those fine young girls, those graceful boys?. They've got it! They've got it! And by my system I can drain them of it—drain it into those of us who know its value. They go to sleep—"

Down and around the driveway and out of sight went the superb black limousine that had brought the supposed Eben Grindel here. Doctor coffin, standing at the window here on the upper floor of Dr. Godoy's vast establishment, saw it go. Also, he had a glimpse of the two big Chinamen in the car, his faithful servants, Ming and Ling.

For a moment Doctor Coffin was following the car still farther in his thought. Down at the entrance gate the car would halt. And there the two powerful Sons of Heaven would—in ways known to themselves and in which they were very skilled—take charge of the gate-keeper there, the one who looked like an ex-policeman.

So far, so good.

"And is it here you—give your treatments?" asked Mr. Eben Grindel with what seemed to be a keener interest.

"Yes!"

It was an uncanny breath that carried the word.

Doctor Coffin felt a touch of nausea, as if he'd been breathed upon by something unspeakably foul. He had to turn aside for a moment. He gazed about the room.

This was that room Arlene Perin had described. A former ballroom, apparently, vast and brilliant, banked with palms, a couple of fountains playing at either end. And a radio, or a phonograph, churning out, very softly, a perpetual stream of music and laughter.

"Don't it kill—the young people?" the disguised Doctor Coffin asked.

"No! They live on—in us!"

"How do you mean, Dr. Godoy?"

"They are absorbed—the vital part of them. It is an old secret—old as the world. Others practice it crudely. Yes! I'll admit. But only I have the quick and sure scientific method." He panted. "Why, I myself have been doing it for years!"

"So?"

Dr. Godoy had let his voice fall to an excited, hollow whisper. He was panting slightly, through his extended, open lips. Even his face seemed to have shrunken—all except his ears. For the moment, even in appearance, he'd become the Vampire that he really was.

He was just turning to say something more when, from somewhere off in the distance of the large building, there came the clanging clatter of a fire-gong.

Without a word, and still with that bat-like look about him, Godoy turned.

"Ah!" he screamed. "I might have known!"

"Known what?"—and the pseudo Eben Grindel maintained his character a few seconds longer. For the clang of the alarm-bell had come as a surprise to Doctor Coffin as well.

"Know what? When I was warned?" Godoy continued to scream. But it was the screaming of a mouse. His voice had become a sort of screeching, minute falsetto. "You're not Eben Grindel. You're—"

It flashed on Doctor Coffin that his prisoner of last night—the one who'd escaped—must have discovered who he was and warned the Man-Bat.

All this was passing not in a series of flashes but as if in a single flash.

"Godoy—"

"You're Doctor Coffin!"

"—I have a pistol aimed—at your stomach, Godoy!"

They stood there facing each other—while things happened elsewhere.

The alarm bell kept up its infernal jangle. From here and there the patients of Dr. Godoy's Vampire Sanitarium came hobbling, tottering, running—as well as old people could run—to the big room where their specialist and the newly arrived old stranger stood confronting each other.

It was like an invasion of ghosts—haggard old specters whose proper place was in the grave, held to earth beyond their time. For it was now late in the day and already they were needing their daily fresh infusions of young vitality again. The elders stared.

There before their eyes they saw what seemed to be a double transformation in progress.

They saw their wonderful Dr. Godoy turning swiftly into the semblance of a huge and terrible but shrunken bat—shoulders hunched, skin gone brown, arms and skinny fingers hooked in a way to suggest a vampire's wings.

Then, in front of him, this man they'd taken to be just another rich old customer like themselves—needing fresh young life and having the money to pay for it: he was turning into something like youth itself—youth aroused, armed, demanding justice and retribution.

Doctor Coffin heard three quick shots from below. It meant that Hughes and Costigan were on hand with their men.

But Godoy also heard that signal.

Swiftly—swiftly as a real bat might have done it—the Vampire had flung himself through the open window. He went out with a certain grace—a flickering, sailing leap.

But he crashed on the cement pavement below and lay there—dead!

Hollywood Ghost

"Everything points to a murder," said Costigan. "Not only that, we know who did it. And he's Public Enemy Number One, so far as Hollywood is concerned. And yet we can't make a pinch. Even if we did we'd be thrown out of court. The body's gone. The witnesses are fixed, Doc, just don't it beat hell?"

Doctor Coffin, Hollywood's leading undertaker, let out the bleat of a mirthless laugh.

"Maybe it's not so bad as you think," he cackled.

The two friends, Chief Costigan, of the Hollywood detectives, and he who was known to thousands of Hollywood residents as Dr. Mortimer Coffin, sat well back in the shadowy interior of the Mortimer Funeral Parlors. Before them were the broad plate-glass windows which commanded a view of one of the busiest sections of Hollywood Boulevard. From where they sat they could see without being seen.

They couldn't have selected a better place from which to observe the passing life of Hollywood. Day and night, to and fro, all the complex human elements of the screen capital flowed by in an endless pageant: actors, writers, producers; queer mystics and plain crooks; financiers and cowboys; then the thousands of the plain and ordinary—the regular crowds of any town's main stem.

And it would have been a safe bet that there wasn't one of those who passed out there but believed that the world had lost its greatest character actor when Del Manning died. Del Manning. The mystery man of the screen. The man with five hundred faces.

Many paused now for a second glance at the funeral parlors, or pointed out the place to visiting friends. It was from here that Del Manning's funeral had been held. A great event. Big as a first night. Traffic jam and all the celebrities on review.

But there'd have been a worse traffic jam right now had word got round that the sedate and elderly "mortician" sitting in there—looking more like a country parson than any actor—was none other than the great Del Manning himself.

Costigan looked at his friend. Even he could hardly imagine that this man seated at his side was a man still young, lithe, powerful—yes, and as handsome as any sheik on the boulevard, too, when he wanted to be.

"Got an idea, Doc?" Costigan asked.

"I used to work for Gresham," said the late Del Manning, still in the tittering voice that was the usual manner of Doctor Coffin's speech. "I didn't love him"—he suddenly changed his voice to an oily, snarling bass—"but I hated Augustus Adolphus Brentwood more. . . ."

"You got Gresham's voice, all right," said Costigan softly, with a touch of fervor.

"Suppose we put on a show," said Doctor Coffin.

II

THE HOME OF THE LATE ALEXANDER GRESHAM, founder and principal owner of the Gresham West Coast Studios, occupied a parklike area on Moscada Drive. It was a big old place, solemn and lonely, especially at night; and doubly so, on a night like this. In the first place, it was one of those rare nights of fog and rain. Then, as if this were not bad enough, along about midnight, all the electric lights in this part of the Hollywood hills went out.

Here and there a candle fluttered. Now and then an auto passed with a flash of headlights. Here and there a night-watchman bobbed along with an electric torch. But that was all.

The night-watchman whose beat was along Moscada Drive saw a man strolling along in his direction shortly before midnight. The watchman put his hand on his gun and flashed his light. Then he laughed and apologized. He'd recognized Chief Costigan.

"That's all right, Jimmy," said Costigan; "walk along with me a way. I'm trying to locate the hide-out of a bunch of crooks. Maybe you can help me."

"At your service," said the night-watchman, flattered. And Costigan led him away.

They were near the Gresham house when they met.

"That place occupied?" Costigan asked carelessly.

"Only by old man Dowd, the caretaker," the watchman answered. "The widow skipped out right after her husband's funeral. I guess Dowd thought more of Mr. Gresham than she did."

"Shouldn't be surprised," said Costigan.

"Funny," the night-watchman went on, "how quick they was to have Gresham's body cremated, without no proper funeral or anything. Folks say he might not have died of indigestion after all."

Costigan let him talk. In the meantime, he'd been listening for something else. He heard it—a faint whistling treble.

The signal had come from a second dark figure, one whom the night-watchman hadn't seen, and who was now crossing the dark lawn of the Gresham place toward the unlighted house.

Dowd, the caretaker of the place, sleeping lightly in the ground-floor bedroom at the rear of the big house, heard a repeated ring at the front door.

He hastily lit a candle, then drew on a ragged dressing-gown and started to investigate.

"Who's there?" he asked.

The voice that answered him set Dowd to trembling. "Jerry—for God's sake—is that you?" The trembling went over Jerry Dowd in repeated waves, alternately hot and cold. The voice was that of his master whom he believed to be dead.

Somehow—both against his will and yet with frantic haste—Dowd got the door open. As he did so, he recoiled. It was with a gasp and a muttered prayer. For he'd caught the sight of a face which was at once strange and familiar—the face of his dead master, a face too long dead; and a hand had groped for the candle, which Dowd had at once let fall.

For a strangling second, Dowd and the apparition stood there in the murky darkness. Then the weird visitant spoke again.

"Don't be frightened, Jerry, I'm not here to hurt you, Jerry. I'm not dead. I'm merely sick."

Gresham's voice, Gresham's figure, a little squat and pouchy about the middle.

"Praise God," said Jerry in a tremolo, "and I'll be lightin' the candle again."

"Don't," said the visitant, "I merely want to talk to you, Jerry, and get some clothing, and then I'll be on my way again. And, first of all, where's my wife?"

Dowd felt an added wave of sickness. There were things that he knew, he didn't care to tell about. He was still in the grip of his original horror, although this was passing away to some extent. You can get used to anything—even to a dead man coming back.

Dowd fumbled and stalled. He led the way along back through the dark hall—spurred and diabolically electrified at almost every step by the touch of an uncanny hand against his ribs.

"Please now, sor," he pleaded; "and I'll be lightin' the candle."

"Very well. But don't bring it too close. No, not too close, Jerry, I've been too long—in the—dark."

When Jerry came back with the flickering candle he saw the grim figure of the visitant seated in a leather easy chair his master had always preferred. And Jerry waited and gaped as if for a sign. He got the sign. He saw the dim figure clasp its pale hands—right over left, left over right—with a recurrent cracking of the knuckles. Mr. Gresham had always done that, especially when he was in a dangerous mood.

Jerry, remembering that warning about not bringing the candle too close, began to look for a place to set it. There was no convenient place except the polished floor. And, having stooped to set the candle on the floor, he decided he might as well stay here, too.

He was on his knees. His thin face and staring eyes made of himself a ghostly presence in the pale and flickering candlelight.

"Damn you," came Gresham's voice; "I ask you again: What have you done with my wife?"

"Nothing, sor. She went away."

"Where to?"

"She was talkin' of Paris, sor."

"Where'd she get the money?"

Old man Dowd shuddered. He was like a man contemplating a plunge into cold and polluted water. But he took the plunge. And, once in, he splashed around.

"Faith, and it was none other than Augustus Adolphus Brentwood who'd put the lady in funds. No check. Cash! A bale of it."

"Why?"

"Because, she claimed, he'd murdered yuh; and him not a denyin' of it either—the swollen, dirthy blackguard. Else why should they have run your body right off the yacht and got it cremated? And you know the nature of the missus when she starts to raise hell. 'I don't give a damn,' she yells, 'how he died or what he died of,' she says; 'but s'help me,' she scrims, 'I won't be left widout enough money to live like a lady—' "

Del Manning, in the sufficient disguise of the late Alex Gresham, let old man Dowd talk on and on. In his own thought he was strengthening his mental picture of what had happened, formulating that bigger show he had in mind.

Gresham and the millionaire Brentwood had started for a weekend cruise on the latter's yacht, the palatial *Carlota*. With them had gone a mixed party of boys and girls. Just Hollywood playmates these were—all except one. The one was the particular girl friend of the millionaire, his latest; one he was grooming for stardom on the Gresham lot.

Caryl Nardac was her name. Del Manning—the sometime Doctor Coffin—knew her. Beautiful; with the brilliant hardness of a diamond.

Champagne—and everything else to drink—absolutely without limit. The *Carlota* loaded her lockers regularly from the Mexican rum row off Ensenada just south of the border.

Had Gresham been shot in a drunken brawl? By Brentwood?

It was pretty well established that Brentwood, Gresham, and the Nardac girl were alone at the moment of the tragedy, whatever it was. In any case, the *Carlota* had been put about at once for the home port; Brentwood had wirelessed his personal physician to meet the yacht with a private ambulance.

Dr. Zitoun. With a private sanitarium that Augustus Adolphus Brentwood had paid for. No wonder the doctor had been willing to oblige.

He'd swear that Gresham had died of acute indigestion. Then, almost before the body was cold, he'd had it cremated. . . .

III

THAT PRIVATE SANITARIUM which Dr. Zitoun operated, with great secrecy and an even greater profit, was also his home. It was a home of which anyone might be proud, even in Beverly Hills, that expensive suburb of Hollywood where so many screen celebrities live. A large pink house in the Spanish style, surrounded by a tropical garden, and the garden, in turn, surrounded by a high and solid wall.

The wall was convenient for two reasons—to keep interlopers out and certain of the shakier patients in.

It was generally suspected that Dr. Zitoun, trading on his professional privileges and the powerful protection of Augustus Adolphus Brentwood, millionaire and politician, got most of his profit from commerce forbidden by Federal laws. But, so far, nothing had ever been done about it. His place was patronized by some of the best-known residents of Beverly Hills, both men and women.

The doctor was asleep—in a bedroom that would have pleased a Spanish grandee—when he was awakened by the ringing of his telephone. He came out of his sleep with a muttered curse. It was one of his strictest rules that he should never be disturbed in the night.

The telephone stood on a table at the side of his ornate bed. Reaching over, he savagely jerked the hook off the instrument a number of times as a signal to the interne downstairs, that he was to be disconnected.

The telephone rang again. This time, he snatched up the instrument and was about to bellow something into it when he stopped to listen. It was the voice that startled him. A voice that he recognized. Suddenly, he was afraid to find himself in the dark.

"Please! Please! Just a minute!" he begged—softly enough, at that; and his hand was shaking as he took time enough to switch on the lace-shaded reading-lamp at the bedside.

Even with the light on, he still hesitated. What was this—a fake? Yet, how could it be a fake? Or a clever, punishing practical joke? He had enemies. Some of them were cruel and clever.

"Zitoun," came the voice; "what do you mean by saying I am dead? What do you mean by trying to cremate me?"

The voice was a slurring bass, devoid of humor.

"I don't know who you are," Zitoun said.

"You do know who I am."

Zitoun had a desperate inspiration, a gust of bleak hope.

"Listen," he clacked. "I have the telephone numbers here in a book. Let me be sure. I will call you back."

"All right. I'll give you one minute, Zitoun."

With a shaking finger, Zitoun ran down his private telephone list. It seemed incredible to him that he should be doing this. Yet the memory of that voice was an ache in his head. And in his heart. He'd always prided himself that he had no conscience. But he had a fear.

His heart was pounding as he found a number and put it through. The response was instant.

"Well, Zitoun?"

"Mr. Gresham!" He couldn't believe the sound of his own voice.

"Yes, I'm Gresham. And I want to see you."

"When?"

"Now. As soon as you can get here. I give you half an hour. Unless you want me to blow the top off."

"Where?"

"Here at my house, you fool! Unless you want me to come and get you with a squad of police and reporters."

Dr. Zitoun found himself dressing with his eyes on the clock. It was just two—two hours past midnight—when he started to dress. It struck him that the minute hand jumped ahead. He dressed with desperate speed. But, even as he did so, his mind was racing ahead. There was a small car in the garage—small but powerful, geared for speed. Should he make for Mexico? No, that would take too long. He might be nabbed before he reached Capistrano. Or a flying-field? That was better.

He still felt as if he were taking part in a nightmare as he went downstairs. Without a word to the watchful interne he went out into the garden and turned toward the garage.

The dial on the instrument board showed two-ten as he turned on the switch. Still twenty minutes leeway. He could be at a flying-field in ten. But as he rolled out of the driveway into the public street he saw a dark car across the way with two policemen in it. He decided to drive for the Gresham house.

Zitoun, like many another man careless of the health of others, had always been careful of his own. He was a man of average build, but powerful. In the glove pocket of the car he found the small automatic that he always carried there. He transferred this to a pocket of his coat.

What had happened? What was about to happen? Many a time in the course of his checkered career he'd been in jams. Some of them pretty tight. Drug addicts. Jealous husbands. Crooks with a delicate sense of self-protection. But never in a jam like this. His fear hadn't left him. But his fear was making him desperate. His desperation was making him reckless. He would see it through. If he had to, he'd shoot it through. The police car trailed him. It had trailed him right on up into Moscada Drive. As he brought his own car to a halt in front of the Gresham home he saw two men standing near the gateway. The electric lights had come back on by this time and he recognized the two men, as they recognized him. One was Chief Costigan, of the Hollywood detectives.

The other was the regular night-watchman of the beat.

Their presence may have made Zitoun a little careless as he passed on through the gateway and started to follow the twisting footpath through the shrubbery.

He had just entered the heavy shadows cast by a group of silver fir when an arm shot out and clamped about his throat. His breath was cut off as if by the yoke of a Spanish garrote. In another instant a hand of steel had caught one of his arms and jerked it back and a knee like a sledge found a place in his back where pressure paralyzed him.

Dr. Zitoun had been in the Orient.

He wondered who in Hollywood had learned this trick of the murder tongs.

Then he was lying on his face in the wet grass. And although the grip on his throat relaxed, still that pressure in the soft of his back kept him silent and paralyzed. So far there hadn't been a sound.

If he thought he'd reached the limit of his terror he was wrong. He heard a voice. It was the same drawling and ferocious bass that had reached him over the telephone—the voice of the late Alex Gresham when Gresham was in a murderous mood.

"I'm a ghost," said the voice; "a ghost of your own making."

From somewhere a bell chimed the half-hour. It was half-past two.

IV

As a limited number of friends were aware, Doctor Coffin was the owner of two oddly assorted and strangely connected houses in Hollywood. One was a large white villa in an expensive neighborhood. The other was an obscure little bungalow up a deep but narrow and heavily wooded canyon which was barred to the public and formed a cul-de-sac in the Hollywood hills.

Between this canyon and the Gresham property were a number of hills and canyons threaded over by only a few narrow trails. Not many persons could have found their way through this maze even in the daytime. Yet the same bell that had chimed the half-hour was striking only three as the "ghost" of Alex Gresham thrust his way over the last ridge and down into the canyon of the hidden bungalow.

He was moving cautiously, for he was bringing a prisoner with him. The prisoner was Dr. Zitoun, curiously tied. Only one of his hands was confined, drawn up behind his back, and the end of the rope then cast in a noose about his neck. That also, he recollected, was a Chinese tie.

And curiously, as yet Zitoun had not seen his captor's face. He had scarcely heard him, except when he spoke. And when he spoke it had been with the voice of that man whom Zitoun knew to be already dead—not only dead but cremated. So that, altogether, Zitoun still had the feeling that his captor might be—must be a ghost, after all.

In the narrow valley, the darkness was intense.

Yet in the darkness a blacker patch appeared. It assumed the shape of a large dog. The dog was silent. Another patch of black appeared. It looked at first, even as Zitoun peered, like a gorilla. Only later his scientific eye told him that this was not a gorilla but a long-armed human hunchback.

It was now the hunchback who held the cord. The dog, still silent, led the way. To Zitoun the way seemed long and tedious. Twice he'd tried to speak. Each time the pressure on the rope about his neck had threatened his wind and warned him to keep silent. He bided his time.

Only some time later was he aware that his original captor had left him. He'd slipped away as silently as the ghost he'd claimed to be.

As a matter of fact, as soon as his faithful servant, Shorty, had appeared to take charge of the prisoner, the late Del Manning had hurried on ahead. The night was far from finished. He still had much to do.

He didn't pause to make a light as he entered the dark little bungalow that had become the scene of so many of his operations, both when Del Manning was still supposed to be alive and later, as Doctor Coffin, when Del Manning's name was carved on a tomb.

Inside the small bungalow, he turned from the hall to a dark parlor. His outstretched hand found the corner of a brick fireplace, and he swung this aside as easily as if it had been a door. He ran lightly down an unseen ladder. Only now he pressed an electric button that threw on the light in a receding series of dim blue globes.

Faint as it was, the light seemed strong after the long period of darkness. It revealed a long straight tunnel. The tunnel was traversed in less than a minute, yet it brought Doctor Coffin to his principal home, the large white villa which lay, to all appearances, in another part of town.

Costigan was there to greet him, and the two friends struck hands.

"Okay so far, Doc?" queried Costigan.

"Okay, so far, Chief," Doctor Coffin answered in his tittering falsetto. And he let out a cry, half in Chinese, half pidgin: "O—og! Chin! Lee! More better catch plenty food! Eh?"

"Everything ready," came a swift answer from the direction of the dining room. "Master come this side!"

Two giant Chinese butlers, twin images of each other in their gray silk robes, smilingly served an ample supper as Doctor Coffin and his friend discussed the development of their plans.

Later, these same Chinamen, in identical black robes and with Chinese masks over their faces, conducted Dr. Zitoun to a seat in front of an ornamental screen where a powerful light revealed every detail of his features.

Back of this screen, himself unseen except by Costigan, Doctor Coffin was once more revealing his genius for portraiture and characterization on that plastic face of his. Zitoun didn't know it, but he was sitting for his portrait. Little by little, there, back of the screen, Del Manning, Doctor Coffin, disappeared. A second Zitoun came into being.

Just before dawn, a sleepy interne heard the tread of Dr. Zitoun's light car coming up the private driveway. The interne saw nothing out of the ordinary a few minutes later when he saw someone whom he took to be Dr. Zitoun himself come in, muffled up in a familiar raincoat.

The supposed Dr. Zitoun spoke to the interne curtly over his shoulder. It was a way the big chief had.

"There are a couple of suit-cases out in the car," he said. "Get them. Take them up to my room. I'm all in."

The interne remembered. He wasn't apt to forget. Those who forgot, when Dr. Zitoun dropped a hint or an order, didn't hold their jobs very long. Yet there'd been something strange. When the interne had come back with the suitcases he'd found the "doctor" still standing in the lower reception room, and he'd motioned the interne to lead the way to his room—that big room upstairs that would have suited a Spanish grandee.

There was something that struck the interne as stranger still.

Less than a half-hour after "Zitoun's" return, two handsome and well-dressed young men—they were fresh-faced and husky and didn't look like patients—drove into the grounds of the establishment and insisted on seeing Dr. Zitoun in person.

It was now almost daylight, and the interne tried to put them off.

They wouldn't be put off. They were so insistent, in fact, that the interne finally decided to take the risk of announcing them. Gale and Peacock, they said their names were.

The interne telephoned up to the owner's room. To his surprise and relief, word came back to send Messrs. Gale and Peacock up.

And that was the last that the interne was to see them. His tour of duty ended at six.

V

AS A MATTER OF FACT, Messrs. Gale and Peacock were two of Chief Costigan's brightest young men, and they'd been sent out to the sanitarium to "bug" the room, as they called it—that is to wire it; and also to lend a hand in case "Dr. Zitoun" should need their assistance.

The first part of their task was simple enough. There were velvets and silk brocades enough in the room to have concealed a thousand wires. A concealed door led into a private bath and dressing room.

While they were doing their stuff, the new Dr. Zitoun was doing his. The two young detectives didn't know who this man was they'd been sent to work with, but they were quick enough to see that he was some sort of an expert. They saw him darken the room with the heavy curtain, then try on all the lights in various combinations.

It wouldn't do to have the room too dark, he explained, especially for people coming in direct from the broad daylight. But he wanted the shadows to fall just so. Plenty of light, so they wouldn't feel uneasy; yet not too much in case the makeup went stale, as all makeup is apt to do after a few hours.

It wasn't until the strange Dr. Zitoun mentioned his makeup that either Peacock or Gale noticed that he had any on. And, even then, it kept disappearing from sight and mind—this made-up face looked so natural and life-like.

The admiration of the two young detectives went keener still when they had a chance to observe the "doctor's" work at the telephone.

First he'd gone into the bathroom and gargled a few mouthfuls of water, rinsing his throat. This accomplished, they saw him shake his head and begin to mutter to himself. At the same time, gradually, his mood was manifestly becoming one of a brooding gloom and fear. This general mood was shot through at times with occasional spasms of staring fright that verged on madness. After this had gone on for a while, the strange Dr. Zitoun began to talk aloud in a muttering and haunted undertone.

"I saw him," he said. "God, but I did! Alive! Still alive! After death! After cremation! I can't understand! I can't understand."

And then he'd break off to stare again, perfectly still for perhaps a dozen seconds; until a faint shudder would begin to get possession of a hand or just one half of his face, and begin to spread, until his whole body was shuddering; when he'd sob a little and begin to moan and mutter again.

It was in the middle of this display of terror that he finally picked up the telephone and spoke into it.

"Get me Mr. Brentwood," he panted.

His voice was so breathless and broken that it brought a little cry from the operator below that the listening detectives could plainly hear over the open line:

"Oh, Dr. Zitoun, are you ill? Can't I do something for you?"

"No, no! And for God's sake, under no pretense disturb me! Get me Brentwood! Brentwood! Keep on trying until you do get him!"

He almost dropped the instrument as he returned it to its hooks.

There was not the slightest change in his mood.

While he was waiting for his call, he continued to walk about, mumbling and shivering. He jerked off his coat and vest and dropped these to the floor, as if unconscious of what he did. He tore at the throat of his shirt. His somber eyes were going bloodshot.

"Back from the dead! Impossible, eh? But I tell you I saw him! Talked to him! He cursed me, laughed at me! Ha! Ha!"

The telephone rang, and he seized the instrument.

"You, Brentwood? You?" His voice had become a stifled whisper. "Yes, this is Zitoun. Listen! I want to talk to you! Listen! Listen! For God's sake, listen! You've got to come! Got to, I tell you! And bring Caryl—Miss Nardac! Bring her, I tell you!" His voice was now going a little raucous, louder, and almost incoherent. "What about? . . . About?" And now his voice sounded like an echo in a cave. "About Gresham! I've seen him! He's alive!"

VI

SOME BRIGHT YOUNG FLAPPER had once told Augustus Adolphus Brentwood that he looked just like his name. He'd forgotten the girl but he'd remembered the remark. It had become the one ideal in his life he'd ever wanted to live up to. And he'd succeeded measurably well. He could see that, every time he looked at himself in a mirror.

He was smooth and powerful, well set-up, over the average height. Besides, he was always perfectly groomed. His valet saw to that. He'd been born rich. He'd never done a lick of work in his life. He'd never been sick—except for a few morning qualms after too much wine. At that, he preferred getting other people drunk to getting drunk himself.

More fun. More self-satisfaction. The more the others drank, the more you could show to them and yourself your mastery of them. It had always been like that when he'd thrown a party on the *Carlota*.

Always, except once. The last time.

And, at that, you only had to slip once to break a leg—or a neck.

"He's got you worried," said Caryl Nardac.

She looked the girl that a man like Brentwood would pick. A swell looker. A blonde doll. Eyes as blue and bright and as hard as colored glass.

"Who? Me?" grunted Brentwood.

But he was worried all right. And he was showing it, although he tried not to.

They were driving down to the beach, where Brentwood had a cottage— at Malibu—for luncheon. They'd just come from that interview with Dr. Zitoun—or him they'd taken to be Dr. Zitoun—at the Zitoun sanitarium.

"He looked," said Caryl Nardac, with no change of expression on her enameled face, "as if he were going crazy. Did you notice how his legs jerked? And he kept hiding his face in the pillow as if he were trying to shut out something he'd seen."

"That bird is crazy."

"But that won't save us if—"

"Shut up! The chauffeur may hear."

The girl's perfect face remained unchanged. But there was an added glitter in her eyes.

"You should have thought of that," she said, "while you and Dr. Zitoun were raging at each other there in his room."

"I didn't say anything," he rasped.

"You said plenty."

"What?"

"That you'd shoot the—you know—again—if—"

There came to Brentwood a glint of ugly recollection. He had said something like that, now that he came to think of it. For a time he sat looking steadily at the back of the chauffeur's head. He could see the chauffeur's pink ears standing out under his cap.

But, after all, there was no chance of the chauffeur hearing what they said. The machine was of the town-car type—a foreign model with an exceptionally long body. Not, for that matter, was it likely that anyone would have been listening in during their visit to Dr. Zitoun.

"I would," he said. "I'd shoot any—"

"Sh!" she warned, wilting against him and putting her manicured fingers against his lips. It was a gesture she'd been drilled in by the director of the last picture she'd appeared in. "How am I to make my career if Tootsums is jealous?"

Brentwood, nearing fifty, was suspicious of baby-talk.

"To hell with a career," he said. "Let's go to China—or Tahiti. The *Carlota's* cleaned and fueled."

Caryl Nardac pouted. "This afternoon," she said, "you're taking me to the Gresham lot."

"You mean on Zitoun's crazy statement that—that Gresham wants to see us there?"

"Yes. He said at three o'clock."

"But Gresham's dead. Zitoun's crazy."

"Jerry Dowd isn't crazy. He says that Mr. Gresham came home last night."

"Then, who was it I shot?" Brentwood demanded. He turned on the girl with a gust of savage passion. "Who was it, then, you were making love to?"

"How should I know?" she drawled. "All of us were so perfectly spifficated!"

Brentwood sank back. For the present he wasn't feeling so very Augustus Adolphus. Not at all! The car purred along for a mile or so and nothing said. Then, Caryl Nardac spoke again.

"You're going to take me to the studio; aren't you, darling?"

To Brentwood there came a swift yet subtle premonition of disaster. It was like a warning voice telling him to say "No"—warning him to keep away from the Gresham studio. That had been the correct hunch he'd voiced a minute ago—to run. The *Carlota* was ready. It was big enough to carry him anywhere. Even now, here from the car, he caught a glimpse of the blue Pacific. China, over there. Shanghai. Saigon.

But as men often will, he said now the thing that was just the opposite of what he wanted to say. He turned to the girl.

"Sure," he told her; "I'll take you."

VII

THE BIG GRESHAM STUDIOS had been practically closed since that queer thing—whatever it was—that had happened to the boss. But even when a studio is practically shut down it still carries a large population and a staggering payroll. But the place seems empty. And never more than at such a time do rumors so multiply and rumble so loud.

This day a number of queer rumors were in circulation. The queerest rumors you ever heard. Coming as rumors do, from no one knew where.

One was, that Alexander Gresham wasn't dead, after all.

Another was, that not even Del Manning was dead.

A third was, that, somehow, the two had got together and had decided to come back.

Did you ever hear such goofy talk!

In any case, there was an air of mystery about the front office. Along about noon, an order had come to the house-cleaning squad to get busy freshening up the president's room, there where the late—if it was the late—Alexander Gresham always held his private interviews. Then the juicers—the electricians, that is—got an order that this same room was to have special lighting effects and was to be wired for sound.

At that, the room had always been silent enough, and almost large enough, to serve for a sound stage—double doors and windows, special ventilation, a room that was long and broad, high-ceilinged.

In any case, something of importance was in preparation; and the work of making ready for it was being rushed through at high speed.

Then, shortly after one o'clock, something of an electric shock ran back and forth and all around the studio, giving a queer, unearthly stimulus to every one who came in contact with it. At least one of those queer rumors had coalesced into fact.

Or had it? Could it be?

Yes, sir. Del Manning himself had been seen and identified. He'd arrived in a closed car with a number of other men. The car had come in through the main gate on a special pass, and Del Manning had been recognized by the watchman there. Old Harrigan. One of the few men Del Manning had ever been intimate with. In person, that is; not in character.

Later on, the juicers were to appear with confirmation of the Harrigan report. Some of the older men had also known Del Manning in person. They'd almost dropped from their perches when they'd seen him down there on the floor of the president's room.

Del Manning! He'd tested the lights. He'd shifted them around—spots here and kliegs there. Still knew his stuff. Had the mike brought down. Didn't care if it did get in the camera.

If it wasn't Del, then Del had a twin brother.

One hour later, another shock went scooting around the acreage of the big studio—through all but deserted stages, into remote shops, stables, draughting rooms. And, this time, it was another of those impossible rumors that had become substantial. Another dead man had come to life, and this time, sure enough, it was Alexander Gresham.

"They're all talking about you, Doc," said Costigan, as he returned to one of the inner offices after a tour of inspection through the studio.

Doctor Coffin uttered a few notes of his cackling laugh—not so mirthless, this time, as it generally sounded.

"They'll have something else to talk about before we call it a day," he said.

He was standing before a long floor mirror surrounded by powerful lights. He was stripped to his underclothes. He was building up his lithe and compact body to fit the clothing he had brought away last night from the Gresham home.

His hands and his face and head were already made up to a living image of Alexander Gresham. It was as if the head and hands of some used up old man had been placed on an athlete in his prime. A prank of the gods. But as the late Del Manning shifted swiftly and skillfully into the borrowed raiment, the athlete suddenly disappeared. It was only the old man who remained.

Even the former Del Manning's character appeared to change. His head was inclined to nod. There was a twitching of one of his hands. To correct this twitching, he began to clasp one hand over the other—first one, then the other—cracking his knuckles as he did so. And when he spoke, his voice came in a low-pitched growl.

"There's an accountant downstairs," he said. "A fellow named Azroth. Been with me since God knows when. Send him up here."

"Do you mean it, Doc?" Costigan asked.

"Sure, I mean it," growled the resurrected president of the Gresham Studios.

He gave another swift survey of himself, then stepped away from the lights and stood, squat and pouchy, his head down, looking at the door.

The door opened and Azroth was standing there, ancient and thin, almost hairless, almost toothless. He stood there staring for seconds, as if not quite able to realize that what he saw was flesh and blood and not just some trick of his senile brain. Then his mouth opened and he was trying to speak, but no sound came, He tried to laugh, but instead he began to cry.

"That's all right, Azzy," the late Del Manning said. "It's only makeup. And I'm offering you fifty bucks to find a flaw."

Azzy wiped his nose, and now he could laugh.

"Your offering me that," he wheezed, "is a flaw—in characterization."

"You win," growled the resurrected Gresham; and he counted out the fifty, while old Azroth stared once more in doubt.

A buzzer sounded.

It meant that two other leading characters had arrived for this day's drama and were headed for the stage.

VIII

DOCTOR COFFIN—Alexander Gresham pro tem.—stood in the shadows and watched Augustus Adolphus Brentwood come on. He had never liked the man. Costigan had pretty nearly stated the truth—Public Enemy Number

One. Just about, so far as Hollywood was concerned. All the money in the world; using it to no good end. A fine presence, health, education, freedom, opportunities galore; all wasted; worse than wasted. Just using them for bait to trap poor kids—all the beautiful and silly girl-kids flocking into Hollywood every month.

Yet he felt sorry for the man—felt a little sick on his account.

He switched his eyes to the girl that Brentwood had brought along. Caryl Nardac. He hadn't dared to look at her too closely—only those few hours ago—when he was playing the rôle of the frightened and soul-sick Dr. Zitoun. Hard! Diamond hard! She could have scratched her name on a pane of glass with her fingernail.

The Greeks made Nemesis a woman. To every man—like Brentwood—his Nemesis—like the Nardac girl.

Then, somehow, a change was coming over the one-time Del Manning and the subsequent Doctor Coffin. He was neither of these two persons. Not even in his thought. He was being submerged by this new personality. He wasn't playing the rôle of the late Alexander Gresham. He *was* Alexander Gresham. He felt an unhealed wound in his abdomen—a wound so real that, instinctively, he clasped a hand over the place and held it there during all that followed.

Yes, it was he who'd drunk too much wine on the *Carlota*. The wine had made him forget his age, his common sense, his remnant of decency. He hated Brentwood for having shot him; but, at heart, he didn't really blame him. He could be cordial, if Brentwood gave him the chance.

He came shuffling out from the shadows, slowly, dragging a little, one of his legs; one of his hands pressing the place where the bullet had struck him; on his face, a placative smile.

"Hello! Hello!" he greeted them.

He saw them stare—and understood.

"So," he rumbled; "you thought I was dead! Didn't Zitoun tell you? He said he had a long talk with you this morning at the sanitarium. He told me everything. Sit down! Sit down!"

Brentwood and the Nardac girl slid down into chairs. The one they'd come to see trudged laboriously around his desk and seated himself near them.

They were like three corpses, not one only, in the green intensity of the klieg lights. So intense was the interest of Brentwood and the girl that they were paying no attention to the lights; or, if they had noticed them, had now no thought except for the specter in front of them.

"Oh, Mr. Gresham!" Caryl Nardac exclaimed.

But there was no hint of a tear, no real feeling in her voice.

"Look out," said the resurrected one, with a loose-lipped smile, "else you'll be making him jealous again. And you know what he told Zitoun this morning—he'd do it again. Am I right, Gus, or am I wrong?"

So far, Brentwood hadn't spoken a word. Now he drew a breath, preparatory to speech.

"Alex," he said, "we always played fair."

"Except when you shot me."

"Alex, if I shot you—"

"Not 'if,' Gus. Shall I show you the wound?"

Brentwood made a swift gesture of repugnance. "Anyway, Alex, you know why I did shoot you." He stopped short and gave a quick look round with sudden alarm.

The pseudo-Gresham smiled.

"Don't be alarmed, Gus," he said. "You have nothing to fear. Nothing more to fear."

"This looks like a trap, Alex," Brentwood said. "What do you mean, nothing 'more' to fear?"

"Why, first of all, Gus, there's Dr. Zitoun. He's told all he knows. Told it to the police and got himself arrested."

"Zitoun? Arrested?"

"Only, I think he got it twisted, what really happened. He says it was our little Caryl here, who fired the bullet."

Caryl Nardac exploded with a little scream. "Why, the dirty liar!" Sudden rage was about the only sincere emotional outlet she possessed—that and hysteria. She turned on Brentwood. "If he says that, I'll show him up good and plenty. If the decent people of Beverly Hills knew one half of what was going on in that dump of his, they'd burn it down."

"Shut up!" said Brentwood with chill emphasis. "When you squawk like that I could wring your neck."

The girl contemplated him with a look of frozen rage. The green light of the kliegs turned her red lips black, spread a cadaverous pallor over the rest of her face.

"I'm through with you," she announced. "And I'll have some stories to tell about you, too, if you try to spoil my career."

The following action of Brentwood was so smooth that it was almost completed before the others saw what he'd done. With a sigh, as of resignation—or of something deeper, of weariness and despair—he'd drawn a pistol from a lower pocket of his vest. It might have been a cigarette case, it was so small and bright.

He'd brought this up a little ways, as if undecided whether he should use it on himself or on the girl, or on both, after taking one more shot at Alexander Gresham.

But at that moment Doctor Coffin had seized him—no longer Gresham at all; rather, the old Del Manning.

Together they came to their feet, fighting for possession of the pistol, the weapon held high above their heads, each trying to outreach and outmaneuver the other.

All this quick as a flash; and then set to the phantom music of Caryl Nardac's screams. She also was on her feet.

"Oh! Oh! Oh!" she piped. "He killed him once and now he wants to kill him again. I saw him do it. And he had a poor sailor killed, too—just because he'd heard the shot! Mr. Gresham! Mr. Gresham! Don't let him shoot you again!"

But now the fighting pair had whirled away from her. There was a shot and a shatter of glass. Then Brentwood had broken loose and had started to run.

For a moment he was out of sight—out of sight of those who still had the light in their eyes.

Brentwood must also have been partly blinded by this sudden bolt into the shadows from the light zone. He found his way blocked in the way he was headed. He turned and tripped over a live power-line, pulling a plug as he did so. There was a jet of electric flame.

He was dead when they got to him. He still held his pistol gripped in his hand and on his forehead was the mark of a jagged burn—a figurative mark of Cain.

All the time that this had been going on, except for the tragic finale, the microphone and the cameras had been recording this unrehearsed drama. Chaotic stuff, most of it; but so is life. And none of it apt to get by the censors, which is also like so much that happens outside of polite scenarios.

But the Hollywood police set great store by the film, such as it is. And perhaps, if you're ever out that way, and happen to have a pull with Chief Costigan, you'll be permitted to see and hear it.

By a curious twist of Fate—really the quite sensible decision of relatives—it was decided that the funeral of Augustus Adolphus Brentwood should be held from the Mortimer Funeral Parlors on Hollywood Boulevard. It would have been uncharitable of Doctor Coffin to have done anything to prevent this plan from going through. But he himself didn't have the heart to have anything to do with it.

The day poor Brentwood was buried, Doctor Coffin was far away in the High Sierras, with his friend, Costigan, who'd also decided he needed a vacation.

They went for a long walk. As evening approached they sat on the brow of a hill and watched the valleys go purple and the snow-crests turn to pink and gold. A star flamed out, whitely, and a friendly ranch dog came and sat between them and also looked at the landscape.

"Honestly, Doc," said Costigan, "you ought to go back to the screen. Some actor!"

Doctor Coffin let out a couple of notes of his mournful laugh.

And no one ever could tell what that might mean.

Manhattan Monster

HE WAS A FINE-LOOKING MAN. He was dressed like a swell—silk hat, tail coat, striped trousers, spats and so forth—but he didn't need the clothes to make him appear distinguished. There was something about the way he carried himself, something in his face.

He was about thirty, average size—maybe a little over; but compact. As he left the taxi in front of the big hotel—one of New York's finest—every movement he made was perfect; like a cat's—quick and graceful—timed to the second, no waste.

But, after all, the distinction was mostly in his face—deep-set, meditative eyes with plenty of space between them. They were eyes to stop you when they looked at you, if only for a moment. Leaving you the impression somehow—although the face was handsome—that you'd been looked at by a skull.

The newcomer had slipped a folded bill to the chauffeur and was already entering the hotel before the six-foot doorman, in gray livery, or the chauffeur himself, knew he was gone.

The chauffeur peeked at a corner of the bill like a careful poker player examining a card. He mastered a start as he saw a five.

There was a question in the big doorman's raised eyebrows, but the chauffeur merely winked and drove rapidly away.

The chief of the house detectives, looking more like a broker than what he was, met the newcomer just inside the entrance and saluted him softly:

"Suite 420. I'll show you the way."

"They're waiting?"

The house detective nodded.

Those who waited in Suite 420 of the big hotel were neither of them ordinary men. Both were famous, each in his own particular field. And both were of about the same age—getting on, well past middle age. But in other respects they were different enough.

One was short and chunky, with a lively, luminous face, above which his white hair rose like a fluffy cloud. When he spoke, it was with a pronounced but not unpleasant German accent.

"I feel," he said, "I haf done a great wrong, Inspector, to disturb the commander of the greatest police force in the world."

The man he addressed as inspector was tall and trim, with the look about him that some active, fighting general has, even when dressed in civilian clothes.

"The greatest police force in the world," the inspector smiled, "asks nothing better than to protect the world's foremost scientist."

"Aha," said the scientist; "so you call me that!"

"Everyone does—even if your theory is too much for them to understand, Professor."

"Maybe," said the little professor, "it would be better, in dat case, we let this Monster kill me, too, as he has already killed so many others. Like that, my fame, it would be safe."

He spoke lightly, with a sort of sad humor. But he was restless.

He took a turn up and down the large richly furnished room—the drawing room of the suite. The inspector sat in a leather easy-chair and watched him. There were no others present.

"We're not going to let him kill you, Professor," the commander of New York's police army said quietly. "You've not only got the whole police force of New York as a bodyguard—and that goes for every man in uniform as well as the fifteen hundred or so who are not. But there happens to be in New York at present one of the best men in the world for a case like this—just such a case as this."

"Ha! Another detective."

"One of the greatest, though an amateur, a volunteer."

"So! A Sherlock Holmes!"

"Not precisely. As gifted, perhaps, though in a different way. A former actor—a motion-picture actor. One who was as famous on the screen as you are—excuse the comparison—among the people who think and read. Perhaps you may have heard of him and remember him. Del Manning?"

"Del Manning! Ach! Surely now! Though I hardly ever go to the movies. I see him only once. Yet I nefer forget him—der 'man of five hundred faces'—"

"That's him."

"But he is dead."

"He merely allows the world to think so—so that he can be free. His fame was becoming a burden—"

"That I can understand!"

"So I asked him to meet us here."

There was a knock at the door, and the inspector sprang up to answer it. He greeted the well-dressed stranger from below. A moment later he'd turned to the world's foremost scientist.

"Professor," he said, "this is the gentleman I was telling you about. Meet Doctor Coffin."

• • •

II

THE TWO MEN SHOOK HANDS. There'd been no waste of words when the three of them—the inspector, the professor and Doctor Coffin—pulled up chairs. Doctor Coffin had been on the point of flying back to Hollywood when he'd got the inspector's S.O.S. The professor was someone who couldn't remain out of sight very long without being missed. As for the inspector, New York was just one long Battle of the Marne for him. There was no time to waste.

"There's a killer loose in New York," the inspector began without preliminaries. "He refers to himself as a monster—calls himself 'the Monster of Manhattan,' and he may be right, at that—and he is now out to kill the professor, here. That's why I wanted to get in touch with you, Doctor Coffin."

"Much obliged," said Doctor Coffin, with his brilliant, deep-set eyes still on the professor.

"It's a dangerous affair," the inspector went on. "This killer is evidently a homicidal maniac. And, like many another maniac, just over the line from genius."

"A genius is what he is," the professor broke in. "As proof of his intellect, he has transformed six of my equations from pure mathematics to pure morals, showing that it is right to kill off at least thirty per cent of the world's population."

Doctor Coffin listened to this with no other emotion than that of a concentrated interest.

"He has already begun?" he asked.

"Has he begun!" the professor cried, with a sudden shake in his voice. His own attitude toward killing people, even in a so-called defensive war, was well-known. He was one of the leading pacifists of the world, besides being the world's most famous scientist.

The inspector explained.

"By his own confession, this Monster—we might as well call him that, for we don't know what his real name is—has already killed more than two hundred people."

"Murdered them?"

"Murdered them—including women, children, infants."

"How?"

"In different ways—and there's where his genius comes in. Fire, poison, jumps or falls from upper floors; explosions, wrecks. In every case, thus far, his killings have been booked, not as homicides, but as accidents or suicides."

"How do you know they weren't?"

"We've been checking up—with the professor's aid. Here of late, each time the Monster pulls off a killing he lets the professor know about it, either by telephone, a telegram in code, or an advertisement in the papers. These notices come in always too late for us to interfere and too early for the Monster to have got the news from another source."

"For example?"

"There are no end of examples. A whole family suffocated by gas in a Brooklyn flat. A young millionaire apparently shot by accident. Another doing a dive from the eighteenth floor. Six children drowned through the ice—"

"Ach Gott!" the professor panted.

The inspector handed him a cigar and helped him light it.

"How did you verify the killings?" asked Doctor Coffin softly, smoothly.

"Fingerprints, mostly," the inspector said. "As soon as we got a line on what was up, we began to look for fingerprints, and we found them—practically in each case where there'd been a supposed accident or suicide. There was confirmation in other clues, furnished by the Monster himself."

"And in all these cases the fingerprints were the same?"

"The same."

"You don't know whose?"

"No hint, although we've sent them to every fingerprint bureau in the world, from Buenos Aires to Shanghai. The nearest we came to it was a return from Zurich, in Switzerland, where there was a certain similarity with the fingerprints of a man who'd been a professor in one of the universities—"

"Hot dog!"

The inspector shook his head. "He's out—unless we have a ghost at work. At least, he died two years ago. Two years, wasn't it, Professor?"

"Almost three. Poor Oscar! He was a friend of mine."

Doctor Coffin took thought.

"But I also am supposed to be dead," he said, and he ripped out a note of cheerless laughter.

"Oscar really died," said the professor. "I was present at his funeral."

It occurred to Doctor Coffin that there were those who could say—who would swear—that they'd been present at the funeral of the late Del Manning. Yet here was he who'd been Del Manning—alive and strong, able to think, ready to act. It might well be that his own case wasn't unique.

The inspector broke in.

"Whoever he is, he's now ready to show himself. He insists on an interview one hour from now with our friend, the professor, here. I don't want the professor to go. I'm afraid of what might happen to him. And yet, if he doesn't go, if the Monster even suspects a trap—"

"What then?"

"The Monster threatens to blow up Radio City tonight."

III

THERE, FROM WHERE THEY SAT, they could look through the tall windows of the room and see the towering heights of Radio City—the world's newest and greatest cluster of skyscrapers. It was as well, the world's greatest amusement center. This was to be the night of the grand opening. Far below those glittering peaks of stone and metal there was the huge cavern of a music hall, seating thousands, decorated like some magic cave in a tale by Sinbad.

Doctor Coffin turned his wrist and looked at the dial of his watch. It was four-thirty. In a few hours now, the crowds would begin to flow in that direction—half the notables of America.

Four-thirty on a rainy afternoon. But, just then, the sun that was going down broke through the clouds and flooded the west and the heights of Radio City with red flame. The ruddy light dripped about the high towers of the amusement center like a bath of blood.

Doctor Coffin's dark eyes caught the gaze of the inspector's clear gray eyes.

"I'm on," said Doctor Coffin.

"It's a lot to ask," the inspector replied with reticence.

Doctor Coffin ripped out a bit of his curious laugh. "You're not asking. I'm offering."

The professor looked at the two of them with an air of trouble. "Excuse me," he said. "But I do not quite follow."

The inspector explained.

"The proposal is this—that Doctor Coffin take your place. He is the one man in the world with the skill to disguise himself to look enough like you beyond the possibility of discovery; the one man in the world with genius enough to play the part of the Herr Professor—the world's greatest scientist."

"Impossible!"

"Not impossible," the inspector replied. "Doctor Coffin has played rôles even more difficult—not only before a camera but in front of a pointed gun."

"Then, what would you haf me do?"

"Return now with Doctor Coffin to the house of your friends. I've already taken the liberty of sending his make-up outfit there. Let him leave there disguised as yourself to keep this rendezvous with this so-called Monster—"

"I shall go myself," the scientist protested. "I am not a coward. This is some scientific madman who wishes to get possession of my brain—who will carry out his threat against that great audience tonight if he is deceived—"

"Before the curtain rises tonight, our madman should be in our hands, dead or alive. Trust us. Trust Doctor Coffin. You yourself, go to the show with your friends tonight as if nothing had happened—"

The inspector got to his feet. Just as he did so, the whole building was as if softly shaken by some subterraneous explosion. At the same moment, there was a ring at the telephone.

It was Doctor Coffin himself who leaped for the instrument. It was with the voice of the great scientist that he spoke:

"*Bitte! Sie wollen—*"

Even those others who stood there, away from the instrument, could catch that muted sinister reply:

"Ha, ha! Just to remind you, Professor! Another accident! You'd better be at the place of rendezvous! This is—*the Monster!*"

There was a heavy click as the instrument at the other end of the line was banged into place.

There had been another one of those mysterious explosions in the sub-basement of a New York hotel. There'd been a number of them of late, each time with a loss of life. Was it mere coincidence that this time the explosion had taken place in that hotel where Doctor Coffin had met the inspector and the professor?

The question was but one of a hundred that turned in the mind of Doctor Coffin when he finally found himself alone. He had just left the broad front door of one of the few fine old private houses that still remained on upper Fifth Avenue. This was the house of those friends who had the great European scientist as their guest.

Anyone passing at that moment would have believed that it was the famous professor himself who stood there now on the steps of the mansion. A mane of white hair fluffed out from under a soft, black felt hat. A long, black cloak of foreign cut shrouded the rather plump, slightly stooped figure from shoulders to knees. The dim face that looked out on the all but deserted avenue was wrinkled and kindly, the face of an idealist and a thinker. The step of the cloaked figure was that of an ageing student rather than that of an athlete as the supposed professor now made his way carefully down to the sidewalk, where he paused to light his pipe.

Night had fallen in the crowded fifty minutes. The clouds that hung low over the swarming island of Manhattan threatening more rain, were luminous with the reflected shine of Broadway's million lights. But, by contrast, this part of Fifth Avenue, opposite Central park, seemed all the darker.

The last instructions from the Monster was that the professor, on leaving the house of his friends, should cross the street to the park and there walk slowly south along the curb and await developments.

The cloaked figure obeyed instructions. There was little traffic. Pedestrians at this hour and place, on such a night, were absent.

Then, just as the disguised Doctor Coffin reached the opposite side of the street, he heard the wail of an ambulance, and he turned to look. The ambulance had swung into the avenue, from a side street.

It stopped at Doctor Coffin's side and he heard a hoarse, authoritative whisper commanding him to come on and lose no time.

IV

IN AN INSTANT, IT SEEMED, the whole stretch of that deserted avenue had come to life. From a dozen points, north and south from where the ambulance had stopped, men were tumbling over the park wall with pistols drawn. From the houses opposite, other men dashed out of areaways. There were three quick shots—then a blare of whistles.

The inspector had laid his plans well, but so far not well enough.

The ambulance was on its way.

That ambush of hidden detectives was only one small part of the inspector's plan.

A dozen radio-equipped police cars had suddenly concentrated on the neighborhood. Just now a number of limousines had turned into various side streets, up and down the avenue from the home of the professor's friends. The limousines had all the appearance of private cars conducting diners to various houses in the neighborhood. But suddenly they were blocking the side streets. The supposed dinner guests also were out and armed.

Anyone would have said that the driver of the ambulance had been supplied with a map of the inspector's plan.

It was a straight dash, so far as he was concerned, and not so far to go. First down to the nearest entrance to the park, which happened to be Fifty-ninth Street, then a skid and a whirl into the park itself.

And here there were details of the chase that were going to make it a tradition in the annals of the New York Police Department for a long time to come.

Barely in the park, the ambulance had jumped a fringe of turf and was off the driveway entirely onto one of the broad footpaths. Later, it was traced along this footpath for a whirling mile or so, where it left the footpath and now raced across a meadow.

Not more than two minutes had passed since the ambulance had picked up its strange passenger on Fifth Avenue. But if it had been swift, so had the police. The drivers of all those police cars, light or heavy, were young men generally bored at going slow through traffic and dying for a race. Sometimes they were up on charges for inventing a race all on their own, just for the sake of a little speed. They were getting all the speed they wanted this night.

Two minutes and a half, maybe, and all the traffic cops in Central Park were stopping traffic and shooing the police cars through. The park from one end to the other—almost three miles of it—was a hoot of sirens.

The ambulance was in sight, then it wasn't.

First one police car, then another, tried short-cuts at sight of the flying ambulance, only to run into trouble.

There was some shooting. But it had to be low. It was known that a friend of the inspector's was in that ghostly car. The ambulance was ghostly, all right. Its own siren made no sound any more. Its lights were out. It slid in and out of shrubbery. It disappeared for long seconds.

It was after one of these disappearances that the ambulance was clearly trapped.

This was when it was discovered sliding down the slope of a lawn toward a road that followed the shore of a lake near the western side of the park. North and south the road was blocked by swift police cars headed toward the ambulance. There were perhaps a dozen cops and volunteers also headed in.

A cheer went up. More shots were fired.

The ambulance plunged on—it reached the road and crossed it—then plunged into the lake—headed out toward deep water.

Not until minutes after that was it discovered that the ambulance at the time of its plunge, no longer had either driver or passengers. Those who'd been in it at time of the dash down Fifth Avenue had made their getaway.

Doctor Coffin, disguised as the world's greatest scientist, and so completely absorbed in his rôle that he'd practically forgotten his own identity, had been warned in advance that an effort would be made to capture the Monster—or those who were the Monster's agents—at the time of the meeting on Fifth Avenue.

But he'd responded to that summons to enter the ambulance as the Herr Professor himself might have done.

He'd made the half humorous inquiry:

"You would take me for a ride?"

"It's a ride. Lookit. I got a gun! Hop in! This ain't foolin'!"

It was a man dressed like an interne who spoke with the husky voice. But a killer. Doctor Coffin knew the type. Still—he was sure of this also—the fake interne was no Monster—no big shot—just a killer.

And not alone. In the ambulance more or less hidden, a strong-arm moll dressed like a nurse. Then another gunman—dressed like any gyp or clip of the big town this time. The chauffeur made four. Manifestly, the bird who called himself the Monster of Manhattan had a regular mob. And some roll. It took heavy money to swing an outfit like this, even in these days when the rum syndicates were going in for fleets of freighters and speedboats.

Anyway, he was still alive, when, somewhere in a dark corner of the park, he was jerked from the ambulance on the run and pushed into a manhole—down a sewer and up to his knees in running water.

"Keep quiet, now," came a stealthy voice, "and stick up your hands!"

V

A LOT HAS BEEN WRITTEN about the sewers of Paris, and nothing greatly exaggerated at that. Besides its sewers, moreover, Paris has its catacombs. Also its subway—the Metro, as they call it—which is like an underground web of such complication that the spider who designed it must have been drunk.

Even so, New York isn't far behind. If behind at all. Ordinary sewers. Trunk sewers. Water tunnels. Subways finished and unfinished. Man-size conduits for power, light, heat, telephone and telegraph, pneumatic carriers.

Before Doctor Coffin could get his eyes adjusted to the dark he could feel himself being searched by at least two pairs of hands. He was glad that he'd found a new place to carry his small automatic, which was close up under his chin.

He was still armed—and there was some satisfaction in that—when they finally told him he could lower his hands. The permission was followed by a command to duck his head and poke ahead. There'd been little enough said—and that little was whispered and swift. All in English, so far. And that was something else to be grateful for. It was going to be just too bad—maybe for others as well as himself—if anyone tried him out in the language of the Herr Professor. He could stagger a little way in German, like most Americans, but not far enough to sustain a bluff like this.

He'd walked ahead, bowed low, for about five minutes, and all this time in a cramped and sloppy darkness, when he made a play for information.

"But I protest," he said.

"Shut up!"

"I vill not shut up. Came as one gentleman to keep an agreement."

The only response was a muttered curse and the unmistakable poke of a gun in his back.

"If you shoot me," he said boldly, slowing his step, "I will be but as another dead man. Have you not enough cadavers without one more?"

It was another voice that put in. It came in a ghostly whisper from the rear. The whisper took on an added ghostliness from the confined space. It was like a voice from the grave.

"You are right, Professor. The Monster has corpses enough."

Doctor Coffin felt a thrill. If this wasn't the same voice he'd heard over the telephone at the hotel it was a perfect imitation.

"Ah, so!" he intoned softly. "Is not this the voice of the Monster?"

The succeeding silence was more impressive than any spoken response would have been.

It was the near voice that finally spoke—after a heartbeat or two of silence—not very long, but long enough.

"Move on!"

"But I choke!"—and Doctor Coffin fumbled at his throat.

The light of an electric torch flickered about him, as if the purpose of his movement had been suspected. Still, he'd managed to palm his small automatic from under his flowing tie. He had it in his hand as the light went out and he was shuffling ahead in the dark again.

Only two—Doctor Coffin meditated—and the Monster was one of them. With luck, he might kill them both. He could surely kill the rat just back of him. About the Monster himself he couldn't be so sure—if it was the Monster. A big shot. Maybe a maniac. A maniac—as it had been pointed out at the hotel—fringing close on genius.

Doctor Coffin was no more anxious to get himself killed than any normal man—than any normal fighting man. Especially here and now. In a slimy sewer. Where his body might lie for months—furnishing New York with one more addition to its already staggering total of unexplained mysteries.

Even so, it couldn't be rightly said that Doctor Coffin's first consideration was what might happen to himself. He held his life in trust. That was all. He had a picture in his mind of that huge music hall in Radio City, of that brilliant crowd of first-nighters who would fill the vast auditorium this night— millionaires, men and women of the people, girls and boys, painters, dreamers, mothers, hearts and brains and imaginations.

His own people!

As a phantom on a moving-picture screen he had appeared before the people like this. They had made him famous—the late Del Manning! They had made him rich!

Sure, he'd die for them if he had to. And that was that. But to let some crazy killer turn their frolic to panic—to mangled suffocation—death—

The thought was nerving him, just as the slimy trough of darkness through which he shambled emerged into some larger passage. He turned the corner, then, timing his blow almost by instinct, brought down the weapon in his hand on the head of the gangster who'd been following him.

The timing was right, but the hat the fellow wore was almost a helmet. And Doctor Coffin had to strike again, then again, before his man was down. But before he was down he'd pumped out two shots, given a yell.

After that it seemed minutes before the echoes rocked away and the dank air was free from smoke. Yet during this time, Doctor Coffin held steady—waiting, holding to his sense of direction in the dark, his gun, this time, ready for a shot.

Suddenly, his pistol hand was paralyzed. It was as if his wrist had been struck by a sledge hammer. Then an arm coiled about his throat and it was as if he'd been taken in the toils of a gigantic snake.

"You fool," came a stifled whisper; "don't you know yet that the Monster sees in the dark?"

VI

As a man gets fragments of the truth in a dream—or glimpses of reality through the clogging vapors of delirium—so Doctor Coffin was getting tatters of information now, while he fought—fought for his life and fought to kill, concerning this creature who called himself the Monster.

The Monster was a maniac. He had gusts of maniacal strength, long spasms of raving. Again, it was clear that he was an educated man—a man who'd been highly educated—educated to a point where he could, in fact, have taken the equations of that white-haired professor from Europe—the world's foremost scientist—and not only comprehend them, but convert them to some crazy system of his own.

The arm about Doctor Coffin's throat tightened to strangulation—to the verge of death—to the point where the black darkness was neither black nor dark, but a red haze shot with white-hot sparks. Then the arm would relax.

To kill first—die afterward.

That was the whole of Doctor Coffin's thought. It was a thought as tough as the coiled steel spring of his life itself. But he was handicaped. His right arm was practically out of commission. He'd been seized at a disadvantage. He had no weapon. This maniac, he discovered, was as skilled in all the tricks of wrestling, mauling, maiming, as he was himself.

The maniac would strangle him into helplessness, then talk.

"Ho," the Monster grunted. "You, the great savant! I was greater until they operated on my brain!"

In that dark, dank battle—when the life-spring almost snapped—the words seemed to take on a wider meaning, calling up pictures, rousing vague memories of things forgotten.

That's right. Doctor Coffin remembered now. There'd been a famous professor, of one of the great universities here in New York, years ago, who'd suffered a fractured skull. That also had been in a fight. There'd been a scandal—hushed up, except to the ears of the police and the underworld. The professor had eventually wound up in an asylum for the criminal insane.

And, after that, Doctor Coffin knew that he was further handicaped. The knowledge came to him by degrees—while he still fought—now down and almost smothered, now up and panting again for mastery. The knowledge was this—that he'd lost the impulse to kill.

"I want your brain," came one of those shreds of whisper from the Monster. "I've already told you that. I'll give you mine in exchange."

Not all at once. Between every word—between the shattered gasps of words that had to be pieced together later—this sort of monologue ran on.

Then, suddenly, Doctor Coffin spoke. Even now he found himself using a German accent.

"Then, for why—for vy—you kill my brain? I stop fighting. I help you."

Even this came slowly, brokenly. It was all strain—hauling, pushing, clinging. And there, for a while, Doctor Coffin knew that the Monster was studying the possibility of an exchange of brains here in the slimy dark.

This was like the twilight of life, then the night. There'd been a swoon of almost complete exhaustion, out of which Doctor Coffin came to discover that he was free, that those terrible, unseen hands were no longer at his throat. He pulled himself together, ready to stagger away.

But again the dread voice reached him, telling him to wait.

The man he'd knocked out as the fight began was regaining consciousness it seemed. For a few seconds there was the dance of blinding light from the electric torch, then darkness again.

There was another danger that Doctor Coffin was quick to recognize. Automatically he felt of his head and face. In all his long career on the screen he'd always used a system of makeup that could stand rough treatment. His fighting on the screen had been real fighting more often than not. He'd fought on land and water, in mud and under water.

He could tell. He was still the Herr Professor—double of that gentle-faced philosopher whose fame was even greater, maybe, than that of the late Del Manning.

The thought steadied him. It was as if he was two men now instead of one—Del Manning himself, then the great professor. It almost made him laugh—in that mirthless way of his. He would have laughed, if his throat hadn't felt so sore.

Now, the gangster he'd knocked out was shuffling on ahead, using the electric torch. But there must have been a gadget on the torch to reduce the glare. The light was dim. Doctor Coffin followed. Back of him, still unseen, came the Monster—whispering, mumbling, falling silent; and, somehow, the silence was worse than the things half-heard—things about an operation—about the old Egyptian method—the way the embalmers had when preparing the mummy—of extracting the brains of the patient through the nostrils.

They had, it seemed, walked miles, through what may have been an abandoned aqueduct—a water conduit with a section like that of an upright, narrow oval.

They came to an iron door no larger than the door of a furnace set in the wall of this.

"Crawl through!" came the Monster's grisly whisper.

VII

STILL WITH NO MORE LIGHT than that of the dimmed electric torch they came up into what appeared to be the sub-basement of a private house. The man who carried the electric torch now guarded Doctor Coffin with a drawn revolver while he who was undoubtedly the Monster unhooked the microphone of a telephone from the wall.

Instantly as he did this the instrument filled the place with a confused humming—a muted roar of traffic, of police whistles and auto horns, of uncounted voices, the muffled stroke of a bell.

Doctor Coffin knew that he was listening to the noises of New York. But of what part of the great city? He knew that he couldn't be so very far from Central Park. The walk through that stifling underground trench couldn't have been so long as it seemed.

Then the shadowy figure at the instrument himself volunteered enlightenment.

"Ha! Radio City!" he whispered with a sinister laugh. "Even now the crowds are beginning to assemble. They do not know that the main feature of tonight's entertainment will not appear on the printed program."

"You mean?"

"That there'll be a wholesale killing."

"But—*aber*—since I am here!" Doctor Coffin protested.

For the first time now he could clearly see his satanic host—a large man, gray-bearded, with bulging eyes which never appeared to be quite in focus. Yet the intellectual type, the former scholar, head of a department in a great university. He was the Monster, all right—and the more the Monster because of his gifted and distorted brain.

The Monster grinned at this semblance of the great German savant who stood in front of him.

"You were in collusion with the police. I warned you that if there was any trickery, any deception, I'd blow up that audience tonight."

"There was no deception," said Doctor Coffin. "Am I not here?"

The Monster reflected.

"Very well, Professor," he said. "We'll see later." He broke off and said something in German: "*Die Rechnung muss bezahlt werden!*—"

Doctor Coffin felt the glint of an inner chill. He'd grasped the meaning of those German words—something about an account that had to be settled— but his knowledge of German was scant. Suppose the madman now insisted on speaking German? That would mean an end of stalling; instantly this disguise would be useless.

But the danger passed.

The Monster was hungry. Would the Herr Professor dine with him? While they dined they could discuss the forthcoming operation. Doctor Coffin assented. He needed time.

At any moment now the opportunity might present itself to escape. An alarm, and this house would be surrounded.

A house, so Doctor Coffin learned, that stood on the fringe of Radio City. There were many such old houses still standing about the great development and some of them still rented. This one and the two adjoining houses, so the Monster said, he'd occupied ever since the work on Radio City—that city within a city—had begun. Then, blast by blast, as the excavations for the huge enterprise went ahead, the Monster and his associates had done some blasting of their own.

There was a tunnel connecting the house with the labyrinth that underlay the new skyscrapers. By means of it, the Monster bragged, he had direct access to the great new music hall which tonight was to have its opening.

"Where'd you get the dynamite for all that blasting of yours?" Doctor Coffin inquired, still careful to speak with his German accent.

"I needed no dynamite," the Monster boasted. "While I was in the State Hospital for the so-called"— he laughed—"insane, I worked out the principle of my new atomic bomb. I have so perfected it, I could shake this town with a grenade no larger than—your head! I'll kill half the congregation in that music hall tonight with a tool that appears no more dangerous than an old-fashioned watch."

He drew such a watch from his pocket and stared at it with his bulging, badly focused eyes.

"Dinner is served!" came the announcement in a whisper.

The whole house seemed to be stirring with servants—madmen and crazy women also, the disguised Doctor Coffin guessed. The house was as full of squeaks and scurryings as if it had been invaded by an army of rats.

Trying to disguise his absence of appetite, keen to learn what he could while there was still a chance, Doctor Coffin asked about those finger-prints that had baffled the police so long.

The Monster reached into his breast pocket and brought out a human hand. He put this on the snowy tablecloth in the center of the table.

"Preserved and electro-plated," he gloated, "also by a process of my own. I use it as a signature for all my little affairs—finger-prints everywhere—and the owner of them in his grave since half a dozen years! Ah, you see, Herr Professor, I also am a genius; and when I have your brains in my head as a more efficient working tool we will startle the world. There is only one thing—"

"What is that?"

"Die Aufgabe, Deutsch zu lernen."

The task of learning German! The meaning of the phrase was filtering into Doctor Coffin's mind. But he could not reply. He—the supposed scientist, with his fluffy mane of white hair, he who was supposed to have spoken German all his life, could not reply.

VIII

WHAT FOLLOWED CAME SO FAST that it already seemed a part of the past even while it was taking place.

For an interval, the Monster had sat there staring across the table at his guest—staring with those disordered, bulging eyes of his—while his face blackened, his eyes went bloodshot and his bearded lips began to twitch.

Then, without other warning, he'd let out a scream of demoniac laughter and scrambled to his feet. He screamed again. He howled. The howl was only half-formed into words, but his meaning somehow came clear enough in the few words that were distinct:

"Trick! Counterfeit! Spy! Emissary of the hated police!"

There was no delay while this was coming out—no more than other elements of a storm delay while the thunder rolls.

Doctor Coffin had seized a silver fruit knife from the table in front of him. It was the only weapon that came to hand.

At the same time, the room was invaded by queer figures, some of whom had been visible before, others whose presence had been merely guessed.

They would have fallen on Doctor Coffin and probably shredded him—as man-sized rats might have done—were it not for some command that had been shrieked in the midst of the fight by the Monster who was their acknowledged leader.

"Keep him! Hold him!" the Monster screamed. "I'll be back!"

The words were coming disjointed—filtered through a heavy web of battle.

Then, a comparative silence; and Doctor Coffin knew that the Monster was on his way—through that tunnel he had mentioned—into the labyrinth of underground passages and chambers that underlay Radio City—there where already the thousands would be gathered for the opening of the music hall.

Doctor Coffin was filled with such a sudden desperation that he himself was fighting like a maniac now. He was fighting in a vortex of whirling bodies and thorny hands. It was like having been caught in a free fight not of men but of wildcats.

Then, somehow, in a way that he would never know, he was on his feet and had his back to the wall. He still had the fruit knife in his hand, and the blade was bloody. The blade was slightly bent, but it had served him so far well enough.

Through the din that was rocking in his brain and assailing his ears, he heard again a scream he recognized.

It was as if a voice had reached him from the music hall itself, telling him to follow and to lose no time.

He was barely on his feet before he'd flung himself in pursuit of the Monster. A door blocked his way. He jerked his shoulder against it and it yielded. With the chase at his back, he plunged down a narrow flight of steps—an old stage-trick, taking a fall like that head-first. It was enough to have killed an ordinary man.

But he was up again, and using his tough body as battering-ram against another door. This also yielded, but grudgingly, stiffly.

Before him he saw dimly a narrow tunnel that had been rough-blasted through the solid rock that here underlay New York. Down that tunnel—divined rather than heard—there was a pound of running feet. Back of him, the crazy horde of servants were in pursuit.

He swung the door shut and was able to bolt it just in time.

So far, at least, he hadn't lost.

He neither paused to reflect on what had passed nor what might come. He was on his way.

And in the meantime, it was as if all the wealth and gaiety of New York, the talent and the beauty, had concentrated to honor the opening of Radio City.

Here was something that the world had never seen before—except, perhaps, in its wildest dreams. A pleasure dome—as the poet would have called it—that seemed impossible as a work of human hands.

Singly and in groups the celebrities had poured in. They'd stood for their pictures before a battery of "still" cameras and motion-picture machines. They talked into microphones, then rolled along to make room for others— bankers, politicians, motion-picture stars and luminaries of the stage, debutantes, famous beauties, diplomats. It was one of those nights when everyone would be there—everyone from the standpoint of the newsreel men and the gossip writers.

Then the hall itself—with a ceiling that looked more like a sky at sunrise than anything manufactured by men. The seats filled up—parterre and balcony.

The murmuring roar of six thousand people all talking at once gave way to a surge of music from a hundred—or two hundred—piece orchestra. There was the folding and unfolding of a stupendous curtain and the show was on.

Six or seven thousand people. And it would be safe to say that about the last thing any of them were thinking about was death—the threat of death— of some one man now fighting for their lives as he was also fighting for his own. And this man one who had been known to them as the greatest character actor the screen had ever known—the late Del Manning—otherwise, that "living dead man," Doctor Coffin, sometimes the leading undertaker of far-off Hollywood.

Yet, suddenly, they were seeing him. There he was again before their eyes. And of all that vast audience, two only recognized him. One was that little German professor with the snow-white mop of hair—the world's greatest scientist. The other was the commander of the greatest police army in the world.

IX

THERE'D BEEN A NIGHTMARE CHASE as Doctor Coffin raced after that fleeing madman who was now bent on wholesale slaughter—first through a maze of underground tunnels, of subterranean power-plants, of huge excavations in the living rock to which as yet no equipment had been brought; then to an electric hoist that had snatched both Doctor Coffin and the Monster to some unguessed height.

All Doctor Coffin could tell at that particular time was that fate or the madman's cunning had brought them to an unoccupied floor far up toward the top of the colossal new skyscraper.

The whole purpose of the Monster, so far, had been, it seemed, not so much an effort to throw off pursuit as to make a display of his genius, his superior strength and cunning. It was a familiar phase of insanity—the insanity of pride.

The Monster shouted it:

"Behold, I have magical powers! I am as one of the gods!"

And before Doctor Coffin could catch up with him, he was through an open window and running along a ledge—so far above the dizzy depths of the streets below, that the streets themselves were invisible except as a misty haze of illumination.

There was nothing to do but follow. The Monster might fall. But the greater menace remained. He would be back again—this time without a pursuer—filled again with his purpose to astonish that vast audience below before consigning it to slaughter.

Doctor Coffin, trained as he was, concentrated on the solid stone beneath his feet—he shut his eyes and his mind to the luminous gulf that opened under his hand—as he ran, then jumped a gap, then ran again along that murderous ledge.

The Monster had disappeared through a dark window. Doctor Coffin followed.

Next—or some time afterward, for in the whirl of events there was no keeping track of things—the chase led down a bottomless well of steps. It was down and down—sliding, falling, scrambling—floor after floor, level under level, turn after turn—until heart and lungs were laboring and the brain was spinning. Then, through a door, which the Monster seemed to know.

All this time, the Monster had carried in his hand that old-fashioned watch. Was this the bomb of which he had spoken? It probably was. In the secret archives of the Police Department—and of the War Department in Washington—were missiles no larger than this that, prepared in a certain way, were known to be capable of sending down a rain of death over thousands. All this time, Doctor Coffin had clung to his stained and battered knife.

They were through another door and onto what, this time, rather than a floor, appeared to be a vast gridiron—a grill of steel joists and bars through which, from below, there streamed up a thousand shimmering slants of light. And on the instant, Doctor Coffin recognized the nature of the place. They were out over the vast stage of the music hall. Down there the stage was covered with a dance of tiny figures—dancers—flooded with light.

So much, and the Monster had panted something in his hollow voice: "*At last!*"

Doctor Coffin sprang to seize him. But as he did so, the Monster himself sprang—he jumped like an ape—and caught the end of a steel cable that hung free. The cable began to unwind slowly from a drum.

Doctor Coffin also sprang, and in a moment the two of them—Doctor Coffin and the Monster—were tangled together at the cable's end, with the stage a hundred feet below.

The cable ran out slowly from the drum. The fighting pair swung lower. Now they were below the flies. Suddenly the whole vast cavern of the auditorium swung into sight; and as it did so, there was one universal gasp from the thousands seated there—it sounded as if the world itself had gasped.

Here was a feature indeed that hadn't been billed. One of the surprises, no doubt. Was it? Was this an accident? Or was it an act? The ballet had stopped. For a moment the big orchestra was jerked out of tune. Then the leader of the orchestra had taken a fresh grip, and a louder burst of music than ever was thundering out. As if this were a signal, the audience began to applaud—a surf of handclapping—a surf like that of a storm.

And then, some masterful stage manager, guessing the truth, turned on the steam curtain and jets of mist came up to conceal the stage—as those two fighting figures—the general opinion was that they must have been a pair of eccentric acrobats—came lower, lower, fighting apparently—apparently squirming in some sham battle of death.

Then, just as the steam curtain concealed them, there might have been faintly heard—through all that music and applause—a slight thud, as one of those dangling actors fell.

It was the Monster who fell.

He'd fallen to his death, and the head of New York's police force himself was there to pronounce the requiem. He was there also to receive Doctor Coffin, as his feet at last found the stage.

The police commander was hard as steel—tempered by a thousand beatings and baths of tragic experience. But all he could do, just then, was to take Doctor Coffin's hand in his own and look the things he couldn't say.

Small Town Stuff

THEY WERE GOING TO REMEMBER later that no one had ever seen him before. But the stranger had looked so much like one of the regulars that he hadn't attracted any particular notice until—there he was with a gun in his hand and giving orders.

"Steady!" he said. "Hands up!"

His voice had sand in it—it grated.

It was heavy but not very loud. And deadly—with something in it to match the heavy blue automatic with which he now slowly fanned the crowd.

"Now, turn round," he said. "Face the wall. Keep 'em up!"

He looked like a brakeman from the near-by railroad yards—husky, supple, dressed in blue woolens. He had on an old soft black hat pulled low and the front brim turned down. But what could be seen of the face matched the voice—matched the gun. There was something about his shadowed eyes and lean, strong jaws to suggest the face of a skull.

There may have been some among those who stood there with their hands up who suspected the truth—that this was Doc Coffin—"Skullface," as he was getting to be better known in the underworld. But if so they made no comment.

There was a shuffle of movement as the crowd obeyed—twenty of them, just about, and probably not one of them who wasn't armed, with a "shiv," a blackjack, or a gun. As tough a mob as you could have run into anywhere. But not one of them now who didn't feel that he personally would get the first slug when that automatic began to spit fire.

They were in the pool-hall back of the Red Indian grill-room, Dartown's principal sporting center. Dartown wasn't very big—not much more than a village according to New York standards. But it was tough, all right.

Doctor Coffin, on special business, had been here a week. It was just a little more than a week ago that Dartown's reform mayor, Jerome Saunders, had been found murdered—sewed in a sack and left in Court House Square.

When Doctor Coffin made his gun play just now the only one in the room to show resistance was Kay Bird.

Kay was in charge of a gambling layout—the only game so far in operation. The time was early night. He made a reach for his gun. He always could think and act as quick as a rattlesnake. Kay resembled a rattlesnake in other respects—wiry and lithe, pure poison to anyone who crossed him.

But before Kay was half-way to his draw, Doctor Coffin shot out his left—quick and hooked like a tiger's claw—and pinched a cord in Kay's neck. A curious grip—one that could not be shaken off, causing a sort of paralysis.

Kay—held like a snake in the hand of an expert—still made a play, but only in words.

"You win, bo," he gasped. "Take the jack and lam. We ain't stoppin' yuh."

Doctor Coffin's only answer was to pull him up and back by that grip on his neck.

There were a number of ways in and out of the gambling rooms besides the front entrance through the grill-room by which most of the Red Indian's customers came and went. Doctor Coffin evidently knew his way about. In a silence that suddenly seemed to have become absolute, Kay Bird was snaked through the room to a back door that gave on an alley. There, Doctor Coffin paused to look back.

Among those facing the wall there had been a movement, preliminary perhaps to a break. Then Doctor Coffin displayed one of those tricks that had made him famous on the screen. Only, when he'd pulled it on the screen, people had thought it was a mechanical trick. But this was no mechanical trick. Standing there where he was, he "threw" his voice.

To those who heard it, the voice seemed to come from right there somewhere in back of them—clear, soft, yet with the same grating menace:

"Hold it, y' bums! Or do yuh want some hot lead?"

II

BUT NOT EVEN DOCTOR COFFIN—"the late Del Manning," he who'd been known and loved as the world's greatest character actor, "the man with five hundred faces"—could control all the forces of a play like this. Not in a complex joint like the Red Indian.

In the partition wall separating the grill from the supposed pool-hall there was a small window through which orders could be served to the gamblers straight from the kitchen. The cook was an ex-convict named Frenchy. As for that, there was scarcely an employee about the place, from the big boss down, who hadn't, at some time or other, been up against the Law or who wasn't quick to smell trouble where ordinary citizens might have overlooked it.

It was that sudden silence in the gambling room that got to Frenchy.

In a moment he'd jerked open the little quick-order window and poked his head through. One look was enough. He jerked back and let out a howl. But all in the same instant he'd grabbed a sawed-off shotgun from the bread-shelf under his counter and poked it through the window.

The door to the back-alley was just swinging shut, but Frenchy let go. The blast and the howl started things.

One of the first to respond was the big boss of the place, "Soapy Jo" Rezner—the Hon. Joseph P. Rezner, to give him the name he preferred; and had a right to, at that, now that he was Dartown's "acting mayor." By a political deal with the reform element, the boss of the Red Indian had managed to get himself elected to the town council at the time the reform mayor, Jerome Saunders, went in. It wasn't long after that before Soapy Jo had himself elected president of the council. He'd become mayor automatically when Saunders was murdered.

Jo had been sitting at a table in the grill with a number of political friends.

He was no hand-shaker, but he had to eat—a whale of a man, built like a heavyweight prizefighter; cold as an iceberg and as hard; "soapy" because he was slippery, that was all.

There's always something impressive about speed in a big man. Jo was out of his place at the table and over at the door leading into the back room before the other politicians at his table could do more than stare.

He stood there now commanding both rooms—cold and steady, not a quaver about him.

"Nothing!" he said, and a nod of his head was cue enough for the waiters in the grill.

They were back on their job, reassuring diners.

Jo shot a glance at Frenchy, and suddenly Frenchy also was back on the job—of grilling a steak, with his sawed-off shotgun out of sight.

But the Big Boss jerked a lot of action into the back room.

As soon as he saw that the restaurant was quiet he was out there and the door closed and locked behind him. His first jump was for the deserted gambling table from which Kay Bird had disappeared. It took but a flick of his eyes to see that no one had tapped the bank. The stakes still lay on the table.

There were a dozen wise ones by this time trying to tell him what had happened.

"He looked to me like Doc Coffin," someone said.

So had Soapy Jo heard rumors that Doc Coffin had come to pay Dartown a visit.

The grapevine telegraph of the underworld had been spreading the news.

While everyone was still talking, Soapy Jo signaled two of the mob with his eyes. They were off on a run—toward the back door—reaching for their guns.

· · ·

III

THE WHOLE AFFAIR, SO FAR, had been a mere matter of seconds—as full of details as a railroad wreck and as swift. Doctor Coffin was out in the back alley with his prisoner before Kay Bird himself came fully awake.

To Kay there was only one answer to what had happened. No one was kidnaping him for his beauty or because they loved him. Someone was taking him for a ride; and if he had to die, it might as well be now. He gave a convulsive jerk and kicked—both feet off the ground—and at the same time reached for his gun.

The gun barked. And the flash that stabbed the dark was where the late Del Manning's head should have been. But the volunteer detective had ducked. Before Kay Bird hit the ground—or could fire a second shot—Doctor Coffin bashed him across the head with the flat of his own gun.

Kay was out. He might have been dead for any sign of life that he gave just then. But Doctor Coffin wouldn't leave him here. He'd come here especially to get this man. From what he'd picked up so far, here in Dartown, Kay Bird could tell a trifle more than anyone else—unless it was Soapy Jo Rezner himself—about the killing of Jerome Saunders.

Up the alley forty or fifty yards away there was a brief hoot from an automobile siren, followed by the whir of an engine as the car started to roll away.

It was the car that was to have picked up Doctor Coffin after he'd made this raid. It had been agreed that a single shot, here in the alley, would be a signal for the car to make its getaway—that the raid had failed.

Doctor Coffin jerked his unconscious prisoner to his shoulder and started in pursuit. Useless, he knew it before he'd taken half a dozen steps. The car was picking up speed.

Then, just back of him, a door jumped open and two men sprang out. They were the gunmen Soapy Jo had sent out to get him.

Instantly, Doctor Coffin jerked off his hat and dropped his human burden. In the dark he called out, smothering his voice:

"Here I am, fellers! I'm Kay! And did I drop this sucker! Come on! Light a match!"

Doctor Coffin stooped low over the still unconscious Kay Bird. The alley was dark. This spot was hot. He knew it was. Those shots had been heard. There were sounds of people approaching from both directions with the jerk and play of flashlights.

The gangsters from the Red Indian had taken him at his word. He didn't straighten up until they were bending low. He struck again, and was careless, this time, whether he killed or not—struck twice, with the intensity and speed of a pneumatic riveter.

One of the gangsters passed out cold. The other twisted over, jerking his trigger-finger and not appearing to care where the bullets went. Doctor Coffin silenced him, this time, with a quick kick in the head, then backed away, dragging Kay Bird with him.

There wasn't much choice of the direction he could take. It was one way or the other and enemies in both directions. He couldn't go back through the gambling room, that was certain. Nor was this a spot to linger on either— getting hotter every moment.

He kept right on in the way he'd started, once more getting Kay across his shoulder. His right hand was free. His hand was on his gun. He was hoping he wouldn't have to use his gun. But he'd use it if he had to. He'd given his promise to certain people.

There was a sharp stoppage to even this flashing thought as the white spear of an electric torch leaped out of a dark doorway and sought his face. It was the face of Kay Bird he maneuvered into the lights instead of his own.

"Who's that?" he demanded.

There was a cautious movement toward him of four or five dark shapes and the foremost of these Doctor Coffin recognized as Captain Fisher of the local police—a stout man with a mean eye and a walrus mustache—who stood in well with the crooked politicians.

"Hello, Captain," said Doctor Coffin. "Hold-up! Down the alley. I'm afraid they got poor Kay. Soapy wants you to help me get him away."

He was shooting it out so fast that Captain Fisher was having trouble to follow him. But it clicked. Soapy Jo's orders; and that was enough for the big policeman. The torch was off and it was dark again.

"Gotcha," he said. "We'll get a jit at the corner."

Just a small town, Dartown; but it was the county seat and the trading center of a far-flung district of mines and mills. This was Saturday night and the town was crowded. Pay-nights like this made the town a prize worthy the attention of any ring of political grafters. These crowds who came in on Saturday nights were liberal spenders and bent on excitement. The concessions, so-called, were gold-mines—bootleg, gambling, and so forth.

No wonder the crooks had bumped off young Jerome Saunders when he'd tried to clean up the place and stop their revenue.

"Where'd you say you was taking Kay?" asked Captain Fisher.

Doctor Coffin held his answer. "Get him into the cab, first," said Doctor Coffin. "Soapy's leery. He thinks this is some sort of a comeback in the Saunders case."

"Oh, he does!"

And where the alley joined the street, Captain Fisher flagged a "jit"—not a regular taxi, just an open touring car driven by its owner for hire. The owner was a shrewd slim young man who looked like a farmer.

"Drive fast," said Doctor Coffin, as he and Captain Fisher sagged into the back seat with an unconscious Kay Bird between them. "Get us across the river. I'll tell you where to go after that."

The car jerked away. Already there was the beginning of a crowd. Then, as they bumped across the main stem where the Red Indian and other signs blared in a riot of electric light, they could see the beginning of another mob—people streaming along toward the Red Indian as to a house on fire.

It took them only a couple of minutes to strike the bridge and there the car spun smooth.

"Where you takin' him?" asked Captain Fisher, with sudden suspicion.

The suspicion was justified. Only the older families of Dartown—members of the "reform party" who'd elected Jerome Saunders mayor—lived on this side of the river. Here the murdered mayor himself had lived.

"I'm taking him," said Doctor Coffin, suddenly slinging out his words loud and clear so that the driver of the car also would hear, "to talk to the man he thinks he murdered."

"Thinks he murdered!"

"Sure! Mayor Saunders isn't dead. You'll be talking to him yourself pretty soon, right over there at his grandfather's house."

Captain Fisher strained around. His mean eyes popped and stared.

"Are you nuts?" he rasped.

And he made an awkward reach for his gun. But before he could get his hand anywhere near it, Doctor Coffin twitched his automatic into view.

"I wouldn't," soothed Doctor Coffin. "You're just an accidental pickup, Cap. But old General Saunders—and his honor the mayor—will be happy to see you, too."

Doctor Coffin leaned over and removed the big policeman's gun. He let out the brief cackle of a mirthless laugh. Just then, in that dim light, his face was like that of a laughing skull.

IV

GENERAL JOHN SAUNDERS—"Fighting Jack," as he'd been known in the army. Going on eighty, now; but still the fighting man all right. Tall and lean, with a shock of white hair and bushy white eyebrows, eyes that were twin blue gimlets.

His big old house lay back from the road in a bit of woods. It was here that his grandson, the murdered mayor of Dartown, had lived with him. There were no other relatives.

But there were plenty of servants—mostly black; and most of them, at that, using the Saunders name as their own—children and grandchildren of slaves who'd belonged to the General's own grandfather who'd lived in this same house before the Emancipation.

The General was polite to Captain Fisher of the Dartown police. And at that the big policeman was inclined to bluster. The General stopped that.

"Captain Fisher," he said, "before God, I'm going to avenge the murder of my grandson and clean up this town if it takes another war. I ask you now. Which side are you on?"

He stood there drilling the policeman with his gimlet eyes.

"I'm on the side of law and order," the fat captain mumbled. "But—"

"But?"

"But this here outsider—"

"This outsider, sir, if you refer to Doctor Coffin, is risking his life for that law and order you speak about."

"He says your grandson's still alive!"

General Saunders seemed to need a second or two for self-control. Maybe not.

His voice was soft and steady when he spoke again.

"Strange things happen, Captain Fisher. You shall see."

Of all the strange things that were slated to happen, this night, some of which and rumors of which were already sending an extra thrill through the Saturday night crowds in Dartown, one of the strangest was happening right now on an upper floor of the old Saunders' homestead.

There, in a room that had been occupied by the murdered mayor, Doctor Coffin, he who'd been known to the moving-picture world as the great Del Manning, was undergoing one of his greatest transformations.

It was a miracle watched with fervor by three Negroes—one of them an old black woman who'd watched the late Jerome Saunders grow up practically from the day of his birth.

Into this room she'd seen come this white man who looked just like any white man who worked on the railroad. Now, here before her eyes, unbelievably, it was young Marse Jerome who was taking the brakeman's place. Marse Jerome who'd been handsome, who'd been elegant, pure quality.

The Negroes had placed on the floor, at Doctor Coffin's suggestion, a wide tall mirror; then, at the side of this, a full-length, life-sized portrait of Jerome Saunders finished shortly before his death.

Before mirror and portrait Doctor Coffin squatted on the floor, cross-legged, with his great make-up box in front of him. That bony yet finely modeled face of his own was like a preliminary portrait sketch that might have been built up into a resemblance to almost any face. Swift, sure—he was the master artist.

At last he rose and stood there in his underclothes and an old bathrobe—studying the portrait, studying his reflection. Gradually he straightened up somewhat, yet his body flexed, became more graceful.

He turned to one of the Negro men and spoke in a soft clear voice copied from that of the old General downstairs.

"Jerry," he said, "tonight I think I'll let you select the costume I'll wear."

"Bress Gawd!" the old woman cried. "It's Marse Jerome his self!"

There'd been a gradual gathering of neighbors—men only—at the old Saunders house in its patch of woods. Young, old, rich, poor—all sorts; but all of them similar in a number of respects. Sober, for instance; not talking much; able and willing to fight; friends of the General and of the General's murdered grandson.

Sitting in a place of honor almost, you would have said, in the midst of this solemn party were the two who didn't belong. One of them was Captain Fisher of the Dartown police. The other was Kay Bird, Soapy Jo Rezner's right-hand man.

Kay was all right again. He'd been well cared-for. He'd got over that crack on the head. He'd even been given a couple of drinks of whisky. But silent, motionless, watchful without seeming to be. The cards were against him—he could see that; and the stakes were high—his life—against what?

Suddenly it was as if everyone was holding his breath. Not a sound. Then a step on the stair—and a sort of gasp and shudder from the crowd in the hall.

It was a sound or a shake—or both—that spread to those in the room where the crooked cop and the crooked gambler sat there side by side. Captain Fisher lurched and stared.

Kay Bird never moved but, almost visibly, he began to freeze.

An apparition of the murdered mayor of Dartown was standing in the door—graceful, handsome, his wavy hair rather long: the late Jerome Saunders come to life.

The late Jerome Saunders now laughed softly.

He spoke with a well-remembered voice:

"How many murder mysteries, gentlemen, might be cleared up if the victims could always confront their killers!"

His eyes were on Kay Bird as he sauntered forward.

Not a sound.

Then a strangled shriek—half curse, half just unadulterated nightmare—

as Kay Bird jumped and tried to run.

But almost before he was out of his chair Doctor Coffin's strong hand caught him by the throat and the gambler had fallen to his knees.

V

SMALL TOWN STUFF—that murder of the young Dartown mayor; but they'd tried to do it in a big-town way. Kay Bird was telling everything he knew— giving names, giving the precise gist of conversations that had preceded and followed the murder.

The chief conspirator in the murder of young Jerome Saunders was Soapy Jo Rezner, the present acting mayor of Dartown, boss of the Red Indian and other illegal joints—there was no doubt about that.

Kay wasn't trying to clear himself. Once he started to lay down his hand, he laid it down—that was all: all his cards on the table and face up, showing no more emotion than if he'd been merely sitting in a poker-game.

"So we got the mayor to inspect the back of the station-house," he said; "one afternoon when there wasn't any prisoners and nobody was around but the captain here."

"You're a liar," said the big police chief.

But his brawn had turned to tallow. He kept tugging at his walrus mustache, which was wet. His mean eyes were popping.

"I'm not lying," said Kay Bird, in his small unshaken voice. "His honor here will back me up."

And there he was, switching his attention to Doctor Coffin—the late Jerome Saunders, that is; the man he was supposed to have helped murder and put in a sack.

The funny part of this is that there wasn't anyone present who seemed to find this unreasonable—not even Doctor Coffin himself, he who might even now be called "the late Del Manning." For a long time anyway, Doctor Coffin, Hollywood's leading undertaker and America's leading nemesis of crooks, himself had been, so to speak, a living dead man. This was no new rôle.

And anyway, this wasn't, as a matter of fact, Doctor Coffin sitting here in front of the murderous little gambler, but the late Jerome Saunders in person. It was always like that—and it had always been like that—when the late Del Manning undertook a rôle. When he played a character, he became that character.

"What you say is true, Kay," said Doctor Coffin—the late Jerome Saunders. "The captain, here, saw everything—knew all the time what was going on."

"You lie!" Captain Fisher pumped.

Old General Saunders jumped up, white and shaking—"Fighting Jack."

"You, sah!" he said. "You give the lie to one of mine! Old as I am, by God—"

And he raised a fist.

One of the younger men present jumped ahead of the General and caught the big police captain by the hair.

Doctor Coffin—the voice of the late Jerome Saunders—called for order, but, all of a sudden, there was lynching in the air. Just now these people had been hearing such a tale of murder that their blood ran cold. In the swift reaction their blood was boiling.

Doctor Coffin saw the danger. He was on his feet—his dark eyes flashing. His voice, still the voice these people remembered, rang out:

"Gentlemen—"

There was a gradual silence.

"When you elected—not me, but the grandson of Fighting Jack Saunders to be your mayor—he pledged himself to put the crooks behind the bars or run them out of town. That pledge is still unfilled. Will you help me carry it out?"

There was a shout of, "Yes!"

"We'll begin by arresting these two—"

That shrewd-faced young driver of the local taxi who'd driven Doctor Coffin, the police chief and the unconscious Kay Bird out here from the center of town a while ago had been scouting about the place in a state of high excitement—up against something that he couldn't understand but just naturally feeling that all hell was about ready to pop.

There were plenty of others roaming about—crowding the porch, peering into windows, coming and going through the woods. Some had come in cars and some in wagons. Everywhere there was talk of a wholesale lynching.

The murderers of the mayor had been discovered. Yet there was the mayor himself. Something no one could understand. And only one thing certain.

Tonight in Dartown there was going to be war—war to the finish, the reformers against the crooks.

The taxi-man sneaked away. Whatever it was, this news was too big to hold any longer. He'd have to spread it. He was on his way—back across the bridge, headed in the general direction of the Red Indian and Court House Square.

As a matter of fact, the news, to some extent, had got there ahead of him. Dartown was in a state of ferment—no one knew just why. Jerome Saunders was alive. The murderers of Jerome Saunders had been discovered—they were going to be lynched.

You would have said that the news spread to the rest of the county and was bringing the people in from other towns and hamlets. Never such a crowd in Dartown had ever been seen—not even on election night. And the two hardware stores doing a rushing trade—selling guns and knives, ax-handles, rope—

VI

SOAPY JO REZNER, COLD AS AN ICEBERG—and as hard—followed all this. If anything, he was even a step or two in the lead of these swiftly developing events.

Right from the start-off, he had not liked the look of things. Kay Bird gone—and Kay knew too much. Gone in a taxi with Captain Fisher—Soapy's own selection as chief of police. And, tie that if you could! Along with the hold-up who, someone said, looked like Skullface—Doc Coffin—the mysterious detective who lately had been giving some of the big-time crooks the run-around. Then, two of his gunmen slugged and left in the alley. That looked like Doc Coffin's fine Italian hand—

As soon as Soapy Jo could get the Red Indian in order and running smoothly—chuckaluck, bird-cage, faro, roulette, craps, and every game crooked—he strolled over to City Hall with some of his political friends, two of them thugs and serving as a bodyguard.

The acting mayor of Dartown and his friends were cooking up the job of putting through the deal for a new million-dollar bridge, about nine hundred thousand of which price would go in cuts, fifty per cent to Jo himself and the other fifty to the lesser wolves.

But even during this short walk there was no getting away from the fact that something was the matter with the town.

"What's the crowd followin' us for?" one of the heelers asked.

"Jo's gettin' popular," another heeler wisecracked.

"Must be that new line of hootch," another politician slid from the corner of his mouth.

But this crowd wasn't drunk—too silent, too watchful, too dense. And no popularity of Soapy Jo was dragging them along—Jo got that before the others did.

The others got it when a sudden voice shrilled out: "Hey, Soapy, need another sack?"

At that, there was a murmur from the crowd.

And not a cop in sight. Not until they were just going up the steps of City Hall and one of the cops supposed to be patrolling the other side of the river came breezing in, breathless and excited, wild-eyed.

"Chief!" he said to Soapy Jo.

He'd never spoken to the acting-mayor before in his life.

"What do you want?" Jo asked.

"He's alive!"

"Who?"

"Mayor Saunders!"

They were standing on the steps of City Hall at the time—the henchmen pressing in and the crowd in the background.

Soapy Jo never winced. He turned and went into the building—others following, the two thugs who served as bodyguard squeezing the cop between them.

But City Hall was already invaded. It was always like that on Saturday nights. This was the place you came to see the big boss—to get a job, to get a license, to fix anything from a summons to a criminal case.

Soapy Jo kept on walking—right on through the front hall to the jail at the rear. It was in that room back there where Jerome Saunders had been shot and his body put in a sack. Soapy knew it, and the knowledge reassured him now. He whirled on the cop.

A new man—sandy, freckled, looking what he was in spite of his misfit uniform, just a clodhopper from the sticks.

"You ought to leave it alone," said Jo.

The cop didn't even understand. "Leave it alone?"

"The hop," said Jo. "You're nuts." And he hauled off and shot a punch at the man's face.

At that, he might not have landed if the two thugs hadn't seized the green cop by the arms at the same instant and shoved him into the blow. The man staggered a little. While he staggered, the thugs relieved him of his gun and "billy." The one who got the blackjack lifted the weapon for a knockout at a signal from Jo.

There'd been many a time when the big boss relieved his nerves with this sort of play.

But the cop, tough as a wildcat, had reached understandingly at last—and not so slow at that.

"I tell you," he panted, "Mayor Saunders ain't dead! He's comin' back! He's comin'—"

"Throw him in," said Jo, and the thug with the blackjack aimed a blow. But the cop dodged. He'd lunged sideways, going to the floor with the man who held the gun. In a moment, the cop had recovered his weapon and—seated there on the floor—shot twice. One bullet caught the thug with the blackjack under the chin—and Soapy Jo jumped back to dodge a squirt of blood. The cop's second shot went through the head of the man on the floor—

as if nailing him there, so that his head held fast while his legs jerked.

Before the second jerk the cop was up and after Jo.

But Soapy Jo—at his first retreat from that spurt of blood—obeyed a hunch to keep on going. There was a back hall leading from the jail-room to the alley at the side of City Hall. It was through this back hall—Soapy remembered—where the sacked body of young Jerome Saunders had been carried.

Just as Jo reached the open air, he heard the surge of a cheer—an overwhelming cheer, and in it some element of madness.

VII

SOAPY JO—ACTING MAYOR OF THIS CITY by right of murder and feeling for the first time some hint that this might not be so good—ran along the dark side of City Hall to see what was going on out there in front. Right then was when he was going to get his first great shock—like going crazy in an instant and yet knowing it—looking at something that couldn't be and yet, there it was in front of your eyes.

The swarm of a milling mob—thousands, and everyone shouting. And there in the center of the mob, under the full blaze of an arc-lamp, the man who'd been murdered and put in a sack, Jerome Saunders, mayor of Dartown.

Just a flash. A glance no longer than the tenth of a second. But unmistakable, everlasting—like the shot of a high-speed camera.

Jerome Saunders himself standing up on the back seat of a big, old-fashioned auto with the top thrown back—unmistakable, dressed in white, waving his Panama hat, just as he had on the night of his election; and the crowd, then as now, going wild.

Jo turned.

He saw the policeman who'd just killed the two thugs come out of the side door—the door Jo himself had just left. The cop still had his gun. He was on the prowl.

Just as Jo started to run, the policeman saw him and started in pursuit. . . .

Even before Doctor Coffin—the Jerome Saunders back from the grave—had started this return of his to the center of Dartown, a posse of volunteers, men who could be trusted, had rushed Kay Bird and Chief of Police Fisher not to the city but the county jail.

The county jail was an old stone building—put to the test before by lynching mobs and shown to be reliable. Yet even from here more elements of the sensation that was setting the town on fire seeped out and did to the excitement what so much gasoline would have done to a regular fire.

Everything else forgotten—movies, speaks, gambling joints, dance halls;

all the elements that usually gave the crowds in Dartown on Saturday nights the excitement they craved.

There was a crowd around the county jail—with rope enough to hang a regiment. That crowd that had followed Soapy Jo and his henchmen to City Hall had swelled.

But even so, neither the crowds at one place or the other felt that they were at the scene of the main event.

Then, suddenly, everyone was running in one direction. How it started no one knew. But the whole town was humming. And the hum was a clamor. You couldn't have heard the firebells.

There was a procession coming over the bridge. It was a procession of the friends of Jerome Saunders. And Jerome Saunders was coming back.

They were yelling it, shouting and dancing it, wigwagging it with their arms. The very absurdity of it was part of the excitement. Something stronger than hootch. A greater intoxication. Like the end of the world.

To Doctor Coffin, standing up there on the back seat of the big old-fashioned car there came a discordant shriek.

One section of the mob had just emerged from City Hall—looking for Soapy Jo himself but finding only one of the politicians who'd dined with him tonight at the Red Indian.

Now the mob was dragging the politician out with a rope around his neck.

Doctor Coffin made a flying leap. He'd been needing something like this to relieve the tension he was under.

The crowd about him fell away and gave him room as if he'd been an actual ghost. In a moment—instantly it seemed—he was surrounded and protected by a sort of flying wedge.

"Not that!" he shouted. "Not now!"

And that was the shout that the mob about him was taking up.

There came another:

"Soapy Jo's the man we want! We want Soapy Jo! String up Soapy Jo!"

Doctor Coffin found himself standing over the politician. The man was flabby, unable to stand. He gave one look up at the man he supposed to be Jerome Saunders.

"I helped," he said. "But Soapy Jo made me!"

It was more by lip-reading than by sound that Doctor Coffin made out what was said. The din of the mob was like the steady, hooting roar of a hurricane—

They got the politician to one of the cars, and the car headed for the county jail. It was in the county jail now, Doctor Coffin knew, that lay Soapy Jo

Rezner's own only hope of escape from a mob like this.

To one of the posse who'd come over the river with him, Doctor Coffin made a swift recommendation and the man was swept out of sight. Had he understood? Did he agree? Would the state troopers come?

Doctor Coffin himself had been swept away—riding that human flood and still controlling it to some extent. He was the miracle man. He was the mayor of this town.

Across Court House Square the crowds bore him. They were looking for Soapy Jo—the man who had murdered their mayor and on whom the murdered mayor would now pass judgment.

VIII

THEY SWEPT INTO THE RED INDIAN. They went into the front door—then through the whole front, as windows were smashed—flattening out everything like a stampede of elephants; then back into the gambling rooms, crashing down the partition, overturning pool-tables, shattering and scattering all sorts of equipment.

Here the crowds split and separated—half to the back and half to the front—as Doctor Coffin, mounted on a counter, shouted his orders.

Even as he stood there, a curtain of flame spread up the wall back of him, there where Frenchy's kitchen had been—

Soapy Jo had been hearing that roar of the mob for many minutes—each minute an hour. He was powerful. He was quick. But for once in his life he'd been caught at a disadvantage in a dozen different ways.

He was out of training. He was unarmed. He was alone. He had no hideout. And—this also for the first time in his life—he felt that he was getting old. He couldn't throw off this young hick—this yaller hound—of a red-headed, freckled policeman who was following him.

Right now there seemed nothing in the world so impossible to Soapy Jo Rezner—not even the return of Jerome Saunders—as that less than half an hour ago—less perhaps than a quarter of an hour—he had been in a position where he could order this man slugged and thrown into a cell.

What had happened?

There were plenty of back alleys in Dartown, all of them dark. But not dark enough. Soapy Jo Rezner ambled from one to another. He went through vacant houses and empty lots.

Always, just back of him, was that killer cop.

Until, at last, Jo was running blind.

And, all this time, that heavy organ music of the mob in his ears—cheering the man he had murdered, seeking now to murder him. And then, gradually, like a part of this murder-dirge, a spread of red in the sky.

Soapy Jo was flatfooting it up a deserted side street now when, suddenly, at a crossing, he saw a billow of flame go up and the whole town shivering in a bright red illumination.

That was the end of the Red Indian. It was the end of a whole row of dives and joints that had paid him revenue. It was on their account that Jerome Saunders had been sentenced to death—

Just back of him Jo heard a cackle of strange laughter. He turned. He was face to face with that apparition he'd already glimpsed over there in front of City Hall.

It was Jerome Saunders—or some specter of him—who stood here confronting him now. The shaking red light that surrounded them—getting brighter—threw over Soapy Jo the spell of a thought that here they were, at the gates of hell.

"I've got you, Jo," said the returned Jerome Saunders.

Soapy Jo panted twice then spoke. "I'm glad," he said, "that it was all a mistake."

Doctor Coffin clicked his peculiar laugh. "It was a mistake, all right," he said. "You're going to burn, Jo. Kay Bird and Captain Fisher have both come clean—all written out and sworn to.

"They'll be waiting for you in the county jail."

Jo lurched. He still had a spasm or two of fight in him. But Doctor Coffin barely moved. He didn't have to.

All the time the brief interview had lasted a capless policeman had been creeping near, a drawn revolver in his hand.

But now, at the end of his desperate chase, the policeman was no longer so interested in Soapy Jo as he was in this spectral presence of Jerome Saunders.

As Jo lurched, the policeman grabbed him and jerked him aside. Jo flopped and hung for a moment to the policeman's hooked fingers, while the policeman still stared.

It was Jerome Saunders who had appointed him to the force less than a month ago. This was his benefactor—returned from the dead. The situation was too much for the policeman.

He stood there gaping and silent, rooted to the spot.

"You're a good man," said Doctor Coffin, in the voice that the cop was never going to forget. "I wish you luck. Now, take your prisoner over to the county jail. Don't rough him. He's all in. And keep him away from the mob. We want to save him for the chair."

The policeman had got back something of his nerve.

He saluted.

"Yes, Mr. Mayor!"

He leaned over Soapy Jo and was glad he hadn't killed him. When he looked up again, Doctor Coffin was gone.

IX

DOCTOR COFFIN HAD GHOSTED DOWN THIS SIDE STREET as far as he could go, then into a country road that would lead, he knew, to another bridge across the river a little below town. He was just headed for this second bridge when he heard a moaning roar far off ahead of him—a swift, smooth roar that instantly grew louder.

He hid in some bushes along the road and watched a company of state troopers whir past on their motorcycles—making something close to fifty miles an hour.

They were headed for Dartown, and already the beacon of a dozen burning buildings lighting them on their way.

As soon as they were gone, Doctor Coffin resumed his lonely walk. He crossed the bridge, then made his way back toward the town on the farther side.

It was not much more than an hour later before he came to the old Saunders homestead in its patch of woods. There was a single lighted window on the ground floor. He looked through this and saw old General Saunders seated there—fully dressed, clean white linen, shiny boots and everything. But asleep. And a smile on his face.

"Fighting Jack!"

"This was his fight, not mine," said Doctor Coffin to himself. "If I hadn't felt tonight that he was my granddaddy I'd never been able to get away with it."

Which is maybe true and maybe not.

In any case, Doctor Coffin let the old gentleman dream on—keeping unspoiled this vision of the grandson who'd come back to him. Doctor Coffin merely roused out, softly, one of the servants. And then, up there in the room that had belonged to Jerome Saunders—why, Jerome Saunders simply disappeared again, and Doctor Coffin came to life—himself a living dead man, headed for he didn't quite know where.

Appendix: The Doctor Coffin Stories
(Bold-face titles are included in this collection)

Thrilling Detective

1	1932 June	**The Living Dead Man**
2	1932 July	**The Murdered Wife**
3	1932 August	**Dead Man Blues**
4	1932 September	**Seven Seconds to Die**
5	1932 October	**Horror House**
6	1932 November	**Hollywood Ghost**
7	1932 December	Crime Canyon
8	1933 January	Sudden Death
9	1933 February	The Black Ram
10	1933 March	The Chinese Alibi
12	1933 April	Skullface *
13	1933 May	**Manhattan Monster**
14	1933 June	Midnight Justice
15	1933 August	The Chicken King
16	1933 September	**Small Town Stuff**

* Reprinted in *Thrilling Detective Heroes* (Adventure House, 2006)

CPSIA information can be obtained at www.ICGtesting.com
Printed in the USA
BVOW03s0832170414

350823BV00003B/857/P